THE EDGE OF FALLING

J. S. COOPER

Contents

Blurb

Am I making a mistake by moving in with my brother and his hot best friend?

Most definitely!

Did my heart start pounding when I saw him in his towel?

No comment.

Did I get all dolled up for what I thought was a date that ended up being a work event?

Can the earth swallow me up now, please?

Oliver James has been in my life since I was seven. As my brother's best friend, he was at my house more often than not. And I loved having him around. In fact, I even had a secret crush on him. Even though he was four years older than me, that didn't stop me from daydreaming. Until I turned seventeen and he broke my heart. I swore I would never interact with him again. And I didn't. But now, it's five years later, and I'm graduating college and all out of options.

With no job and no prospects, my parents have stated I can move back home or I can live in New York with my brother. Obviously, New York is the better option, but my brother's roommate is Oliver. Oliver with the gray-blue eyes that have haunted my dreams. Oliver with the kissable lips that smirk whenever they see me. Oliver with the steely tongue that lives to boss me around. I've told myself that I'm older now. I'm not going to let him bother me.

But then he picks me up at the airport, and I know that staying away from him will be a lot harder than I thought. Oliver James isn't happy that I've been ignoring him for years, and now he's determined to make me his. But the joke's on him because I'm never going to fall for him again.

The Edge of Falling is a standalone romance.

Rosalie,

We need to talk. I'm done playing games. I may be your brother's best friend, but I'm not a schmuck. If we're going to continue living together, we need to set some ground rules. Meet me in the kitchen at 7am and have the espresso machine on.

Oliver James

Oliver,

You are a schmuck. Make your own coffee. I'll see you at 7am.

Rosalie

Chapter 1

Rosalie

> From: Rosaliesloane@firstuniversity.edu
> To: Fostersloane@kingofbanking.com
> Re: Coming to stay
> Hey Foster,

Dad told me he talked to you about me coming to live with you in New York. I've got a plane ticket for next week. Can you pick me up? Also, will I have my own bedroom and bathroom? Also, thanks for the graduation gift. So generous of you! (That's sarcasm, by the way).

> Your loving little sis,
> Rosalie
> From: Fostersloane@kingofbanking.com
> To: Rosaliesloane@firstuniversity.edu
> Re: Coming to stay

Rosalie,

Dad did call me and ask if you could stay, and I said no. Oliver and I live in a 2 bedroom/2 bath, and there isn't room for you. I suggest you go back home and see if you can find a job with that expensive English degree of yours.

Foster

From: Rosaliesloane@firstuniversity.edu

To: Fostersloane@kingofbanking.com

Re: Coming to stay

Foster,

I'm not going back home. I'm twenty-two. I am coming to New York, and if you say no, I will tell Mom and Dad that you're the one who stole Dad's Porsche that summer and smashed it.

Your loving sis,

Rosalie

From: Fostersloane@kingofbanking.com

To: Rosaliesloane@firstuniversity.edu

Re: Coming to stay

Really, Rosalie? And you wonder why I didn't get you a present for graduation? I will speak to Oliver and let you know. I can't pick you up from the airport because I'm going on a work trip for two weeks. Which I told you about when you called last night.

Foster

I stared at my brother's latest email and tried to

ignore my thudding heart. *He was going to speak to Oliver and let me know.* I hated that I was in this position. I didn't want to stay with my brother and his best friend any more than Foster wanted me to stay. But it was a much better option than living with my parents, who still treated me like I was a twelve-year-old preteen as opposed to a twenty-two-year-old adult woman. I decided to call him as I knew that emailing would not change his mind.

"Rosalie, I'm busy." Foster sounded annoyed as he answered the phone, but I wasn't going to let that deter me.

"Does Oliver have to pick me up?" The words rushed out of my mouth before I could stop them. Foster didn't know how much I disliked his best friend, and I didn't want to play my cards before I even moved in.

"What?" I could hear the subway in the background and ignored them. I didn't want to give Foster an excuse to hang up.

"Can't you pick me up?" I pleaded. "Can't you postpone or cancel your trip?"

"It's not like I'm going on a bachelor party to Vegas. I'm going on a work trip, so no, I won't be canceling. Unless you want to go on the work trip for me?" Sarcasm dripped from his voice as if he wanted to rub in how successful he was. The model child to my black sheep.

"But..."

"But what? You're the one coming to stay with me. In my two-bedroom apartment."

"You can afford three bedrooms," I said softly, and I giggled as I heard him gasping. Of course, I didn't expect him to get a three-bedroom place just to accommodate me, but I loved egging my brother on.

"Rosalie, I'm going to give Oliver your number and—"

"No," I cut him off quickly. "Give him my email address...I'm, I'm busy today, so email will be better."

"Busy doing what?" He didn't sound like he believed me. "Shopping with Mom and Dad's credit card?"

"I have to pack and figure out what I'm bringing with me to New York City and—"

"Don't bring too much, Rosalie." His voice croaked with worry. "You're going to be sleeping in the living room. Your bags will go in my room, but I don't have that much space."

"I'm not going to bring a lot. I'm just going..." I paused.

"You forget, I've known you your whole life." Foster sighed. "You are not a light packer...oh, and please tell me that Alice will not be joining you."

"No, why would you think she's joining me?"

"Because she's your best friend, and you do everything together."

"I mean, I would love for her to move to New York as well, but we're going to wait until I get a job and my own place, and then she can live with me while she looks for a job."

"Sounds like a losing plan." He chuckled, and I glared into the phone.

"Thanks for the support, Foster. You're such an *amazing* big brother." Sarcasm dripped from my voice as I gripped my phone.

"Is that your way of saying thanks for letting you live rent-free in my Manhattan apartment?"

"Yes, and thank you. I love you. I'll let you go now," I said quickly. I didn't want Foster to call our parents and tell them I wasn't welcome after all.

"Wait..." He paused. "Is Alice actually coming with you or…"

"What? No, don't worry, Foster. I don't expect you to put Alice and me up."

"She's welcome to visit if she wants."

"Aw, there's my big bro I love." I laughed. "I'll let her know. Also, Foster..."

"Yes, Rosalie?"

"What did Oliver say when you told him that I was going to move in with you guys?"

"Nothing." My brother sounded nonchalant. "He just nodded and said fine."

"Oh okay." Disappointment coursed through me, but I wasn't sure why. Well, that was a lie. I knew why. Oliver James was the bane of my existence. The one who got away, even though we'd never dated. He had been my first crush, the subject of my first daydream, his was the name I always put in teen quizzes about who you're going to marry when you get older. Oliver was the first man to make my heart race and, if I was honest, the first face in my mind when I fantasized about exploring sexually. However, Oliver hadn't seen me like that. He'd thought that he was too good for someone like me. I wasn't sure if he knew just how much I'd crushed on him, and I knew he didn't know why I'd stopped talking to him, so it hurt somewhat to know that he hadn't even asked any questions about why I was now allowing him back into my life.

"Why? What did you expect him to say?" Foster sounded confused.

"Well, seeing as I haven't spoken to him in years, I figured he would have had something to say."

"You haven't spoken to him in years?" Foster sounded shocked. "What?"

"Don't tell me you haven't noticed." My voice rose in surprise and slight anger. "Oliver didn't mention anything?"

"I don't even think he knows." Foster laughed. "Why haven't you spoken to him?"

"I have to go," I said quickly, questions coursing through my brain. How had neither of them noticed I'd been ignoring Oliver? I'd skipped Thanksgiving dinners and even a Christmas Day lunch just so I didn't have to see him. He hadn't even noticed? I was pissed. I'd hoped he'd been sad and depressed about my pointed avoidance.

"Um okay, well I will have…" Foster continued speaking, but I didn't want to listen to him anymore. I was too upset. I took a couple of deep breaths and looked around my childhood bedroom, then walked over to my single bed and took a seat. I stared at a poster of Harry Styles on my wall. I'd been a huge One Direction fan, still was, but I didn't admit it anymore. I lay back on the bed and stared up at the ceiling. It felt weird being back home. It was comforting and homey, but I felt like I was regressing in life. I was twenty-two years old and already a failure. I had no idea where I was going in life. No idea what I wanted to do. And all I could think about was how upset I was that Oliver hadn't even noticed that I hadn't been in his life for years. Jerk! I pressed my lips together as I thought about him. Was I making a mistake by moving to New York? How would I feel being around him? How would he react when he saw me? I chewed on my lower lip, wondering what I would do if I saw him naked in the shower or something. I sighed and picked up my phone to text Alice

9

when I saw I had an incoming text from Oliver. My heart froze as I sat up and opened it.

*O*liver: Hey, Foster told me you're moving in...and need me to pick you up?

Rosalie: I don't need anything from you.

Oliver: So you have a ride from the airport?

Rosalie: I will get a taxi.

Oliver: You have $75 to waste on a taxi? I thought you were moving in because you're a broke ass. :P

Rosalie: Very funny, Oliver.

Oliver: It's a joke. Just send me the flight info, and I will be there.

Rosalie: Fine. Thanks.

Oliver: No worries. It will be good to see you. It's been a while.

Rosalie: Has it?

Oliver: A few months or so...

I stared at his message and stuck my tongue out at the phone. There was no way in hell that he really thought it had only been a couple of months. Did he?

. . .

*R*osalie: Yeah, something like that.

Oliver: You got a boyfriend?

Rosalie: What?

Oliver: Just wondering if we will be expecting visitors.

Rosalie: I will ask before I have anyone over.

Oliver: Just saying, you're sleeping on the couch, so you won't exactly have privacy...

Rosalie: Thanks for your concern, Oliver.

Oliver: No worries, Rosy. :)

I stared at his nickname for me and took a deep breath. I wasn't ready to be all friendly and comfortable with Oliver again. I didn't want him using nicknames with me, reminding me of the fact that we grew up together.

*R*osalie: I'll send you the flight info. Thanks.

Oliver: Just don't bring too many My Little Ponies with you...

Rosalie: I'm 22...not 12.

Oliver: And??

Rosalie: I'm not a little girl anymore. I don't play with My Little Pony anymore.

Oliver: I guess you're into rabbits now?

Rosalie: Huh?

Oliver: Nothing. Don't want to corrupt you.

Rosalie: Have a nice day, Oliver.

Oliver: See you soon, Rosy. I've missed you.

*M*y heart thudded as I threw my phone down onto the mattress. What the hell did that mean? He missed me? Did he really miss me? Or was he just typing that to be polite? I wanted to scream. I felt like I was fifteen-year-old Rosalie obsessing over every little thing a boy said to me. Obsessing over what Oliver said to me. Fantasizing about him wanting to kiss me or take me on a date. Hoping he'd realize he loved me. Wanted to marry me. Have babies with me. It had been a child's fantasy. He hadn't been interested in me at all, but that hadn't stopped me from hoping. Until that night...and then I'd never spoken to him again. He had to realize I've deliberately been ignoring him? Hadn't he?

Chapter 2

Rosalie

"So what are you going to do when you see him?" my best friend Alice asked me as I waited on a bench in the airport for Oliver to pick me up.

"I don't know. I guess I'll say hello," I said, trying not to think about it too much. As if I hadn't spent the past forty-eight hours obsessing over how our meeting would go.

"That's it? You're not going to tell him off?" She sounded surprised.

"What would I tell him off about, Alice?"

"Rosalie, this is Oliver James we're talking about."

"Yeah, I know it's Oliver James."

"And you hate him." The words sounded so matter of fact that I didn't even flinch. Alice knew exactly why I hated him, and she also knew I'd had a crush on him.

"I know I hate him."

"And you're going to be living with him."

"Well, I'm going to be living with him and my brother."

"Same difference, Rosalie." She paused, and I swore I could hear her thinking. How are you going to live with the man who made you cry for a week straight?

"Yeah, so?" I pretended to be clueless. I didn't want to talk about the past. It was done, and I didn't care about Oliver anymore.

"You haven't spoken to him in five years."

"And I wouldn't have spoken to him in a billion more years if I didn't have to. I can't believe my parents only gave me two options." I let out a deep sigh as I stared into the crowd of people, my heart racing. The truth of the matter was that I was not ready or prepared to see Oliver James again. He had been my brother's best friend since I was seven years old, and I'd always thought he was amazing. In fact, he'd been my first real crush. I had followed him and my brother around everywhere, and I'd daydream that one day we would be together. Until I was seventeen and the absolute worst thing happened. I hadn't seen him since, and I never wanted to see him.

However, I just graduated from college, and I didn't have a job, and I didn't have many prospects. I guess that was what happened when you studied English literature for a major. My parents had given me two options. I could go and live with them in Sarasota, Florida, which I really didn't want to do, or I could move to New York City and live with my brother and his best friend, Oliver. Neither one of the options had really been something I was interested in, but I figured New York City would give me a new start in life. Maybe I'd find a good job and, hopefully, could afford to move out of the apartment as soon as possible.

"Hey, Rosalie," Alice said, her voice sharp in my ear.

"Sorry, what?"

"You're not daydreaming about him already, are you?" There was a tinge of amusement in her voice, and I frowned.

"Why do you ask me that?" I asked sharply.

"Because I was speaking to you for the past couple of minutes, and you didn't respond."

"Yeah, sorry. I was just thinking about what I'm going to say to Oliver when I see him..."

"I thought you just told me you were going to say hello."

"I mean, I can't just say hello, though." I started to feel agitated. I hated him. He was a jackass. He didn't deserve me at my friendliest self. "Oh my God," I whispered into the phone. "I see him." And there he was, tall and muscular, his dark brown hair long with a slight curl. I could see his blue-gray eyes looking around, and my heart thudded as I stared at the profile of his handsome face. He hadn't shaved in a while, and I could see a beard and mustache growing. Oliver was no longer a boy. He was a man and a very sexy man at that. "Oh, shit. Oh, shit," I whispered into the phone. "Oh my God, Alice, what am I going to do?"

"I don't know. I wish I was there." Alice's voice sounded sweet and calm. More than anything, I wished she was taking this journey with me.

"Me, too. Why couldn't you move to New York?"

"Because I don't have a brother who's going to let me stay there for free," she groaned. "And my parents want me to work at Dad's laundromat." Alice was my best friend, and we'd gone through elementary school, high school, and college together. We'd both studied English literature. She also didn't have a job, and she was back home in Sarasota with her parents, hoping to find a way to get out as soon as possible. She was lucky, though.

Her parents lived near the beach, so at least she had a great view.

"Oh my God. He's looking around. Oh my God. I think he just saw me," I said and swallowed hard. Oliver was heading toward me. "What am I going to do, Alice?"

"Just put on a brave face. Don't let him faze you," she said quickly. "Okay? Remember, you're beautiful and kind, and he only wished he could be with someone like you."

"Okay. I've got to go." I hung up quickly and put the phone into my handbag. I sat there and waited for Oliver to approach me. I wasn't going to jump out of my seat. I wasn't going to make this easy for him.

His eyes met mine, and he gave me a small smile. I didn't smile back at him. I looked up again a couple of seconds later, but he was no longer walking toward me. I frowned slightly. Was he pissed off that I hadn't smiled back at him? What was his game? And then confusion entered my brain as I watched him walking up to a girl sitting a couple of rows away from me.

"Hey," he said. "What's going on, Rosalie?"

The girl blinked and looked up at him. "Sorry, what?"

"Aren't you Rosalie?" He gave a wry smile and shrugged. "It's me, Oliver."

"Um, I don't know who you are. My name's Barbara." She jumped up, and I held in a giggle. Now that I looked at her, she did resemble me slightly, but she resembled a teenage me, the me who had been slightly overweight with bleached-blond hair. I no longer dyed my hair, so I had my natural brunette locks. I'd slimmed down in college, but I guess Oliver didn't know that as we hadn't seen each other, and it was unlikely Foster had told him anything. It was unlikely that Foster had even noticed that I was now fifty pounds less than I'd been when I started college. I wasn't exactly a model now, but I was happy with my womanly figure. I would never be a rail because I liked fries and cupcakes way too much.

I watched as he blinked and looked around. "Oh, sorry. I thought you were my best friend's sister. I'm picking her up from the airport."

"Well, I'm not, but if you want to take me home..." The girl flirted with him, and I just rolled my eyes. Typical! Women always fell all over Oliver. Life was so easy for good-looking men.

"Um, sorry. I better look for her. Her parents will kill me if I don't find her." He continued to look around then, a small smile on his face as he surveyed the crowd. I could tell that he had absolutely no idea who I was. I let out a deep sigh and stood. I walked over to him. He gave me a warm smile.

"Hello," he said, his eyes twinkling. There was a flirtatious smile on his face and I smiled back, loving the way he was looking me over. Then I remembered that I hated him and didn't care if he was looking at me like the most beautiful woman he'd ever seen in his life.

"Oliver?" I said coldly, ignoring my beating heart.

His face froze for a second, and he looked at me, blinking in surprise. "Rosalie?" His silky voice sounded so familiar to my ears, and I felt butterflies in my stomach as our eyes connected.

"Yes, it's me." I shrugged my shoulders and held my head up high.

"Oh, wow," he said, and I watched as he looked me up and down. He ran his hand through his hair and licked his lips slightly.

"Well, I never…" he said. He shook his head as he gazed at me, a devious glint in his captivating eyes.

"Hello, Oliver. My bags are over there." I nodded back to my previous seat. "I'm ready to go whenever you are. You're ten minutes late." I wasn't going to let myself fall under his spell again. I would not do that to myself.

"Well, nice to see you again, Rosalie." He reached his arms open for a hug, and I just stared at them and stepped back.

"I don't think we'll be hugging," I said, glaring at him. He blinked at me a couple of times and shook his head with a smirk on his face.

"Well, well, well. I guess you're still angry with me for whatever I did to make you avoid me, huh?"

"You guessed right, Oliver James. Now let me tell you a couple of things before we even get back to the apartment," I snapped. So that answered one question. He had known I'd been avoiding him.

He started laughing then, and it was my turn to frown.

"What's so funny?"

"You are," he said. "You might not look like the old Rosalie, but you certainly have the same attitude."

"What's that supposed to mean?" I glared at him.

"I just mean that even though you're a woman now, you still act like a petulant little kid."

"You're such a jerk, Oliver."

"That's the Rosalie I remember," he said. "Now, come on. Let's get going. You're going to help me with these bags?" He stared at the three suitcases and duffel bag with a raised eyebrow.

"No, I'm not. Isn't that why you go to the gym and lift all those weights? Isn't that why you have so many muscles?"

"You think I have muscles, eh?" He raised an eyebrow, and I just shook my head. He started laughing then. "Welcome to New York City, Rosalie. I have a feeling that we're going to have a really good time."

"I doubt it." I picked up the duffel bag and turned away from him, so he couldn't see the blush on my face at his words. What did he mean by having a good time?

"Rosalie, wait." Oliver's voice sounded amused as he said my name. I stopped and looked back at him, raising one single eyebrow.

"Yes?" I said succinctly, trying not to let him see how much he was affecting me.

"You really can't expect me to carry all three of these suitcases, can you?" He looked at my three huge suitcases, a wry smile on his face as he looked back at me. "Did someone give me Superman powers and not tell me?"

"I thought you were strong and macho." I flexed my muscles as I stared at his biceps. "I guess I was wrong." I watched his lips twitching at my words, and I couldn't stop myself from staring at them for a few seconds. My lips twitched slightly in response as he started chuckling, a deep warm sound that made my heart flip. "Fine. I guess I can pull one of them, or would you rather me pull two?" I stepped toward him and stared into his eyes, mine challenging him.

"Well, they are your suitcases," he said, grinning. "If you want to pull two, I won't argue with you."

My heart sank at his words. My suitcases were heavy as hell.

"Yeah, but you're the big, macho man. And I'm just a—"

"I thought you were a feminist, Rosalie." He grinned as he cut me off.

"I am," I said. "Why would you even question that?"

"Well, if you're a feminist, wouldn't you want to carry all of your bags yourself? Why would you want a strong, macho man to have to help you?"

I stared at him for a few seconds and just shook my head. "Very funny. That's not exactly what I was saying."

"Well, I'm glad I'm making you laugh." He cocked his head to the side and surveyed my face with a wide lazy smile.

"Does it look like I'm laughing, Oliver?"

"No, but I guess you've become a bit of an actress."

"Really?" I stared at him, raising my eyebrows. "Why do you say that?"

"Because I know I'm funny, and I know you want to laugh. You're just not doing it. So the only reason you wouldn't be doing it is because you're acting and—"

"Really, Oliver?" I broke into a grin. "Are you analyzing me already?"

"I seem to remember that you used to love it when we analyzed your every move...remember all those quizzes we took in that magazine you loved? What was it called again? *Seventeen*?"

"*Seventeen* and *Cosmo*?" I giggled. I had loved taking those quizzes, and oftentimes, Oliver would take them with me. I'd forgotten about that.

"So I thought..." He paused as I rubbed my stomach. "Everything okay?"

"Can you please just grab two of my suitcases so we can go to your car? I don't have time for this." I could hear my stomach then, and he started laughing.

"Are you hungry?"

"I mean, a little bit. The flight wasn't that long, but they only gave us peanuts. I mean, would it have hurt them to give us a meal as well?"

"You weren't in business class, were you?"

"No, I was in economy, but should that make a difference? Is it right that only rich people get to eat on planes?"

"I don't think it's right," he said with a small smile, "but that's just the way it is. You get what you pay for."

"Well, my parents paid for this ticket begrudgingly, so it's not like I could really say much." I looked at him for a couple of seconds. We grabbed the suitcases and started walking. "So you're an attorney now, huh?"

"Yep." He nodded. "The suit didn't give me away?"

"I mean, you could have been a broker like my brother."

"No, I'm not interested in finances and stocks and stuff."

"So what sort of law do you practice?"

"Corporate law."

It was my turn for my lips to twitch. "You study corporate law, but you're not interested in finances and stocks and—"

"Hey"—he shrugged—"I deal with tax cases involving the Federal Tax Code. It's not fun, but it pays well. And—"

"You're boring me," I said, yawning.

"Oh sorry, I didn't want to bore someone like you." He raised his eyebrows and pressed his lips together. I felt confused and annoyed at the same time. Was he being condescending?

"What do you mean someone like *me*?"

"I mean someone who's living a life of luxury, someone who doesn't have to worry about getting a job."

"Of course, I have to worry about getting a job." I glared at him. "That's why I'm here. To look for a job and figure out what I want to do with my life.

But I don't want to be a lawyer. And I don't care about finances or taxes or—"

"So I guess that rules out H&R Block from your list."

"Um, who?"

He started laughing then. "The tax firm? They prepare your taxes at tax time so you can get a tax refund. You've never heard of them?"

"I've never gotten a tax refund. My parents have always claimed me," I admitted guiltily. I knew I had lived a sheltered life, but my past didn't matter now because I was on my own. At least financially. My parents had given me a thousand dollars and told me that any further money I needed had to be made by myself. They'd even taken away two of my credit cards and only left me with an AMEX for emergency purposes, which they'd told me would be closed if I used it for anything other than an emergency. These were hard times. I knew I was spoiled. Not that I'd admit that to Oliver James, though.

"Ah, makes sense."

"What's that supposed to mean?"

"I'm just saying it makes sense. You've never had a job so you wouldn't pay taxes."

"You think I'm an immature little girl, don't you? You think..." I stopped and glared at him.

"This isn't really the place to have this conversation, Rosalie. Maybe we can wait till we get to my car?" He raised an eyebrow as he looked around at the crowds of people walking beside us. "But if you want to throw a tantrum, I'd wait until then..."

"Do you think that I'm still twelve years old or seventeen years old? I'm twenty-two now. I'm a woman, and you can't talk to me like I'm a little kid. I'm not going to stand for that. And just because I'm staying with you and Foster doesn't mean that—" I was angry, and I wasn't going to shy away from letting him know how I felt.

"It's fine." He held his hands up. "I was just teasing you, Rosalie. That's what friends do."

"I didn't realize we were friends," I said sarcastically.

"Well, true. You have been avoiding me for a long time, but..." He shrugged. I stared into his eyes, and he stared back into mine. "Are we going to talk about it?" he asked softly.

"Talk about what?" I could feel my heart racing.

"Why you stopped talking to me?"

"So you did know I stopped talking to you!" I knew he had to have known.

"I mean, it was kind of obvious, don't you think? You were literally around all the time, and then you just disappeared off the face of the earth." He shrugged. "I'm just curious as to why."

"Because..." I said as I ran my hands through my long dark hair.

"If you don't know, then..." He stared at me for a few more seconds wordlessly. He rubbed his forehead and then sighed. "Come on, we're close to the car now.."

"That's it? That's the only conversation we're going to have?"

"I mean, you didn't seem to want to say anything else about it." He licked his lips. "And your stomach is growling, so you're hungry. Let's get out of here, go and get you something to eat, then we can go back to the apartment. Foster said that you can sleep in his room while he's away, but don't get used to it because you will be on the couch."

"Wow. How generous of him. You'd think he'd let me sleep in his room the whole time."

"Why?" Oliver shook his head. "It's not like you're his mom or his girlfriend. You're his sister."

"Yeah, I'm his baby sister. His one and only baby sister. He should be treating me like a princess, like a queen, like royalty."

"Um, I think you need to find yourself a boyfriend if that's what you're looking for, Rosalie."

"What's that supposed to mean?" I stared at Oliver, scorn on my face.

"I'm just saying that if you want someone to treat you like a princess, that should be your man or your dad. And you decided you don't want to live at home with your dad, so you're living with Foster and me. And neither one of us is going to treat you like—"

"I know, and it's fine. You're both jackasses."

"Hey." He held his hands up. "What's with the animosity? I took off work so I could come pick you up."

"And I appreciate it, though I did tell you I could catch a taxi."

"With what money, Rosalie?"

I chewed on my lower lip. "I'm not completely broke, you know. I have some money."

"So you have enough money to just blow seventy-five dollars for nothing?"

"Well no, but—"

"But nothing. Come on. Do you like Mexican food?"

"Yeah, who doesn't?"

"Lots of people don't, but I know a cool little Tacqueria I can take you to. And—"

"Yeah?" I asked him.

"If you really want to show me how much of an independent woman you are, you can pay for the tacos."

"What, me?" I stared at him, wide eyes, already thinking about how quickly the thousand dollars in my bank would be depleted.

"I'm joking." He started laughing. "It's on me. Welcome to New York City."

"Well, thank you, Oliver. I do appreciate it."

"I can be a nice guy sometimes." And then he gave me a long, warm smile. I could feel my heart flittering as I stared at him. "Yeah, I guess you can. Come on, let's go," I said, quickly walking ahead of him. I wasn't sure how I felt. It was like old times the way we bantered back and forth. Yet there was another level to our conversations that had never existed before. An understanding and intensity, a chemistry that hung in the air between us. If I wasn't mistaken, Oliver was attracted to me and that provided a buzz like I'd never felt before in my life, but I wasn't going to act on it. I wasn't going to let him think that just because I'd slimmed down and was hot now, he could have a chance. He didn't want me back then, and he certainly wouldn't be able to have me now. No matter how badly my body wanted to get to know him better.

Chapter 3

*R*osalie Sloane, fuck. I was in trouble. She looked hot as hell.

I clutched the parking ticket in my hand and went to the meter to pay. Rosalie was sitting in the passenger seat of my Honda Pilot, and all I could think about was how she'd blossomed into a beautiful butterfly. Not that she'd ever been ugly. I'd never thought that, but shit, I hadn't expected her to be a fucking bombshell.

I took a couple of deep breaths and put my ticket into the machine and waited for it to tell me how much I owed. I was in fucking trouble. Rosalie was going to be living in the apartment with me, and for the first couple of weeks, Foster wasn't even going to be there. I knew I could not make a move. No matter how hard she made me. Foster would absolutely kill me. He'd made it clear since we were kids that his sister was off-limits, and I had to respect that. He was my best friend. And more than that, he was like my brother. "Fuck," I mumbled under my breath as I pressed the buttons to pay, waiting for the machine to return my card and the parking ticket.

I hadn't seen Rosalie in so long. She'd stopped talking to me, and I'd never really been sure why, but I hadn't reached out to find out. I'd figured it was for the best. She was off-limits in my life. And as she'd grown older, it had been harder and harder not to kiss her, not to tease her, not to flirt with her, not to grab her and pull her into my arms.

She'd always been a true romantic as a teenager. Always talking about what her first kiss would be like and how her first love would sweep her off her feet, dancing under the moonlight while listening to Frank Sinatra. She was a true romantic who loved old movies. And I'd always felt slightly sad for her, knowing that her idea of love would never come true because there was no perfect relationship. There was no perfect man. No man was going to sweep her off her feet.

I wondered if she'd ever found that with anyone. I wondered if she had a boyfriend. I hadn't wanted

to ask Foster, and he never volunteered any information about his sister. It wasn't that he didn't love her
or care about her. It just wasn't a topic of conversation. Yeah, he told me when she was going home
and how she was doing in school, but nothing more
than surface level. Walking back to the car, I opened
the door and slid into the driver's seat. I looked over
at Rosalie, who was glaring at me, her brown eyes
full of an emotion I hadn't seen in a long time.

"What's wrong?" I said, turning the ignition and
starting the car.

"I'm..." She paused and chewed on her lower lip.
I stared at her plump, pink lips. She must have put
on half a bottle of lip gloss in the last five seconds
because it was practically oozing off her lips. And
the car smelled like strawberries. I smiled to myself.
That was something she hadn't grown out of. Rosalie
had loved strawberry everything. Strawberry sham-
poo, strawberry body wash, strawberry lip gloss,
strawberry body spray. I chuckled.

"What's so funny, Oliver?" she said, glaring
at me.

"You know, if you keep glaring at me, your face
will stay like that, and everyone's going to think
you're a grump." I stared at her pouting lips. All I
wanted to do was kiss them and see if they tasted like
strawberries as well.

"I'm not glaring at you. I'm just..." she sputtered, her eyes narrowing.

"You're just what? Why are you pissed off at me?" I looked in the rearview mirror and made my way out of the parking lot. "We haven't seen each other in years, and you have a little attitude."

"I don't have an attitude. You didn't even know who I was."

"Yeah. So you've changed a little bit." I licked my lips and smiled to myself.

"I haven't changed that much, Oliver. I just can't believe you went up to another girl and assumed she was me."

"Is that why you're so upset?" I raised an eyebrow, turning to look at her as I made my way onto the freeway.

"I'm not upset. I'm just..."

"I'm sorry. I didn't know. You'd blossomed into a beautiful butterfly in the months I hadn't seen you."

"You know it's been more than months," she said, and my lips twitched at the indignant tone in her voice. I wanted to grab her neck and pull her toward me and kiss her. But I knew that would be the biggest mistake I could ever make. We'd barely seen each other for thirty minutes. There was no way I could do anything untoward. For all I knew, she'd call her brother and then her dad right away and get me in hot shit. And I didn't need that right now. I didn't need that ever.

"Uh-huh, whatever you say, Rosalie. Can we start afresh? It's going to be a long couple of months if you're going to be mad at me the entire time." I looked over at her and noticed her staring at my face, wearing an inscrutable expression. I wasn't sure what she was thinking, and I didn't like that. I could normally read Rosalie like a book.

"So are we going to go and get those tacos or what?" she said, finally looking away and rubbing her stomach. "I'm hungry."

"I thought there was something else you wanted to say to me."

"No," she said in a long-drawn-out tone. I shook my head and decided not to pursue it.

"How much was the ticket?" I watched as she opened her wallet and pulled out a five-dollar bill. I started laughing when she handed it to me.

"Honey, that ticket was twenty dollars."

"Twenty dollars? But you were barely there for a couple of minutes. I..."

"Welcome to New York," I said, beaming at her. She bit down on her lower lip and reached into her wallet again.

"It's fine. You don't have to pay me back. I think I can cover it."

"Are you sure?" she said, sighing.

"I'm sure."

"Well, I don't want to owe you anything."

"You're going to be living in my apartment rent-free. I think you owe me a lot more than twenty dollars."

"I'm not living rent-free. Foster pays half the rent, and well, he's just covering my part."

"I don't really think it works like that," I said, laughing. "But okay."

"Do you not want me living there, Oliver?" The indignant tone was back in her voice. I licked my lips slowly and turned on the radio without answering her. I could hear her huffing and puffing in the passenger seat next to me. I stifled a laugh because I didn't want her to think that I was enjoying the situation even though I was. It felt really good to be back in her company. It felt like home. I'd watched her growing up. She'd followed Foster and me around for years with her best friend, Alice. And even though she'd been annoying at times, she'd always been a ray of light and brightness in my life. She made me laugh. She irritated me. She elicited all sorts of emotions in me. Though I didn't really need or want her to elicit *all* of the emotions. Certainly not the ones that made me shift in my seat.

"I can't believe you turned on the radio when I was having a conversation with you."

"I thought you might like to listen to some

music." I tapped my fingers against the steering wheel as I pulled out of the airport.

"I don't listen to this music," she said, a slight attitude in her tone.

"What music is this?"

"Exactly," she said. "What is this crap?" She wrinkled her nose as an old man sang about his one-eyed pig.

I started laughing then. To be honest, I didn't even know who was playing.

"You can choose the radio station if you want. I don't mind."

"Do you have Bluetooth? Can I connect my phone and play some tunes?"

"Sure. Just press the buttons, and you can connect."

"Okay." I watched as she leaned forward, pressing her manicured nails against the buttons on my dashboard. She connected her phone and pressed play. And I heard the sound of Pink shouting through the speakers in my car.

"You can turn the volume down a little bit, please," I said, looking over at her. "I don't want to lose my hearing today."

"I didn't realize that the volume on my phone was so high," she said, quickly pressing the buttons on the side of her phone. "That's better."

"Yeah," I said. I halted as we were in traffic and

then turned to look at her. "It really is nice having you here, Rosalie. I know you've been upset at me about something, but hopefully, we can work past that. And hopefully, we can become friends again."

"Uh-huh," she said, shaking her head. "Whatever you say, Oliver."

"Whatever I say, huh?" And then it struck me that little Miss Rosalie Sloane was being impertinent and bitchy on purpose. And even though she was Foster's sister, I would not let her get away with it. I had an idea to bring her to her knees. And while playing games with her wasn't the nicest thing for me to do, I knew I wanted to. I'd never called myself a nice guy. I'd put the plan into motion, and hopefully, she would fall for it. Then maybe, just maybe, she'd understand that she was never going to get the best of me. That she was never going to be in control of whatever the situation of our relationship or friendship was. I didn't like the way she was making me feel as we sat here in the car. All of a sudden, the song changed, and Ed Sheeran blared out of the speakers.

"I love this song," Rosalie said. She started singing along and shimmying in her seat as she talked about looking at a photograph. "Oh my gosh, he's so romantic. I would absolutely love it if a guy sang this to me," she said, forgetting that she was supposed to be angry and pissed off at me. I smiled warmly at her. So she was still a romantic at heart.

"So have you been in love yet, Rosalie?" I asked her softly, cocking my head to the side and observing her face. She looked at me, her eyes flashing something that I didn't quite recognize. Then she shook her head vehemently.

"No, never been in love, but I'm sure I'll meet Mr. Right in New York."

"Hmm, there are a lot of men to meet in New York, that is for sure." I pressed my lips together. "I'm sure you'll meet plenty of men. Will one of them be Mr. Right? I don't know..." I didn't want to tell her that she had to be careful of the men in NYC. "Most men here are after one thing."

"Yep, I'm sure they are. But I just need one guy who falls in love with me and wants me. I'm sure he's just waiting for me. *All* of me." She sighed dreamily as she looked out of the car window, and I decided to keep my mouth shut. I was pretty sure they'd want all of her as well. But I was pretty confident her definition of all of her didn't include anal and doggy style, and I didn't need her to get angry with me again. She'd figure out the truth soon enough. True love was a construct created by corporations to make money. There was no one love or soul mate for anyone, no matter what she wanted to believe.

Chapter 4

ROSALIE

"Wow, you were right. These are the best tacos I've ever had," I said, licking my lips before taking another bite of my steak taco. "I can't believe they taste so good."

"I'm glad you're enjoying them," Oliver said with a laugh.

"I didn't even think I liked cilantro and lime, but wow." I looked at him, and I could see his eyes crinkling as he stared at me. "What? What's so funny?" I asked self-consciously as I grabbed some chips and dipped them into the tastiest salsa I'd ever had in my life.

"I just really enjoy watching you eat."

"That sounds weird." I wrinkled my nose. "What do you mean?"

"I mean, here in New York City. A lot of the women who I meet don't like to eat."

"What do you mean they don't like to eat? How do they survive?"

"On lettuce and cucumbers and protein shakes." He chuckled, and I shook my head.

"I guess that's why I'm never going to be super skinny or a model because I enjoy food way too much."

"I know," he said. "I still remember what you used to say as a teenager."

"And what is that?" I asked him curiously, not sure what he was talking about.

"You used to say, I live to eat. I don't eat to live."

"Oh yeah." I nodded. "Alice and I always used to go back and forth on that."

"How is Alice, by the way?" he asked, tilting his head to the side. "I'm surprised she didn't come on this cockamamie journey with you."

"She wanted to." I laughed. "I wanted her too, but you and Foster don't have a big apartment. And her parents were not willing to give her even a penny to come. They're so mean."

"I don't think they're mean. They're probably just wondering why they spent so much money on her education when she..." He paused. "Well, I guess I shouldn't continue with that sentence, should I?"

"And why is that?" I said, putting my food down and folding my arms across my chest. I stared at him with narrowed eyes. I wanted him to think I was angry with him, but I wasn't. I mean, it was true. Everything that he was saying was true. Alice and I had gotten an expensive education, and it hadn't led to jobs. We'd followed our passion, and now we were jobless without many professional options.

"I don't want to get in trouble with you again, Rosalie," he said, shaking his head. "I think I'll keep my lips shut."

"Were you going to say, like my parents wasted money on my degree?"

"Well, what is it you're doing with your English literature degree?" He shrugged. "Has it been helpful at all?"

"I'll have you know that I know things about British authors that you would not even believe."

"Okay, then try me."

"Okay. What do you want to know?"

"Hmm," he said. "How many times was Jane Austen married?"

I stared at him for a few seconds, blinking. "What?"

"You said you know everything about British authors. Right?"

"I mean, not everything."

"Well, Jane Austen's a pretty popular and famous British author, right?"

"Yes," I acknowledged.

"So how many times was she married?"

"I don't know if this is a trick question, Oliver, but Jane Austen was never married."

"Oh," he said, raising an eyebrow. "Really?"

"Really," I said, staring at him, wondering did he know the answer to that? And was he trying to see if I knew, or was he really that oblivious? "She was in love, though, probably," I said, rubbing my forehead.

"Oh, and what was his name?"

"Oliver," I said with a small smile, "Oliver Twist."

He started laughing then and shook his head. "Very funny. I do know that Oliver Twist is a character who Charles Dickens created."

"Well, kudos to you, Oliver."

"Yeah, yeah. So you were saying, Jane Austen was in love."

"Yeah, she was in love with one of her neighbor's nephews. His name was Tom Lefroy. But"—I sighed—"it wasn't to be. Circumstances kept them apart."

"Oh?" he said, raising an eyebrow.

"Well, he wasn't of the right stock. A marriage seemed impractical between the two because neither of them came from money. Quite sad, really." I took another bite of my taco.

"Yes, that is sad," Oliver said, and I couldn't tell if he was being facetious or not.

I watched as he ate part of his quesadilla, then grabbed his cerveza from the table. He chugged it down, and I tried not to look at the way his fingers gripped the bottle. So strong, and tan, and manly. I could feel my stomach twitching as I gazed back into his face. His blue-gray eyes surveyed me curiously.

"So you do know nonsensical facts, then."

"They're not nonsensical. They're important."

"They're not so important that they will help you get a job."

"I mean, I could get a job if I really wanted to."

"So then why don't you? Why are you living with Foster and me?"

"I just got here. I haven't been able to find a job yet."

"And what do you think you'll try to do?" Oliver was starting to get on my nerves with all of his questions, and I figured I'd play around with him.

"I'm going to be an actress," I said. "I think I'd like to be on Broadway."

He stared at me for a few seconds, and I could tell he wasn't sure if I was serious or not. "Um, an actress? You don't say."

"Or maybe I'll be a singer. I heard some auditions for *America's Got Talent* and *American Idol* are coming up." I paused, took a sip of water, and then cleared my throat. "La-ti-do-so-fa-re-me," I sang quickly, my voice cracking on the higher notes. His eyes widened, and I stifled a smile. "Doe, a deer, a female deer, ray, a drop of golden sun," I sang even louder and slightly out of tune.

"What?" His eyes looked incredulous, and it took everything in me to stop from laughing out loud.

"That's the song I'm going to sing at the audition. Or should I sing something else? Maybe Whitney Houston? What's that really famous song that Dolly Parton wrote? I know, 'I Will Always Love You.'" I started singing, and my voice cracked with every note." I rubbed my forehead and stopped. "Oops, I guess I ate too many tacos today. It ruined my throat."

"Um, Rosalie," Oliver said with a look of panic on his face. I knew that he was debating whether or not to be honest with me about my singing skills. I also knew that I wasn't going to be able to hold my laughter in for much longer.

"Yes, Oliver?" I smiled innocently.

"I don't want to have to tell you this, but..."

"About what?" I said, staring at him with wide innocent eyes. "Do you think I'll make it to the top ten? Maybe I'll be on TV. Would you come to the audience to support me?"

"Um, look, girl, you can't sing. You couldn't sing when you were young, and you can't sing now. You're not going to make it onto TV." He cleared his throat. "I'm sorry. I hate to do this, but if you really think you're..."

I burst out laughing then. "Oh, Oliver. It's so easy to wind you up."

"What?" he asked, frowning.

"I know I can't carry a tune to save my life. But I wanted to see how you'd react if I said that was my career goal."

"Oh my God, you had me so worried." He chugged the rest of his beer. "I think I need to get myself another Corona. You want anything?"

"Maybe a glass of the red sangria."

"Okay," he said. "You sure? Anything else?"

"And maybe that tres leches cake they were telling us about."

"I thought you said you weren't doing sweets right now," he said with a teasing expression on his face.

"Well, I changed my mind. Because if that cake is anything as delicious as these tacos, I cannot resist."

"Okay, and do you want any more tacos?"

I looked down, and I still had one more taco on the plate. "No, I'm..." I paused and looked up at him. His eyes were glittering down at me. "Okay, fine.

Two more carne asada tacos with just the cilantro, onion, and lime."

"Wow, you're a New Yorker already."

"I know," I said. "Maybe I should move to Mexico. I didn't realize I would love the food this much."

"Girl, you cannot live on tacos alone," he said, shaking his head.

"How do you know? I might be able to live on tacos, beans, and rice."

"You cannot live on tacos, beans, and rice alone. Plus, you don't have money to buy that every day."

"I could make it," I said. "Or I can marry a man who could make it for me."

"So that's your standard for marriage?" he asked, his lips twitching.

"What?"

"A man who can make you tacos, beans, and rice?"

"I mean, I have other qualifications that I look for," I said, rolling my eyes at him.

"Oh really? Well, this I'd like to know."

"Why?" I said. "What do you care?" I took another bite of my taco and then finished my glass of water. He was still standing there looking at me. "What are you looking at?"

"Just admiring how much you enjoy your food."

"Oliver, that's creepy."

"I know," he said. "But you've missed out on years of me being creepy. I have to catch up."

"Uh-huh," I said. "Well, just don't watch me when I sleep, okay?"

"I don't think I'd do that," he said, shaking his head, but there was a weird silence between us as we gazed at each other. His eyes were on my lips, and my eyes were on his face. "Why would I want to watch you sleep?" he asked, finally. "Anyway, I'll be back. Let me go and get the stuff."

I watched as he walked away, and I could hear my heart beating in my ears. I wondered if it was so loud that everyone in the restaurant could hear me. I looked around. I hadn't even paid attention to anyone since we'd gotten here. Which was unusual for me because I love to people watch. My phone beeped, and I saw that Alice had texted me. I pulled my phone out and stared at her message.

"Hey, what's going on? Call me ASAP. I want to know all the tea."

I started laughing as I shook my head. I quickly fired back. **"Just having tacos with Oliver. I'll call you as soon as I can. Miss you."** I could see that she was typing back a response. But Oliver was headed back toward the table, so I put my phone back in my handbag.

"Who was that?" he asked, nodding toward my handbag.

"Just Alice."

"Ah, she's checking up on you. I bet she must miss you."

"I miss her too."

"This is the longest you guys have gone without seeing each other?"

"No. When she went to Europe for two weeks, we didn't see each other then."

"Oh, two whole weeks. What are you going to do without each other?"

"I don't know." I sighed. "It's going to be hard. She's like my sister. And well, I really wanted to start this adventure and journey with her."

"I know," he said. "When I moved to New York with Foster, I wasn't sure..."

"Sorry, what?" I asked him curiously. Was he about to admit that he wasn't the strong man he portrayed?

"I mean, when I moved to New York with your brother, Foster. I was really happy to have someone to explore the city with. And he made new friends, and I made new friends, and some of them came together. It's a really cool bonding experience to have your best friend in the same town as you."

"I know, so I really hope Alice can come soon. That's why I have to get a job as soon as possible."

"So you don't just want to freeload on our couch?"

"No, I don't, Oliver. And that's not even funny."

"I'm just teasing you, Rosalie, you know that. So what are your real options? And please don't say that you're going to be a tap dancer or a ballet dancer because we both know..."

"I know," I cut him off. "I can't dance. I can't sing. I was thinking maybe I'd try to get a job as a librarian or at a coffee shop. I don't know."

"Hmm," he said. "Well, we should really think about this."

"What do you mean *we* should think about this?"

"I'd like to help you figure out what you want to do. Remember when we were younger, I always used to try to help you troubleshoot and fix your problems."

"Oliver, that was problems like, should I have two cookies or one? Or should I play soccer or basketball? Or should I wear a black blouse or a white blouse? It wasn't, what am I going to do with the rest of my life?" I stared at him, and all of a sudden, I realized that I had absolutely no clue where I was going in life. My lower lip trembled, and I stared up at him. "I just can't believe that I'm twenty-two years old, and I have absolutely no clue what's next."

"Don't look at it like that," he said, reaching over and squeezing my hand. He paused for a couple of seconds as I pulled my hand away from him. His warm skin against mine had almost electrocuted me.

I couldn't just sit there, letting him touch me, feeling the way that I did. "Look at it," he continued, "as an opportunity to figure out what you really love, what you really want to do. And then go for your passion. This is probably the only time you'll have this opportunity in your life."

"You think?" I said.

"I mean, I don't know." He shrugged. "But this is a great time to figure that out because it's really hard once you have a job and you're making money to leave it, to figure out the unknown."

I stared at him for a few seconds, wondering if he was talking about himself. "Do you not like being an attorney?"

"It's fine," he said. "Is it what I dreamed about doing when I was younger? No. Does it fulfill me a hundred percent? No. Does it pay me shit tons of money? Yeah. But you, Rosalie, you're special. You need to figure out what you want to do that will make you happy. And not think about the money, and not think about anything else. And I want to help you find that."

"Thanks. That's really nice of you, Oliver," I said, and I meant it. I was surprised at how heartfelt his words were and how much they really did mean to me. "I guess we can have a conversation or something in the coming weeks while I try to figure it out."

"Sure," he said. "Whenever you're ready." He smiled. "And didn't you say you had a date tonight or something?"

I stared at him and rolled my eyes. "Well, I've got to download the apps and start swiping first." Part of me wanted to set up a date for the night just to show him that I had options.

He started laughing then. "Oh, Rosalie, you make me laugh."

"Well, at least I'm making someone laugh," I said and then looked away from him because the intensity in his gaze was starting to make me feel nervous. The last thing I needed was to feel close to him again. I didn't want us to start bonding and enjoying each other's company. I didn't need to fall for this man yet again.

Chapter 5

ROSALIE

"Welcome to my casa." Oliver opened the front door to the apartment. "Or rather, our casa."

"Thanks." I stepped inside and looked around in awe. I was taken aback by how large it was. Immediately to the right was a large open-plan kitchen. I dropped my bags on the ground and walked over to the giant marble island. "Wow, this is lush." I looked behind me at the stainless steel french doors of the fridge, the top-of-the-line oven range, and the twenty-four-bottle herb-and-spice rack attached to the wall. "Wow." I saw Oliver grinning at me, but I didn't care. I couldn't believe my brother and his best friend had such a nice place. I turned around and walked into the living room. A huge plush white sectional was pushed up against an exposed brick wall. On the other side was a huge TV mounted on the wall with speakers on either side. I walked past the couch toward the sliding doors, opened them, and stepped out onto a balcony. My jaw dropped as I looked over at Central Park. "Did you or my brother win the lottery and not tell me?" I turned to look back at Oliver, and he just laughed. He joined me on the balcony and stared out at the view.

"I forgot how beautiful the view was." He stepped forward. "I don't get to spend much time out here."

"Too busy on dates?" I asked him, wanting to know more about his love life.

"Too busy at work." He chuckled and pressed his lips together as I raised an eyebrow. "I'm not saying I don't date...I'm not a monk."

"So no girlfriend?" I asked casually, pretending I didn't care about the answer.

"Who wants to know?" He peered into my eyes, and I blushed as I turned around and walked back into the apartment.

"Where's the restroom, please?" I looked around and saw several doors, but I had no idea which one to go into.

"You can use the one on the far left." He

nodded, and I smiled my thanks as I made my way to the door. I opened it, stepped in, and closed it behind me quickly. I gazed around, my jaw dropping as I noticed the pedestal bathtub, separate shower, toilet, and bidet. "A frigging bidet...what is this place?" I mumbled under my breath as I walked toward the sink to wash my hands. I stared at my reflection in the mirror and made some faces at myself. I was feeling out of my element and totally overwhelmed. This apartment was amazing, Oliver was acting friendly and nice, and I had no idea how I was going to keep him at a distance. We'd already fallen into our old pattern, and it was so comfortable. He was teasing and slightly condescending, and I was bratty and grateful. I didn't want that to be our dynamic anymore. I was no longer teenage Rosalie, the impressionable kid who just wanted to be loved. I was adult Rosalie now, the woman who demanded respect as an equal. Just because I was trying to find my way in life didn't mean I needed to be treated like a little child.

"You've got this, Rosalie. Believe in yourself." I pointed at my reflection and squared my shoulders. I could feel a rumbling in my stomach, and my head was starting to hurt. I was beginning to feel anxious and overwhelmed, and it had nothing to do with Oliver. I was out of my comfort zone. I missed my bedroom at home, I missed Alice, I missed my parents, I missed the world I knew. I was able to navigate that world easily. And while it wasn't exciting, it was comfortable. "I wanna go home." I pressed my lips together, and I could feel my eyes welling up. I wanted my mom to put her arms around me and tell me everything was going to be okay. I took a couple of deep breaths and shook my hands out. I pulled my lip gloss out of my handbag, reapplied it, and smiled at my reflection. I walked over to the toilet, flushed it, and then counted to five before leaving the bathroom.

Oliver was in the kitchen, standing in front of the fridge, and he turned to look at me as I walked toward him. "You want anything?" he asked, holding up a beer, and I shook my head. "You okay?" He frowned as he opened his beer and came toward me.

"I'm fine. Why?"

"You look a little low." He took a sip of his beer. "You sure everything is okay?"

"I'm good. Maybe a little tired, I guess." I shrugged and looked away from him.

"It's more than that." He walked closer to me, and I felt him stopping in front of me. "Rosalie, what's wrong?" The softness of his voice made my heart jump, and then I felt his fingers on my face, lifting my chin up so I looked into his eyes.

"Nothing," I said quickly, blinking rapidly.

"Don't lie to me," he said. His eyes looked super

blue in the light, and I swallowed hard at the intensity of the gaze. "We may not have seen each other in years, but I still know your every expression and emotion."

"No, you don't," I said quickly, feeling embarrassed that he could read me so easily.

"You forget I've known you since you were little, Rosalie. What is it? You can tell me."

"I just feel like I made a mistake moving here," I admitted. "I don't know the city. I have no friends here. No job. No prospects. No money. I feel out of my—"

"Rosalie, you do not have no friends here." He shook his head, frowning. "I'm your friend. Foster is your—"

"Foster is my brother, and you're his best friend." I sighed. "It's not the same." He pressed his lips together at my words and dropped his fingers from my face.

"Rosalie, I'm more than just your brother's best friend. I'm your friend as well," he said earnestly, and I could hear the hurt in his voice.

I stared up at him in surprise, slightly taken aback. "Really? You consider yourself my friend?"

"Yes," he said, "and I would hope that even if I wasn't best friends with your brother, that we would..." He paused then. "I don't know. Have some sort of relationship, meaningful interaction, whatever you want to call it."

My heart thudded at his words, and a part of me didn't even believe what he was saying. "Really? You'd be friends with someone like me, a nobody?"

"You're not a nobody, Rosalie. You've never been a nobody. You're the most effervescent, bright, happy, warm-spirited person I've ever been around. You and Alice light up a room when you're together. You're fun, and I enjoy being in your company. You don't think I would've said yes to Foster about having you stay if I really didn't enjoy being around you, did you?"

"I don't know." I shrugged as I mumbled, "Maybe."

"No. I pay far too much rent to just put up with someone I don't like."

"So you're saying you like me?"

"I'm saying I like you, Rosalie. You're fun. And I know it's difficult being in a brand-new city, and it's scary, and you feel like you don't have anyone, but you have me. And like I told you earlier, I'll help you figure out what you want to do. I'll help you look for jobs. I'll help you go over your résumé. Whatever you need."

"Why are you being so nice to me?" I said, blinking at him with surprise in my voice.

"Maybe because I don't want you to go."

"But I just got here. What do you care?"

"Maybe I wasn't lying when I said I missed you. Maybe I've been waiting for this day for the past couple of years."

"Oh," I said, staring at him, wanting to question him more and figure out exactly what that meant. Why was he being so nice to me? Why was he telling me he'd missed me? He had grown in maturity. The last time I'd known and seen Oliver, he'd been an obnoxious, cocky prick. Yeah, he'd always been fun, and he'd always been handsome, but he'd gotten so bigheaded, and he turned into someone I hadn't recognized. Yet I was seeing a difference in him. He was someone who I could really like, someone who reminded me of all the reasons I'd fallen for him as a teenager. "You've changed, Oliver."

"Funny you say that," he said with a small smile. "I was about to say that about you as well."

I ran my hands through my long hair and blinked, not knowing what else to say. "Thanks. You've made me feel better. I should go and set up my bed now," I said, looking at the couch. "It does look comfortable."

"Foster said you could sleep in his room while he's out of town if you want."

"No," I said, shaking my head. "I don't want to get accustomed to his bed when I'll be sleeping on the couch most of the time. I mean, if he was a good big brother, he would've offered me his bedroom for—"

Oliver started laughing. "Don't push your luck, Rosalie. You know he loves you, but he's not going to give up his bedroom."

"I know. I already had this conversation with him," I said, sticking my tongue out at him.

He laughed at my childish antic, and my heart warmed as his eyes crinkled. "Come on. I'll show you to the couch. Maybe we can watch a movie."

"Are you sure?" I said. "You don't have plans for tonight?"

"I'm good," he said. "And you know what? I'll even let you choose. Just no—"

"What?" I interrupted him. "You can't say you're going to let me choose and then give me a caveat."

"You don't know what I was going to say."

"You were going to say no rom-coms." I raised an eyebrow at him. "Am I right, or am I right?"

He started laughing. "Fine. You were right. You know I'm not really into rom-coms."

"I know, but they're fun sometimes."

"Well, let's see."

We walked over to the couch, and I sat down and leaned back. The cushions were firm yet soft enough to be comfortable. "This feels good so far," I said, smiling.

Oliver handed me a remote control, and I

pressed it and turned the TV on. "Thanks," I said. "Do you have Netflix?"

"We have everything." He chuckled. "Netflix, Hulu, HBO Max, and cable."

"But do you have Disney Plus?"

"I didn't finish." He grinned. "We have Disney Plus and Apple and—"

"Whoa, you really do have all the channels," I said, scrolling through.

"We do. You know your brother loves TV, so..."

"What? You don't like TV anymore?" I said. "For years, you and Foster talked about being TV screenwriters and showrunners. I remember listening outside your room as you talked about the different TV shows you were going to make."

"True. I really did think I would go into TV," he said. "Huh. I'd almost forgotten about that."

"So why didn't you?"

"I guess my parents weren't really enthused by the idea when I told them I wanted to study TV screenwriting and producing. So I studied politics and then went to law school."

"I heard you went to Harvard," I said.

"Yeah, well, you know." He gave me a cocky wink.

"What?" I said, laughing.

"Smart men usually do go to Harvard."

"Oh my gosh, Oliver," I said, grabbing a pillow

and hitting him in the shoulder. "You're so full of yourself."

"What? How am I full of myself? It's true, right?"

"Fine. Yes. Congratulations on going to Harvard and graduating suma cum laude. Oh my gosh. Oliver?"

"What?" he said, giving me a grin. "Would you rather I flunked out and worked at a crappy-ass job and made no money and lived off your brother?"

"You mean like me?" I said, giggling.

"Well, you didn't flunk out of college, right?"

"No, but I am living off him. In fact, I only have nine hundred and ninety dollars in my bank account and no other money coming in." I bit on my lower lip. "I'm nervous, Oliver. I don't want to go home with my tail between my legs."

"Don't worry. You live here for free." He grinned. "Plus, I'm sure you can eat here for free, too."

"Um, I doubt Foster is going to—"

"Don't worry," he said softly. "I got you for meals."

"No, no, no. You can't do that, Oliver. You can't."

"I can, and I will. You'll pay me back."

"I mean, I wouldn't count on it. Whatever job I do get, I'm not sure how much—"

"I didn't say it had to be money," he said,

winking at me, and I felt my entire body growing warm. I didn't even ask him to explain what he was talking about. Was he flirting with me? Was this his way of coming on to me?

"Have you decided what you want to watch?" He interrupted my thoughts, and I shook my head.

"Um, what about... Let's see what movies are on Netflix," I mumbled quickly as I pressed the button to take me to Netflix.

"Okay," he said, leaning back. "You want popcorn or anything?"

"I wouldn't say no, actually. And maybe some wine if you have some."

"Okay. I thought you didn't want anything to drink."

"Well, I'm feeling better now, so..."

"Okay," he said and jumped off the couch. "I'm going to go to the kitchen, get some wine, and make some popcorn. And I'm just going to change out of this suit into something more comfortable."

"Oh, good idea. Maybe I'll brush my teeth and get ready for bed, just in case I fall asleep watching the movie."

"If you'd rather just sleep instead of watching a movie, we don't have to," he said quickly.

"I don't want to sleep yet. It's fine, Oliver. I'm grateful for the company. Plus, I'm totally choosing a rom-com, so I can't wait to make you watch it with me."

"Very nice of you to treat me this way." He started laughing. "Oh well. It's your first night here. Whatever you want."

"Wow. This does not sound like the Oliver I've known all these years."

"Yeah, well, don't get used to it, Rosalie. I'm being good tonight, but who knows what I'll be like tomorrow."

"Oh, what are you going to do if I try to put a rom-com on tomorrow?" I said, laughing.

"Ah, wouldn't you like to know?" He winked at me, and I watched as he started unbuttoning his shirt. I swallowed hard as I stared at the brief expanse of naked skin. Shit. I was in trouble. Big, big trouble.

Chapter 6

Oliver

I quickly took my shirt off and unbuckled my pants as I got ready to watch the movie with Rosalie. I thought back to the conversation I'd just had with her, and my heart melted for her. I'd seen a vulnerability in her eyes that I hadn't seen since she was ten years old and her pet dog had died. I felt bad that she was in such a stressed-out place in her life, but I knew that it would pass the longer she stayed in New York City and the more she got to know her surroundings. Once she had a job and made new friends, she'd be having the time of her life and soon forget how upset she'd felt tonight. I sat on the edge of my bed as I took off my shoes, and I thought about how she'd smiled at me as we debated back and forth on whether to watch a rom-com. Her brown eyes had been laughing at me, and I'd felt the familiar tug of warmth and happiness as she gazed at me.

And then there was the way she played with her hair, twirling, pulling, and teasing me. She'd grown up to be a beautiful woman, tantalizing, sexy, a vixen almost. And I knew I couldn't let her or Foster know how I felt. I pulled down my pants and looked around for a pair of shorts and a T-shirt. Normally, I walked around in just my boxers, but I didn't want Rosalie to be uncomfortable with me wearing next to nothing. I wondered what she was going to wear to bed. My thoughts immediately went to an image of her in a silky black lacy negligee, and then I groaned, knowing full well there was no way she would wear something like that.

"Are you coming, Oliver?" She banged on my door, and I laughed at her eagerness.

"I'm coming. What's the rush?"

"I want to watch this movie, and I want to make sure I see the end of it before it ends."

"What do you mean you want to see the end of it before it ends?" I asked, walking out the door. I pulled on my T-shirt, and she stared at me wide-eyed as I grinned.

"I mean, I want to see the end of the movie before I fall asleep."

"What movie are we watching?" I asked her curiously.

"*Just Go With It*, it's with Adam Sandler and Jennifer Aniston."

I groaned, "That sounds like a rom-com and not a good one either."

"What do you mean? It sounds amazing. Alice told me about it years ago. She said it was really good, but I never got to see it, so now we can."

"Since when is Adam Sandler in good rom-coms?" I raised an eyebrow. "I mean, he was in *The Waterboy*, and that was fun, but that wasn't really a rom-com."

"He was in *50 First Dates*," she said, glaring at me. "That was the most amazing movie. I loved him, and I loved Drew Barrymore, and it was so romantic. Oh, I wish I could go—."

"You wish you could go on fifty first dates with someone?" I asked her, raising an eyebrow.

"No, Oliver, that's not what I was going to say, but anyway, you wouldn't understand."

"What wouldn't I understand?" I asked her curiously.

"You wouldn't understand what it is to be in a romantic relationship and to woo a woman."

"You don't think I know how to woo a woman?"

"I'm sure you know how to get a woman into bed."

"And you don't think that I have to woo her before I get her into bed?"

"I don't know." She shrugged.

"So you think I just go up to them and say, 'Hey, would you like to come to bed with me'?"

"Maybe you're good looking enough." She made a face, and I couldn't stop the rush of pleasure that compliment gave me.

"Oh," I said, grinning. "So you think I'm good looking?"

"Where's the wine?" she asked, blushing and turning away from me.

"You didn't answer my question, Rosalie."

"What's the question, Oliver?"

"Do you think that I'm good looking enough to—"

"Not having this conversation. Let's watch the movie."

She ran toward the couch, and I laughed as I followed her. I opened the bottle of wine and poured a glass for her and then a glass for me.

"Where's the popcorn?" she asked, looking around. I put my glass down on the table and walked back to the kitchen. "Let me put it in the microwave. I forgot. Do you want butter on it?"

"Of course," she called out. "Who doesn't want butter on popcorn?"

"I know some girls who are trying to watch their weight don't like butter."

"Are you trying to tell me something?" she asked in a deadly voice.

I realized I'd messed up. "No, I was just asking if..."

"Just hurry up," she said coldly.

The microwave beeped, alerting me to the fact that the popcorn was done, and I melted some butter and poured it over. I walked back to the living room and sat next to her on the couch and handed her the popcorn bowl. She dipped her fingers into it and grabbed a couple of kernels and munched on it.

"Not bad," she said. "Not bad."

"Are you mad at me? Because I asked if you wanted butter?"

"No," she said, glancing at me with a fire in her eyes I hadn't seen before.

"Are you sure? Because you certainly seem like you're mad."

"I just don't think that only fat people eat popcorn with butter."

"I don't think I said that, did I?"

"Well, that's what it seemed like to me."

"I don't—"

"Whatever. I'm watching the movie now."

She pressed a button, and the credits on the screen started. I stared at her for a couple of seconds, wondering exactly what I'd done to piss her off. We'd just been in such a great place not less than ten minutes ago, and now she was giving me the cold shoulder. I reached over and grabbed some popcorn, and our fingers touched for a couple of seconds. She yanked her hand away quickly as if I'd burned her. I glanced over at her face, and she turned to look at me. Her eyes narrowed. "Is everything okay, Rosalie?"

"Oh my gosh. Are you going to ask me that every single day? It's annoying," she snapped.

"What? I was just—"

"Stop asking me if everything's okay. If everything's not okay, I'll tell you. Okay."

"Okay." I pressed my lips together and shook my head. Why was it that women were so emotional and so temperamental? It was so hard for me to keep up. I'd never lived with a woman before, and I wasn't sure how I would like it. Rosalie took a couple of sips of her wine and relaxed back into the couch.

"And this is really good. Thank you."

She looked at me and gave me a small smile. "Okay. I'm glad you like it." I wasn't sure if my comment would get her started again, and she let out a sigh.

"I'm sorry, Oliver. I didn't mean to get all pissed off. I overreacted slightly."

"You don't say," I said, smirking.

"Don't get me started again, Oliver."

I held my hands up. "I'm sorry. I didn't mean to."

"Okay," she said, "well, thank you for being there for me today and thank you for picking me up at the airport, and thank you for letting me stay, and thank you for making popcorn and opening this amazing bottle of wine, and watching this movie with me. It really means a lot."

"You're welcome," I said. I stared at her lips, and all I wanted to do at that moment was lean forward and kiss her. But I knew that I couldn't. "So we are going to watch Adam Sandler get all these hot women?" I said, laughing as I leaned back on the couch and stared at Jennifer Aniston on the screen in a long white lab coat. "Don't tell me she's a doctor."

"No, she just works in his office." She giggled next to me.

"Okay, because that's even more believable."

"Oliver, don't ruin the movie."

"I'm sorry. I'm just saying, is it——"

"Oliver."

"Okay," I pressed my lips together and tried not to laugh as I watched the screen. I put my hand back into the popcorn bowl and grabbed some popcorn to munch on. I wasn't really paying attention to the movie. Instead, I was looking at Rosalie's legs on the couch. I'd noticed that she was wearing a pair of boy shorts, and they were riding up higher and higher. Every time she moved or laughed, the thin material moved up her thighs. Her long tan legs looked delectable, and I was having a hard time looking away from her silky smooth skin. I wanted to touch her and see how she would react if I slid my fingers up and down her legs and caressed her.

"Oh my gosh. Can you believe that?" Rosalie said, interrupting my dirty thoughts.

"Sorry, what?" Blinking, I looked up at her, wondering if she'd noticed me checking her out.

"I said, can you believe that Brooklyn Decker wants him now? Like both of these gorgeous women want to be with him? Like, yeah right?"

"Yeah, that's what I was thinking," I said, having no idea what she was talking about.

"Uh-huh," she said, staring at me. "Are you okay, Oliver? You look kind of dazed and confused."

"I'm fine," I said, blinking, but I wasn't. She'd moved, and I could see that she wasn't wearing a bra under her T-shirt, and it was making me feel some sort of way. I shifted slightly on the couch as I felt myself growing hard. *Fuck it*, I thought to myself. This was the last thing I needed.

"What is going on?" Reaching over, Rosalie

touched me on the shoulder and shifted slightly against me.

"Sorry, what?" I blinked as I glanced at her.

"I said, what is going on? Now Brooklyn Decker just slept with him on the beach."

"Yeah." I stifled a groan. "Sorry, I wasn't paying that much attention to the movie."

"It's okay, Oliver," she said softly. She snuggled next to me, and her head was now on my shoulder. "Do you mind?"

I looked down at her and shook my head. "Of course not." She beamed at me sleepily and yawned slightly.

"Thanks, Oliver. You're the best." She yawned again. "Oh no, I hope I'm not falling asleep."

"Are you tired, Rosalie? I can go to bed if you're falling asleep."

"I'm not tired." She yawned as her eyes gazed up at me, her lips begging to be kissed. "I'm watching the—"

I couldn't stop myself from leaning down and pressing my lips against hers. Her eyes widened as she kissed me back, and I shifted her body so she was now facing me. My hand ran down her thigh, and she shivered slightly at my touch. I grabbed her face and kissed her passionately, my tongue slipping into her mouth. She reached up and touched the side of my face softly before her fingers made their way into my hair. My right hand slipped up her T-shirt, and my fingers lightly pressed against her nipple. She gasped as she shifted against me, and I moved back into the cushions. I lifted her slightly so she was on my lap, and she moved her hips so that her sweet spot pressed against my hardness. I groaned against her lips as she gyrated on my lap, and she pulled back slightly and grinned.

"Is that a baton, or are you just happy to see me?" she asked with a teasing, seductive glance, and I pulled her back toward me so I could kiss her again. My hands ran up and down her bare back, and I was about to pull her top off when she reached down and rubbed my cock through my shorts. I grunted and closed my eyes at her touch. Fuck, this was going too fast. I knew if we kept it up, I would have her on her back in my bed within minutes. And as much as I wanted to be inside her, I knew I couldn't do it. No matter how badly we both wanted it. Grabbing her hips, I shifted her off my lap and kissed her firmly one more time before pulling away.

"We should watch the movie," My voice sounded low as I tried to ignore the blood rushing through me.

"Okay." She nodded, looking slightly dazed as she rubbed her lips. "I'm not sure what just happened," she said, glancing at me. And all I could do was stare back at her because I had no clue what had happened either. It had felt nice. It had felt right. And as I sat there gazing at her legs and feeling the warmth of her body against mine, I knew that the last thing I needed was to feel attracted to Rosalie because I didn't want her brother to kill me. And if I slept with her, I would definitely find myself in an early grave.

Chapter 7

ROSALIE

My body was tingling as I opened my eyes. I sat up slowly and looked around the apartment to see if Oliver was in the kitchen. My brain was buzzing from the night before. I couldn't believe that Oliver had kissed me, and I couldn't believe that I'd responded, but when I'd felt his soft lips pressing against mine, I hadn't been able to resist. I reached down and grabbed my phone and quickly called Alice. There was no way that I could start the day without telling her what happened and trying to figure out what it meant.

. . .

osalie: Are you up?? Wake up?

Alice: What's going on?

Rosalie: You will not believe what happened to me last night?

Alice: OMG, what? Call me!

Rosalie: I can't call you right now!

Alice: Why not? Is your phone broken?

Rosalie: The walls have ears...

Alice: What?

Rosalie: Oliver is still at home. I can hear him in the shower.

Alice: Okay and?

Rosalie: We KISSED last night!

Alice: WHAT??? NO WAY!! Oops, sorry for caps.

Rosalie: No worries. :)

Alice: So you and Oliver kissed. How was it?

Rosalie: Amazing. His lips, his hands...ugh...I nearly came...

Alice: Haha, oh Rosalie.

Rosalie: Sorry for TMI, but it felt amazing. His fingers were under my shirt, playing with my breasts, and I felt like my entire body was on fire.

Alice: Shit, hot!

Rosalie: I just don't know what it means.

Alice: Did you sleep with him?

Rosalie: No, he stopped the kissing so we could watch the movie, and then he went to his own bed.

Alice: You didn't sneak in to join him?

Rosalie: No, of course not! I can't even believe we kissed. Girl, he was hard...

Alice: Oh shit. Do you think he's going to be your first?

Rosalie: I don't know...maybe...I'm still mad at him

Alice: But you're still attracted to him, yeah?

Rosalie: Girl, I wanted to pull his cock out and suck it like a lollipop last night, so yeah.

Alice: OMG, Rosalie! HAHA.

Rosalie: I know...also, he doesn't know I'm a virgin. I can just imagine how that conversation would go.

Alice: Are you going to tell him?

Rosalie: We'll see. If it gets to that point, hehe. It's not like I can say, Oliver wanna be my first, my brother never has to find out.

Alice: Lmao, true. Could you imagine banging Oliver, and your brother comes walking through the door?

Rosalie: No, omg, I would die.

· · ·

"*W*hat's so funny?" Oliver's deep voice was right next to me, and I looked up from my phone, the laughter dying on my lips as I stared at him. My throat went dry. Oliver was standing there in just a towel, his chest dripping wet.

"Oh." I swallowed hard as I stared at his muscles. "Morning."

"Good morning, Rosalie." His blue-gray eyes teased me as they took in my messy hair and rumpled clothes. "Laughing at something on your phone?"

"I was just texting with Alice...um, what were you doing?" I wanted to hit myself in the face for my stupid question.

"Just took a shower." He cocked his head to the side and gave me a lazy smile. "Getting ready for work."

"Cool, cool." I nodded. "You're getting the floors wet. Maybe you should go into your room and change?"

"It's my apartment." He grinned as he came and sat next me. I was about to respond when I felt his lips close to my ears, whispering, "If you weren't my best friend's sister, I would ruin you right now."

I could feel myself blushing, and all I wanted to say in response was, "I wish you would." But I knew I couldn't.

"What, what did you say?" I licked my lips nervously.

"I said, if you weren't my best friend's sister, I would ruin that T-shirt you're wearing right now." He grinned as he nodded toward my Green Day top. "That band sucks."

"Uh, okay." I blinked at him for a few seconds. Had I heard him right the first time? I wasn't sure. His eyes looked at me intently. "Don't you have to get ready for work?"

"I do." He nodded as he gazed at me. "So your brother was telling me that I should occupy your time so that you..." Oliver paused and smirked. I stared at the expression on his face, and I kept my lips in the same position. I didn't want to ask him what he was going to say because I had a feeling it would irritate me. "Don't you want to know what your brother said?"

"Nope," I said, shaking my head and leaning back into the couch. "I can occupy my own time, thank you. I have Netflix and Hulu, and..." I looked away from him, just so he couldn't see me blushing. I was thinking that I had thoughts of his sexy body to occupy my time as well. My stomach did somersaults, and I tried not to let my limbs tremble. Why was Oliver so good looking, and why was he such a tease? He was going to be the death of me. Or at least, he was going to be the death of himself because if he kept teasing me and getting on my nerves, I was going to kill him. And then, my life would really be in shambles.

"So do you want to go out tonight?" he said, running his hands through his short, dark hair. I looked into his blue-gray eyes, confused.

"What do you mean?"

"I mean, would you like to go out with me tonight? There's an event." He paused. "Well, I'd like to take you to the Ritz."

"The Ritz?" My eyebrows rose. "Like the Ritz Hotel?" I couldn't believe my ears. Was he suggesting what I thought he was suggesting?

"Yeah," he said silkily. He leaned forward, his eyes gazing into mine. "The Ritz Hotel. I hope you have something nice to wear."

"Um, I..." I licked my lips nervously. Was this really happening? Was he really going to take me to the Ritz Hotel? Was I about to lose my virginity sooner than I thought?

"Let's just do it," he said, standing up with a smile. "I think it will be an amazing night." He looked down at me. "Wear your nicest dress," he said.

"But are you sure? I mean..." I cleared my throat as I stared at his pecs.

"Hey, I mean, if you don't want to..." He shrugged. He looked away for a second and then back at me. "But I think you want this as badly as I do." I swallowed hard and nodded.

"I mean, I hate to admit it, but you're right."

"Good," he said, with a devious little smile. There was a glint in his eyes that I hadn't seen before in my life, and it made me shudder. If he looked at me that way when we were in the bed together, then I would absolutely lose my mind.

"So I guess we're going to the Ritz tonight," I said, giggling.

"Yeah. Beats Hulu and Netflix, right?"

"Sure does." I jumped up. "I'm going to go and shower."

"Okay, I should get ready for work anyway," he said as he stood as well. He looked at me for a couple of seconds. "I'm glad we're on the same page here, Rosalie."

"Me too, Oliver."

"Good," he said. "I'll see you later." I watched as he walked back to his room and then I grabbed my phone. I called the numbers quickly. I hoped Alice was sitting down because she was not going to believe what was happening.

"Hey, what's going on?" she asked breathlessly. "You didn't respond to my last few texts."

"Oliver was talking to me."

"Oh shit...and?"

"You will not believe what just happened." I

giggled into the phone.

"Oh my God, you just gave him a blow job."

"No, I didn't give him a blow job, Alice."

"He went down on you." She gasped, and I giggled.

"He didn't go down on me in five minutes, Alice."

"What happened? Just tell me."

"He just invited me out."

"He what? On a date?"

"I don't know if it's a date so much as a... Well, you know."

"No, what?"

"Like, a hookup."

"He invited you out for a hookup. What?"

"Yeah, he said he wants to take me to The Ritz-Carlton and to wear a dress. He said a nice dress, but I'm pretty sure he meant sexy, and he gave me that look that told me he was undressing me with his eyes. I mean, I know we have sexual chemistry even though I can't stand him."

"Why doesn't he just do you in the apartment?" Alice sounded confused.

"I don't know. Maybe he's scared my brother will find out. Maybe he wants it to just be a one-time thing. There's obviously something between us. Did I tell you that I think he told me he was going to ruin me this morning?"

"What?" she shrieked. "What does that mean?"

"I don't know, but I want to find out."

"So you're going?"

"Yes, I'm going. It's just going to be a one-time thing, and then I'll be able to get him out of my mind."

"I don't know. Rosalie. That sounds..."

"Sounds what?"

"I mean, he's a jerk. You didn't speak to him for years, and now you're just going to bang him?"

"Girl, I'm not just going to bang him. I'm going to give him the best bang of his life. It's going to be so good that he's going to regret that he's never going to get me again."

"Oh, Rosalie. This doesn't sound like a good idea."

"It's going to be fine. Trust me. Now, should I wear my red dress or my silver dress?"

"Hmm, did you take the little short black one?"

"Yeah, but I can't wear a bra with that."

"So?" She giggled. "Easier access for him."

"Alice, you're wicked."

"No, Rosalie, that's who you're trying to be."

"Am I making a mistake?" All of a sudden, I wondered if I was moving too fast with Oliver. "I mean, I haven't seen him in years, and now I'm going to let him deflower me?"

"You have wanted him for years, but yeah, make

him work for it, girl." Alice paused. "Maybe tease him a bit and then make him beg you."

"He's not going to beg me." I laughed. "He's Oliver James, not some high school loser like Stephan Dimam."

"True." She giggled. Stephan Dimam was a skinny guy we'd gone to high school with who thought he was the best-looking guy in school. He tried to hook up with every girl in our class, and when we all turned him down, he tried begging us all. "So you're going to..." I didn't hear the rest of her comment because I quickly put my phone next to my body when I saw Oliver exiting his room in a pinstripe navy-blue suit.

"I'm off now." He held up his hand and gave me a dazzling smile. "I'll text you and let you know what time to be ready tonight."

"Okay." I nodded. "Sounds good."

"See you later, Rosalie."

"Bye, Oliver." I watched as he walked out the front door and then pulled the phone back up to my ear. "Sorry about that, Alice."

"No worries, this is the second time today you've left me hanging, though."

"I'm sorry, this is what being around Oliver does to me."

"You love him, you want to kiss him, you want to marry him, you want to..." Alice stopped singing and started laughing. "Sorry, I just can't believe you've only been there for twenty-four hours, and you're already having the most amazing time."

"I know." I agreed with her. I felt like I'd been in town for months already. "I wish you were here, Alice."

"Me too." She sounded sad. "But maybe I can get a part-time job and save enough money to visit you."

"Foster said you're more than welcome to stay here if you do decide to visit," I said excitedly.

"He did?" Alice sounded slightly giddy. "Well, hopefully soon."

"Yay." I headed toward the kitchen. "Well, I'm going to make some coffee and get ready for the day. I'll call you later."

"Yes! Call me and let me know how your night of passion at the Ritz is..." She paused for a few seconds and then continued. "Don't do anything I wouldn't do."

"Oh well, tonight, I think I'm going to have to do many things you wouldn't do," I said with a small laugh before hanging up the phone and heading to the kitchen. I was hungry, and I needed caffeine. I smiled to myself as I looked around my new home. It was nice here, and I felt like I belonged. Maybe it would all work out amazingly after all.

Chapter 8

ROSALIE

*S*hort black dress. Check.

High, almost impossible to walk in shoes. Check.

Red, sultry lipstick. Check.

Black mascara that made my eyelashes look longer than sin. Check.

Silver shimmer eye shadow that didn't quite work. Check.

Sexy panties. Check.

Confidence boosted. Check.

Ready to get laid. Check.

Slight self-doubt. Check.

. . .

I stared at my reflection in the bathroom mirror. I looked like a frigging bombshell, and I could feel the excitement running through my body. Oliver would be home any minute to pick me up and take me on this date. Not that it was an official date, of course, but I knew. After the night we'd had last night, he wanted me. And I wanted him. Yes, I had to forget why I'd been so upset with him. But I had a plan. I would allow myself one amazing night of hot passionate sex, and then I'd blank him. I'd pretend the sex was bad and that his breath smelled of onions, and I'd wrinkle my nose if he even suggested doing it again. Because that was what he deserved. Sure, maybe he'd matured from who he had been years ago, but I hadn't forgotten how he'd hurt and humiliated me. I would never forget that.

I sprayed some of my favorite perfume in the air and walked through it, then exited the bathroom. I'd hoped that Oliver would be there waiting for me when I walked out, but he wasn't there. I'd wanted to stun him with my look. I decided to walk to the kitchen to pour myself a glass of wine while waiting for him to arrive. We still had some red left from the night before, and I poured myself a generous portion. I took a large gulp and then walked to the balcony to people watch. A woman was walking a dog, and I laughed as he pulled ahead of her, trying to sniff and pee on every lamp post she saw. Even from this distance, I could tell she was frustrated by the dog. I wanted to shout down to her that she should take him to a trainer and that would stop the pulling issue, but of course I didn't.

"What are you laughing at?" A warm deep voice sounded from right behind me, and I turned around slowly, my eyes widening as I took in his handsome sexy appearance. His pupils dilated, and a wicked smile crossed his face as his eyes moved up and down my body. "Very nice." He grinned at me, and I blushed.

"A woman was walking her dog." I pointed down toward the park. "He was trying to sniff every piece of concrete, and she was growing increasingly frustrated." I laughed. "It was like the dog was walking her."

"Aw, the tale of dog owners with dogs who've never been properly trained on how to walk in the street."

"That's exactly what I was thinking," I nodded enthusiastically, excited that he had the same thoughts as I did.

"Dogs are amazing, but you have to let them know who's boss..." Oliver bit down on his lower lip and stared at my lips. "You have to let them know who the alpha is."

"Yes, you do." I downed the rest of my wine. "You have to put them in their place."

"They have to know who's in control." He continued, taking a step toward me.

"They have to know that they can't just take something when they want it." I took a step toward him. "They have to wait until it's offered."

"If it's ever offered." His eyes were mere inches from mine now. I could feel the warmth of his breath on my trembling skin.

"Well, it will probably be offered," I said, lowering my eyelashes seductively. I pressed the palm of my hand against his chest and held it there for a couple of seconds. I could feel his body stilling at my touch and the power I felt immediately made me feel like Superwoman. Finally, I dropped my hand, looked up again, and gave him an impish smile before heading into the apartment. I could feel his eyes on my back as I walked away from him.

"So is it time for us to leave?" I said, glancing back at him. He stood there with a dazed expression on his face, and I wondered what he was thinking. I wish I had the ability to read his mind. I wish I could tell what was going on in his head and what he was feeling in his heart. If he was as turned on as I was. If he was as excited to go to the Ritz Hotel and have the most magnificent night with me as well.

"Sure," he said, walking back into the apartment

slowly. He closed the sliding door and then stood there for a couple of seconds. "So I think I'm going to change really quickly."

"Why?" I said, looking at him in his smart suit. He looked hot as hell, and I could picture him taking off every item of clothing before he made love to me.

"Don't you think this is a little formal?" He pulled off his suit jacket and draped it over his arm. Then he undid the top button of his shirt, and I had a feeling he was teasing me.

"I don't mind," I said, twirling around in my dress, letting the soft material flutter against my legs. "What do you think about what I'm wearing?" I finally stopped and placed my hands on my hips.

"Do you really have to ask that question?" he asked me, gazing at my legs. I shimmied slightly in my heels and moved my head back and forth.

"Well, I just don't know if it's too much." I laughed coquettishly and moved closer to him.

"Yes, it's too much"—he laughed—"but I don't mind." He walked up to me slowly, and I felt his eyes on my lips. I wondered if he was going to kiss me. I wanted him to. I wouldn't say no. In fact, I was tempted to reach up and put my hands around his neck and pull him down toward me. His blue-gray eyes looked amused as he stared at me.

"What are you thinking about, Rosalie?" he asked me softly.

"Wouldn't you like to know?" I said with a soft little smile.

"Yes. I very much would like to know." His voice was deep and hoarse now. I could see him swallowing as I took another step closer to him. My fingers reached up and undid the next button on his shirt.

"I was thinking that…" I paused and licked my lips as I undid another button and rubbed my fingers against the exposed chest hair.

"Continue." His voice was hoarse, his eyes dark with desire as I offered him an impish little smile.

"I was thinking that if you're going to change…" I stepped back and pulled my fingers away from his chest. "Then you should do it quickly. I'm ready to get out of here. I'm ready to go to this Ritz-Carlton."

"Okay," he said, nodding, his eyes narrowed. "I will change then."

"And maybe we can dance?" I moved my hips back and forth and started to dance seductively, but of course, my stupid heels got in the way, and I tripped on my own feet and fell forward. Oliver deftly caught me in his arms, laughter in his eyes as he helped me gather my balance.

"Perhaps." He smiled at me for a couple of

seconds and then walked past me into his room. I took a couple of deep breaths as I watched him close the door behind him. Holy shit, that had been hot. The banter that we had turned me on more than anyone else had ever turned me on before in my life. I'd had boyfriends. I'd gone to second base and even third base. I just hadn't gone all the way yet. I wasn't sure why. It wasn't like I was saving myself for marriage or anything like that. I guess I'd just been waiting for the right man. The man who made me feel sexy and wanted and turned me on more than anyone else.

If I was honest with myself, I always compared men I'd met to Oliver because even though I couldn't stand him and even though I hadn't talked to him in years, the way he made me feel was still the gold standard in any relationship. And I'd never even dated Oliver. He had just been my brother's best friend, but there was something about the way he looked at me. He had always been able to make my blood pressure rise and skin tingle.

I stood there waiting on him to come out of the room. He'd changed into a pair of black slacks and a crisp gray shirt. I stared at him, not knowing what to say. He looked handsome no matter what he was wearing.

"Ready to go?" He looked at his watch.

"I am," I said. "Are we walking or taxi or are you driving?"

"Taxi." He grinned. "I don't think tonight is a night for driving." We walked toward the door, and he grabbed my hand. "Hey, Rosalie, I wanted to say something."

"Yes, Oliver."

I looked up at him, my heart pounding. This was it. This was the moment he was going to tell me that he was so glad I was here and that he'd been waiting for this moment all his life. I was here for it. I couldn't wait.

"So..." He paused.

"Yes," I said softly.

"I just wanted to say I hope you have a good time tonight."

"I'm sure I will," I said, winking at him.

"Good because..." He cleared his throat, and I realized that whatever he wanted to say was not going to be the romantic moment I'd been waiting for my entire life.

"Don't worry, Oliver. Let's not talk about it. Let's just enjoy tonight, okay?"

"Okay," he said, glancing down at my cleavage. He bit down on his lower lip. "A part of me doesn't even want to go."

"I know," I said, giggling. "I mean, we don't really have to go. We could stay here. Though I do like to be wined and dined."

"Yeah, of course," he said cocking his head to the

side and smiling. "What lady doesn't?" We walked down the corridor toward the elevator. "So…"

"Yes?"

"What happened to your date yesterday?"

"Very funny, Oliver. You know there was no date. I was going to download a dating app and see if I could meet someone, and well, I figured it was late when we got in and—"

"And then what?" he asked, interrupting me.

"Well, you wanted to watch a movie."

"That movie was a solid five out of ten." He chuckled. "Good choice, Rosalie."

"Wow, thanks, Oliver. That really makes me feel good."

"What can I say? A rom-com with Adam Sandler and Jennifer Aniston. Hmm, not exactly my first choice."

"I heard you laughing a couple of times."

"Did you, though?" he asked, raising an eyebrow. "Was I laughing with them, or was I laughing at them?"

"Oliver, you are such an idiot sometimes."

"Hmm. Am I? I wasn't an idiot when you were kissing me, though," he said.

My eyes widened. So the conversation was about to happen. The dinging of the elevator doors alerted us to the fact that the elevator was now on our floor. We walked in, and I was about to ask him what made him kiss me when an old lady hurried into the elevator with a little Russell terrier in her arms.

"Hello," she said in a creaky old voice. She looked at Oliver. "Oh, it's you."

"Hello, Mrs. Jewel."

"How do you know my name?" she asked quickly, frowning, her purple hair bobbing as she looked back and forth between Oliver and me.

"I've met you several times." His voice was polite.

"Oh yes." She blinked, and then she looked over at me disdainfully. "Another one, I see."

Oliver pressed his lips together, but I couldn't stop myself from asking.

"Another what? Sorry, I'm not sure what you're talking about."

"You are another woman of the night that he has going to his apartment, and you're dressed in even less clothing than the last one was." There was disgust in her voice, and I tried not to react or say anything rude in response. She was my elder, after all.

"No, you misunderstand. I..." I licked my lips nervously as she glared at me.

"I mean, I know I'm of the older generation, but really, have some class." She looked at Oliver. "Why would you bring all these women back to your place? Really?" She looked at me. "And why would you demean yourself so much to date a man who has a woman every different week?"

"Sorry, what?" I frowned.

"He has a different woman every week," she repeated as if she hadn't just got the line wrong.

"Okay." I looked over at Oliver, and his eyes were laughing at me.

"Well, how are you doing, Mrs. Jewel?" he asked. "Did you—"

"Did I what?" she asked, looking at him through narrowed eyes.

"I was just going to ask if you got that new TV set up. You were—"

"I was what?" she said, interrupting him again. She looked over at me. "I tell you, in my day, gentlemen did not assume to—"

The elevator dinged again, and I stepped back, grateful when an older man and a young girl walked into the elevator.

"Hi, Oliver," he said. "Mrs. Jewel." He nodded.

The little girl waved at Oliver and made a face at Mrs. Jewel. She looked over at me curiously and then walked up to me. "Hi, I'm Maddie."

"Hi, Maddie. I'm Rosalie. Nice to meet you."

"That's my granddad."

"Hi." I nodded at him.

"Hi. Nice to meet you. I'm Richard. So Oliver, you going to any Red Sox games anytime soon?"

Oliver started laughing. "You know I'm not a Red Sox fan, Rich."

Rich started laughing. "I'm still trying to convert you."

Mrs. Jewel just stood there clutching her dog and glaring at everyone. Well, wasn't she a nice treat to have in the same building? However, I did wonder about what she'd said. Was it true? Did Oliver really have a different woman every week? And if he did, was he going to be bringing them over to the apartment? All of a sudden, I felt uneasy and unsure. I mean, it was one thing for me to hook up with him and walk away from him. It was another thing for me to hook up with him, and then him be happy that I was walking away.

I didn't think he'd been celibate. He was a gorgeous, virile man, but I didn't realize he was such a player. I chewed on my lower lip. Thoughts were scrambling in my brain, and all of a sudden, I wasn't sure I was making the right decision.

The elevator dinged again. "This is our stop, Rosalie," Oliver said. "You first. Mrs. Jewel."

"Hmm," she responded and walked out with her dog.

I watched Oliver and Rich give each other a look, and I smiled at Maddie.

"It was nice meeting you. I hope you have a fun evening."

"Oh, I will. My granddad's taking me to Shake Shack so I can get a burger and fries." She licked her lips. "Yummy, yummy. My mommy doesn't know that because she doesn't let me get burgers and fries, but..."

"Let's keep it a secret, Maddie," Richard said with a little laugh. "Kids, they'll get you in trouble all the time," he said.

I looked over at Oliver, and he nodded and smiled. "That is true."

Oliver held his arm out and gestured for me to leave the elevator first. I walked into the lobby, and he followed me. I felt his hand on the small of my back.

"So," I said, looking up at him, "is it true?"

"Is what true?" he asked, his eyes innocent as we headed toward the front of the building.

"Do you have a different woman every week? Are you a player?"

"Oh, Rosalie. Wouldn't you like to know?" His eyes were twinkling at me, and I glared at him. He was going to play that game, was he? I wasn't going to let him get the better of me.

"Not really," I said, smiling. "I don't care how many women you have. As far as I'm concerned, you could have a billion women because I'm about to have a million men."

Chapter 9

Oliver

I almost felt bad that Rosalie had the wrong impression about our upcoming evening together. I'd figured out fairly quickly that she'd thought that this was going to be some sort of romantic evening or date. I hadn't wanted to dissuade her, though now I was starting to feel a little bit guilty. We were only five minutes away from the hotel, and I wasn't quite sure how she was going to react when we walked into a work function. She was about to meet all of the partners at my law firm and several of the associates I worked with. Not exactly the same thing as going to a romantic dinner.

I wasn't sure what she thought was going to happen after that. But given the way she was dressed, well, I shifted in the back of the taxi. Fuck, I was hard already. I looked at her thighs that were glistening in the artificial light that was shining through the window. She looked over at me and gave me an impish smile.

"So there was one thing I wanted to tell you, Oliver." She chewed on her lower lip, and all I wanted to do was kiss her.

"Yeah. What is it?"

"Well, if we're going to..." She paused. "I mean, so there's one thing you should know..."

"And that is?"

"Well—"

"Don't tell me all of your million men will be there tonight?"

She froze slightly, her eyes narrowing. "That's not funny."

"What? You're the one who said you're going to have a million men. I was just joking."

"Just because you're a male ho doesn't mean I'm going to be a female ho."

"Wow. I'm quite offended. Why am I a male ho?"

"Do you or do you not have several women come into your apartment every month?"

"Doesn't mean I'm sleeping with all of them," I said, shrugging.

"Really? You're not sleeping with all of them?"

"No." Which was true. There were two I hadn't slept with, but I wasn't going to tell her that number.

I mean, I was a man, and I liked sex. What was wrong with that?

"So why do you have them over if you're not planning on sleeping with them?"

I blinked and stared at her face. "Is this what you were going to tell me or...?"

"Forget it. I don't have anything to tell you. I just hope the dinner's going to be really good."

I stared at her for a few seconds and wrinkled my nose. "Well, the hors d'oeuvres will be good."

"What do you mean the hors d'oeuvres will be good? Oh, you mean the appetizers before the meal?"

"Yeah, you could say that." I pulled my phone out and saw that Billy, one of my associates at work, had text me, asking where I was. Supposedly, one of the partners, Kramer, was looking for me. Fuck, I was going to have to schmooze as soon as I got there.

Rosalie didn't know anyone, so she wasn't going to feel the most comfortable, and if she was in a bad mood, who knew what she would say and do? Maybe I hadn't really thought this through all the way. I thought it would be fun to take her with me so she could get to know people. Maybe she'd be interested in being a legal secretary or a paralegal. I just wanted to expand her world and let her meet some new people, but maybe I shouldn't have asked her right after we'd kissed.

Fuck, I thought about the night before and the way she'd ground back and forth on top of me when we'd been on the couch. The way her lips had pressed against mine, the way her fingers had eagerly played with my hair and ran up and down my back. I wanted Rosalie Sloane very badly, but I knew I couldn't have her. I'd known that since I was a teenager when Foster had told me to never lay a hand on his sister again.

I sighed. I still thought about the kiss we'd had when we were younger. I wondered if Rosalie did. I wondered if she ever fantasized about me the way I fantasized about her. I closed my eyes and turned to look out the window. I could feel myself starting to get even more horny, just being in her presence was potent to me.

"So Oliver." She touched the side of my arm, and I turned around and looked at her.

"Yes, Rosalie," I said patiently, resisting every temptation to pull her into my arms.

"Well, I think that you owe me an apology because—"

I stared at her and tried not to start laughing. Sometimes she was absolutely ridiculous. And then, because I couldn't stop myself, I reached over and ran a finger up her leg. She froze, and her lips parted slightly.

"What are you doing?"

"This," I said before leaning over and pressing my lips against hers. She kissed me back eagerly, and I moaned as I cupped the side of her face and ran my fingers through her silky dark hair. She tasted like peppermint, and I shifted in the seat to touch more of her body. She shifted closer to me as well, and I felt her hands on my arms, squeezing my muscles.

"Like that, do you?" I said against her lips, and she started giggling as she pulled away.

"You're so full of yourself, Oliver."

"I'd rather you be full of me," I said, smiling at her, teasing her.

Her eyes widened as she realized what I said. "Really? You're going to..."

"I'm gonna what?" I said, pressing my lips against hers again.

"You're just going to say something like that and—"

"And what, Rosalie? Do you want me to pull you onto my lap and fuck you right here right now?" Her lips parted, and she started trembling. I grabbed her hips and moved her slightly so she was almost on my lap. "Do you have any panties on?" I whispered in her ear. "Have you ever fucked in the back of a taxi before?"

"Oliver," she said sharply, looking at me. My hand slid up the front of her dress and cupped her breasts.

"I could take you right here right now. Is that what you want from me? Is that what you were going to ask me?"

"Oliver," she said, pushing me away slightly and shifting back onto the seat fully. I could see that she was blushing. "I-I…"

"You what, Rosalie?"

"I think that our first time should be somewhere else." She gave me a seductive little smile, and my jaw dropped. That hadn't been what I'd been expecting her to say. I'd been expecting her to tell me off and go off on me. But this was a Rosalie that I was not used to. She was very aware of her sexuality, and she was obviously aware that I wanted her very, very badly. Yet I knew that if I acted upon it, it would complicate everything. I also knew that I couldn't risk losing her from my life again. The last few years had been horrible without her in it. And I didn't want anything to happen that would cost me that time with her again.

Chapter 10

ROSALIE

$\mathcal{I}$ stared up at Oliver in shock. I could still feel the imprint of his lips against mine. "What was that?" I gasped at him.

My mind was reeling with the words he just said. He'd asked me if I'd ever had sex in a taxi before. I hadn't because I'd never had sex in my life, but it sounded hot as hell, and I wondered if he'd ever done it.

"Oliver, can I ask—"

"We're here." The taxi screeched to a halt, and the driver looked back. "That's going to be twenty-four dollars, please."

I watched as Oliver pulled a couple of bills out

of his wallet and handed them to the driver. He opened the door and jumped out and held it open for me. "We're here," he said.

"I can see that." I blinked at him. "I can't believe you just asked me if—"

"If what?" he asked, grinning at me, his eyes teasing me.

"You know what, Oliver. I—"

"Hey, Oliver, there you are," a deep voice sounded. And I turned around. Two guys came hurrying out of the front of The Ritz-Carlton and I frowned.

"What were they talking about, here you are?"

"Hey, Billy. What's up? Mark, good to see you."

"Dude, we have been waiting on you. Kramer is with Passenger, and they are really—"

"Huh?" I stood at Oliver in confusion. "Who's Kramer? Who's Passenger? Who's Billy?"

"Rosalie, I would like you to meet my work associates. This is Billy, and this is Mark, and Kramer and Passenger are two of the partners at the law firm."

"Oh, okay." Huh. They decided to come to The Ritz-Carlton today as well? I was confused. Why were his work associates here?

"Kind of. Look, Rosalie, there was something I was meaning to tell you and—"

"Dude, they're going to be handing out the awards soon," Billy said. "Come on, let's go."

"Awards?" I looked up to Oliver, and he made a face. "What's going on?" All of a sudden, I could feel my heart sinking as it suddenly dawned on me that we weren't here for a dinner date. This wasn't a date at all. This was a work event? I walked inside and saw a sign showing where to go for check-in and then a huge placard for the law firm of Kramer, Passenger, and Associates.

"Oliver," I whispered, tugging on his shirt, "what is going on?"

"My firm had an event today and I thought it would be fun for you to meet some of my work friends." His voice faded as he saw the anger in mine.

"You led me to believe that this was a date."

"I never actually said it was a date, Rosalie. You just—"

"So you knew I thought it was a date, yet—"

"I was going to tell you. I—"

"Look at me." I stared down at my two-inch heels, my short black dress, my heaving bosoms. "I'm not dressed appropriately to me."

"It's fine," he said. "No one will notice."

"Hey, there you are." James, a tall, older man, walked out with a booming voice. "I was wondering if you were going to make it." He held his hand out. "Good to see you, son."

"Hello, Mr. Kramer. I'd like you to meet Rosalie. Rosalie, this is my boss. He's a partner at the firm."

"Hello, dear." I could see Kramer's eyes looking me up and down. "Well, now, I didn't know you were seeing anyone, Oliver."

"He's not," I said quickly. "I'm Foster's sister. Foster, his best friend and roommate."

"Foster, Foster. Does he work at the firm?"

Kramer blinked. "No, he's in finance. You met him at the golf event last year."

"Oh. Vaguely remember him," Kramer said and smiled at me. "So what brings you to New York City?" he asked in a deep voice.

"I've come to find a job and—"

"Oh, okay then. And you thought coming to this event would help you?"

"I mean, I don't know. I just graduated."

"Oh, you just graduated. Have you passed the bar yet?"

"The bar? No. I—"

"What law school did you go to?" he interrupted me.

"I didn't go to law school."

"Oh." He looked over at Oliver. "She didn't go to law school. How's she going to take the bar if she didn't go to law school?"

"I'm not taking the bar," I said loudly. I was feeling frustrated and infuriated that he wasn't paying attention to what I was saying, and I was still pissed off at Oliver, who seemed to be very amused by the conversation I was having with his boss.

"She was thinking maybe she could get a job as a legal secretary or a paralegal, maybe even a receptionist."

All of a sudden, I glared at him. "Actually, no, I wasn't. I—"

"Well, you can check with HR tomorrow. I don't know what positions we have open."

Kramer shook his head. "Now, come on. Let's go inside. They're about to start the awards, and I've heard that you might be receiving one, Oliver."

"Thank you, sir," he said with a smile. "We'll be right on the way. Would you like a drink, Rosalie, before we sit?"

"A drink?" I hissed at him after Kramer walked away from us. "What the hell is going on here? I thought I was coming out for oysters, and steak, and champagne and a night in a penthouse suite, not to your work event."

"Sorry," he said, his lips twitching. "Would you still have come if I told you it was a work event?"

"I don't know, but maybe you should have led with that instead of 'want to come to The Ritz-Carlton'?"

"So you only want to hang out with me if it includes a free dinner and a bang in a hotel room?"

My eyes narrowed as I stared at him. "You are disgusting."

"How am I disgusting? I'm just stating the facts. Did you or did you not think that you were coming to bang in a hotel room?"

"I'm not even going to answer that question, or what do you lawyers say?" I thought for a second. "I plead the Fifth."

"Okay, then." This time, he started chuckling. "You plead the Fifth. I see, but I have one question for you, Rosalie."

"Yes," I said, attitude in my voice.

"If we were going to bang, which, I mean, you know I would definitely do..." His eyes twinkled as he gazed at me, and I glared at him.

"What is your question, Oliver?" I said in a short, sharp tone.

"Well, if we were going to bang, why wouldn't I just bang you at home? Why would I spend hundreds of dollars taking you to this hotel?"

"I don't know. I thought..." I bit my lower lip and looked away.

"Tell me, Rosalie."

"I thought you didn't want to do it in the apartment because you would be nervous about what Foster would say if he found out."

"But I wouldn't be nervous about what your brother would say if he found out that we did it at a hotel? Wouldn't that make it cheaper?"

"You know what, Oliver? I am so done with you. I should have known that you hadn't changed. I should have known that you were full of shit."

"Hey, what's going on?" He held his hands up. "You're that mad that we're not banging right now?"

"I'm not mad that we're not banging. I'm mad that you didn't actually set me straight on what was going on tonight. You led me to believe..." I trailed off. I was feeling more and more embarrassed by the moment. This couldn't get any worse.

"I led you to believe what?"

"You led me to believe that something else was happening tonight." I didn't say anything else. I could feel tears welling up in my eyes. It stung because this was exactly how I'd felt all those years ago after we'd kissed, the first and only time we'd kissed when I was a teenager. He had a way of making me feel like nothing. Like I didn't matter, and I hated that he could affect me like that. I was stupid to have fallen right into his arms right away. I was stupid to think I could ignore who he was as a person just because I was so attracted to him.

"I still think you're hot, Rosalie. I know you're not mad at me because I invited you to attend a work event with me."

"It doesn't matter," I said. "I'm going to go and get something to drink." I looked around wildly. I started to make my way out of the hotel, and he grabbed my arm.

"No, you're not leaving."

"What do you mean I'm not leaving?"

"You don't know your way around the city. You don't have much money. You don't have a key to get back to the apartment and in fact, do you even know the address for the apartment?" I bit down on my lower lip. He was right. I had no clue where he and Foster lived.

"I know it's a tall building that overlooked Central Park."

"We're in New York City, Rosalie. Many buildings look over Central Park. Come on, let's go and get a drink. Sit through this award ceremony and—"

"And nothing. I don't want to sit through an awards ceremony. I don't think you deserve an award."

He shook his head then. "I don't really think I deserve an award either." He sighed. "Fine. What do you want to do?"

"What do you mean what do I want to do?"

"I messed up. I admit it. I should have told you that this was a work event. I understand why you're mad. You look hot as hell, though, and honestly, if there wasn't a work event here, then I would've loved to have taken you to dinner, wined you and dined you, and then taken you up to the penthouse suite and had my wicked way with you." He grinned. "I even have some condoms in my wallet."

"Oh, yay. I feel so happy about that." I rolled my eyes. "How romantic and sweet of you."

"Rosalie, I don't know what you want me to say."

"I don't know. Maybe you should apologize."

"Apologize for what? I'm sorry. I should have——"

"No. You should apologize for what happened five years ago."

"I wish I knew," he said. All of a sudden, his expression changed, and it was serious. "While I really want to have this conversation, I don't want to get fired from my job. Can we please have this conversation later?"

"Sure. Why not? It's always what you want."

"Rosalie, I don't even know what's going on here." He ran his hands through his hair. "Please, can we just have it in an hour? As soon as the ceremony is done, I'll take you to dinner and we can talk."

"Whatever." I rolled my eyes. "Fine."

"Hey, come on," Billy shouted from the doorway. "We're waiting on you, Oliver.

Oliver looked at me and then at Billy inside. "Are you sure we're okay, Rosalie? Are you?"

"Go."

"Are you coming?"

"No. I really don't care to go in there. I don't want to be a fucking paralegal or legal secretary." I rolled my eyes. "And I sure don't want to be your receptionist at the law firm you work at."

He let out a deep sigh. "Are you going to hate me? If I go in there and leave you?"

"No, not any more than I already hate you anyway. Just go," I pushed him. "Don't worry, I'm not going to leave the hotel. I'll just sit here and wait. I got my phone. I'll speak to Alice or something."

"Rosalie."

"Oliver, you coming?"

Oliver looked over at Billy. "Go inside. I'll be there in a second. Okay?"

"Okay. You know Kramer will be pissed."

"It's fine." Oliver blinked and then looked down at me. "What's going on, Rosalie? Why are you so mad? This isn't just about tonight. It can't be. Why did you stop talking to me all those years ago? Why..." He let out a deep sigh. "Why did this have to happen tonight?"

"I don't know why it had to happen tonight," I said, "but I'm mad at you because five years ago, you snuck into my bedroom and you spent the night with me. We kissed all night long and then..." I bit down on my lower lip. I could feel the tears starting to well up. "Well, then you broke my heart, Oliver, and I don't know if I'll ever be able to forgive you for that."

"But what did I do, Rosalie? What did I do that was so bad that you would stop talking to me for all those years?"

"You know, Oliver. You know exactly what you did."

Chapter 11

ROSALIE

"So, Rosalie, was it really that bad," Oliver asked me, a hurt in his eyes that I'd never seen before.

"What are you talking about? Was what really that bad?"

"My kiss," he said. "That's why I kissed you last night, you know."

"What? What are you talking about?"

"Five years ago, I spent the night in your bedroom, and we kissed, and then the next day you disappeared, and I never saw you again. And I just can't help but think that the kiss disappointed you so much, that..." His voice trailed off, and he shrugged.

"What? What are you talking about?"

"The reason you stopped talking to me was because you didn't like my kiss, right?"

"No. Oliver. That night was amazing to me. I thought it was the best night of my life."

"So then what?"

I took a deep breath. "Alice heard you the next day."

"She heard me what?"

"She heard you in the bedroom."

"You're going to have to clarify this for me, Rosalie. I don't know what you're talking about."

"She heard you with Foster, when Foster said, 'Would you ever want to date my sister?' You said, 'Do fat pigs fly?'" My lips trembled. "Yeah, so I was a little chubby and overweight, but do you know how much that hurt me to hear? Do you?"

"Oh my gosh, Rosalie." He looked at me shaking his head. "Please tell me you did not stop talking to me because of a conversation Alice overheard me having with your brother."

"Did you, or did you not say that?" I stared at him, the pain still inside me.

"Yeah, but not for the reason that you think."

"Okay. So you're trying to say that you didn't think that I was a fat pig."

"Of course not. Why would I have spent the night in your room, kissing you, and telling you that I wanted you to have the best experience in college and that I wanted us to date afterward?"

"I don't know. Just so you could get into my bed."
I rolled my eyes.

"No, Rosalie. I liked you, but Foster was getting suspicious, and he said to me, he'd always said to me, 'Hands off my sister.' We were best friends, and, well, I didn't want to come clean and tell him that I was falling for you, that I had feelings for you. There was an age gap, and you were on your way to college and..." He shrugged. "So I said what I thought he wanted to hear. It was just a joke. I never meant that."

"Words hurt, Oliver."

"I never intended for you to know or hear that. I never felt that way about you."

"Well, that's why I stopped talking to you. That's why I felt betrayed. That's why I hated you. I spent the night with you, the best night of my life, and then to hear that you were calling me a fat pig the next day devastated me. I felt used, I..." He grabbed my shoulders and pulled me into him.

"Rosalie, you are the most gorgeous woman I've ever met in my life. You were then. And you are now. How could you ever think that I would...?"

"You always used to tease me. You always used to say that I was a cow or a fox or an elephant."

"That was for fun. I never meant any of those things. You used to tease me too, you used to call me

Mr. T, and you used to call me the not-so-smart Brady son. Remember?"

"I did, but I was just joking, I..." I chewed on my lower lip. "So you didn't think I was a fat pig?"

"No, of course not."

"So then, you enjoyed kissing me?"

"Yes."

"And you thought the reason I stopped talking to you is because I didn't enjoy the kiss."

"Yes. Why do you think I never brought it up? Why do you think I never told Foster? I was embarrassed. I thought I had come off too eager, I thought I turned you off, or... I don't know what it was. That's why last night, I wanted to kiss you again when you seemed to be into me. I wanted to see if you would feel differently. I wanted to see if there was a spark, if..." He sighed. "I don't know. I just don't know, Rosalie. I'm devastated that you thought I would say something like that and mean it. That what I felt for you wasn't real."

"Yeah. I mean, I'm not surprised that you thought your kiss was the reason I got turned off." My lips twitched, and he just gave me a look.

"Really?"

"What? I mean, I'm sure I could teach you a thing or two about kissing."

"Uh-huh, You could teach me a thing or two

about kissing." He smiled then. "So are we better now? Is that cleared up?"

"I guess so." I smiled at him willingly. "I mean, if you didn't call me a fat pig, and you were really worried that I thought you were a bad kisser..."

"I was."

"And then I suppose..."

"You suppose what?"

"I suppose I can forgive and forget, and we could move on."

"Great," he said. He pulled me in for a hug. "Thank you. That means the world to me, Rosalie. You don't understand just how much I've thought about that night and how I've wanted to ask Foster how you're doing, and what you're doing, and if he knew why you weren't talking to me, and why you were avoiding me, but I just couldn't."

"It's okay. So where do we go from here," I said, chewing on my lower lip. I noticed that Oliver was looking toward the door. "We can have this conversation later if you want to. I know you're missing your award ceremony and all that good stuff."

"It's fine," he said, "If you want to have it now, then..."

"No, you should go. I'm okay."

"And you're still not going to come with me."

"I'm kind of embarrassed to go in there. I look a little slutty."

"I think you look hot."

"Thank you," I said, "but I'm not dressed appropriately for a work function."

"No, you're dressed more appropriately for a 'let's bang one out tonight' function." He winked at me, and I groaned.

"Really, Oliver?"

"What? It's true. Right?"

"Do you really have to say 'Let's bang one out?'"

"Oh, sorry. Would you rather me say a make love night?"

"No, that's not what I'm saying. I just think that..."

"You just think that what?" he asked with a wide smile on his face.

"I just think that you should know that..."

"Before you go any further, Rosalie, there's something I need to tell you."

"Oh." I raised an eyebrow. "What do you mean?"

"Something else that I haven't quite told you about."

"Well, you've told me about this event, and we've cleared up what happened all those years ago, so what else could it be?"

"Well, I..." He took a deep breath.

"Don't tell me. You really did get a penthouse suite, and you do want to spend the night with me." I grinned at him. "You know, you're going to have to work a little bit harder now, Oliver."

"No, that's not..."

"Oliver." A shrill voice sounded from across the room. I blinked and turned to it, along with Oliver. I could feel him steeling next to me. "Oliver, there you are." A tall, statuesque blonde headed toward us. She had eyes only for Oliver. I wasn't even sure if she'd noticed me. "I have been looking all over for you."

"Have you?" he asked with a small smile.

"Yes. In fact..."

"Diana, I want to..." He grabbed my arm.

"Oliver. We should go in."

"Diana, I want to introduce you to someone." Then she looked over at me, her blue eyes cold as she assessed me.

"Who are you?" she asked in a distasteful voice.

"I'm Rosalie."

"Rosa-who?" She stared back at Oliver. "Who is this, darling?"

Darling, I thought to myself. Why was she calling Oliver darling?

"Diana, this is Rosalie. She's Foster's younger sister."

"Oh, the one that didn't have a job and was begging to come and stay with you." She looked at me again, dismissively. "I see you made it, but darling, word of advice, we're in New York City now, not Atlantic City. You really shouldn't dress like a hoochie."

"What!?" I said, my jaw dropping. Who was this bitch? "And how do you two know each other?" I asked, staring at him with wide eyes. Rosalie pressed her hand against his arm and looked back at me with a smile.

"So darling, you haven't told her about us?" I froze. My eyes met Oliver's, and I could see a look of contrition in his eyes reflected at me.

"Rosalie, I was wanting to tell you, this is Diana."

"Yeah, I got her name," I said, "And who is she exactly?"

"I'm his partner," she said with a small smile. "And I hope one day to be much more." My jaw dropped as I looked at Oliver for confirmation. This couldn't be real. Could it? He had a girlfriend, and he hadn't told me?

"But that's not exactly true, Diana," he said quickly. "Rosalie, Diana and I, well, we dated for a little bit, but we're not in a relationship now."

"Only because I told you I didn't want to be in a relationship right now," she said with a small tinkle. Her blue eyes turned to me, cold. I almost shriveled up on the spot. "But now that I've had a couple of months to think about it, I do think it could be a good idea for us to move in together and further our relationship. Now, come on, dear. I was just speaking to Kramer, and not only are they awarding you with a prize but they're officially giving you a fellowship."

I stared at Oliver and tried not to let the tears fall from my eyes. Fifteen minutes ago, I'd been the happiest woman in the world. And now I felt like the world was about to end. I bit down on my lower lip and stared at Oliver, hoping he would deny it, but he didn't say anything. He let out a deep sigh and ran his hands through his hair. "Diana, go and let Kramer know I'll be right there."

"But, darling, I..."

"Please," he said.

"Fine, but don't be more than a couple of minutes, or I'll come back and get you."

"Okay," he said. He looked at me and shook his head. "I'm sorry, Rosalie. That's what I was trying to tell you. Me and Diana, well, it's complicated."

Chapter 12

Oliver

The look Rosalie was giving me should have turned me to stone. I felt like shit. I couldn't believe Diana had found us and been the one to drop this bombshell. I knew it sounded worse than it was. I knew from the look on Rosalie's face that she was absolutely horrified and disgusted with me. I mean, the facts of the matter were true. Diana and I had dated but only for six months. We'd broken up because we'd both been really busy with work, and while she fit in my circle, she wasn't someone who lit my body on fire.

We continued seeing each other casually once a month or so. I guess some people would've called it friends with benefits. I had suggested to her that we make a decision to either get back together or move on. I wasn't the sort of guy who was used to casual sex. She had told me she'd let me know. I hadn't thought much of it until Foster had told me that Rosalie was going to come and stay with us. As soon as I'd heard that, Diana had been the furthest thing from my mind.

I'd been excited. I'd wanted to see Rosalie, talk to her, figure out what had happened all those years ago, see if she hated me, if she was disgusted by me, and as soon as we'd seen each other in the airport, the sparks had flown. I smiled to myself. She thought I hadn't recognized her when I'd gone up to that other lady, but I'd just been playing a joke on her. I was going to tell her, but she'd been so infuriated and incensed that I figured that hadn't been the time to let her know. And now, now she was infuriated with me yet again.

"You don't understand, Rosalie. It's not as black and white as Diana is trying to make it seem."

"Did you date her?" Rosalie said, ice in her voice.

"Yes, but not—"

"Did you have sex with her?" she cut me off. I let out a deep sigh.

"Of course. We were dating. Rosalie, that—"

"Did you ask her if she wanted to get back together again?"

"Yes, but that was before——"

"I can't right now. I can't believe you kissed me last night, and you have whatever it is you have with that horrible woman." She sniffed, and I bit back a smile. It was true, of course. Diana, while beautiful, didn't have the warmest personality, but I hadn't dated her because I wanted someone warm. She was a fellow attorney and kinky as hell. There had been many nights when we'd worked late and then gone back to her place or my place and fucked like bunny rabbits just to get out the anxiety and frustration of the case.

I'd never loved her. I didn't even particularly like her. She was just there, but I knew Rosalie wouldn't understand that. She still had an idealistic view of love and relationships and sex, and I didn't think it would make it better if I told her that the only thing Diana and I had in common was our love of doggy style and reverse cowgirl. That was something I would never share with her.

"Please, Rosalie, just let me explain. I didn't kiss you last night because——"

"You already told me why you kissed me last night. You told me last night..." She blinked. "I don't even know what I'm saying right now," she mumbled. "I'm so upset. I can't believe that you cheated on your girlfriend with me."

"She's not my girlfriend, Rosalie. You know that."

"I can't believe you cheated with someone you want to be your girlfriend. I just can't believe this. I never should have come. I should have just stayed at home. I should have just found a job at a local store, saved money, and Alice and I could have moved to LA or something."

"So now you don't even want to be in New York?" I stared at her.

"I don't know," she said. "I can't believe this."

"Rosalie, please let me explain."

"Look, they're waiting for you in there. I don't want someone else coming out saying, 'Oh, please come, Oliver, we need you so badly.'" She rolled her eyes. "Like frigging a, can't they just do whatever they got to do without you?" I pressed my lips together. She didn't know that the sole purpose of the event was the award ceremony and that I was the only recipient of an award, so they kinda were waiting on me. I didn't want her to think I had a big head or that I thought I was important because none of that mattered to me right now, not as long as she was upset. "Just go, Oliver."

"I don't want you to—"

"I'm going to call Alice and talk to her. I'll be sitting over there." She pointed at some seats in the lobby. "Do your thing, and we'll speak later."

"Okay," I said, nodding. I stepped forward to grab her hands, and she pushed me away.

"Oh, no way. Don't even think about touching me," she said. "You're an asshole, and as far as I'm concerned, assholes don't belong in my life." And with that, she turned around and headed to the couches. I let out a deep sigh. I wanted to follow her and explain that Diana meant nothing to me, and it was her that I wanted to get to know and explore better. As soon as I was able to have a private conversation with Diana, I would tell her that it was over. I didn't even care if Foster was upset. I'd have a conversation with him and explain. We were best friends, so he had to know I was a good guy. Well, maybe not the best guy, but at least I wasn't the worst guy in the world. I heard the sound of her voice again and looked up. Diana was standing by the door.

"Oliver, they're waiting," she said in her shrill voice, and as I looked at her, I saw a glint in her eyes that I recognized as malice. She'd done that on purpose. She'd wanted Rosalie to be upset. I pressed my lips together. It was my own fault. I should have ended things with Diana a long time ago, or at least as soon as I'd found out Rosalie was coming to town.

Chapter 13

ROSALIE

*M*y fingers pressed the buttons on the phone clumsily as I attempted to call Alice. I needed to talk to my best friend. My emotions were all over the place, and I was pissed at Oliver and myself.

"Hey girl, what's going on?" Alice said, answering the phone as soon as I called.

"Oh my gosh, Alice, I miss you." I burst out immediately in a garble.

"What? I can't understand what you're saying," she said. "What's wrong?"

"I miss you, Alice."

"Where are you? I thought you were going to

have a wild night of sex with Oliver tonight."

"Oh my gosh. I'm such an idiot."

"Oh no. What happened?"

"He..."

"Oh my God, don't tell me he came within five seconds."

"No, that's not what I'm trying to say."

"Ten seconds?"

"No, Alice. We didn't have sex."

"Oh no. Don't tell me he..."

"It wasn't about sex in the first place," I almost screamed. I looked up and noticed two very distinguished-looking men staring at me, so I lowered my voice. "He has a work event. He brought me to the hotel for a work event."

"Oh," she said. "But I thought you said he asked you on a date."

"Well, I mean, he didn't technically ask me on a date. He asked me if I wanted to go to The Ritz-Carlton. And he said to wear a nice dress."

"Okay. And then what?"

"I guess I just assumed he was saying wear a nice dress because it was a date and we were going to hook up."

"Oh, Rosalie." She sighed. "And so you made a move on him and..."

"No, I didn't make a move on him. We showed up, and there were, like, people waiting on him. And they were like, 'Hey Oliver, hurry up. We want to award you a prize.'" I rolled my eyes.

"Oh, wow. What prize did he get?" Alice said.

"Not important."

"Oops. Sorry. So continue."

"Anyway, we finally had it out..."

"About him getting a prize?"

"No, about what he said about me all those years ago."

"Oh wow. You finally asked him."

"Yeah. I mean, it just came up. Anyway, turns out he wasn't actually calling me a fat pig. He was just saying that so Foster would think he wasn't interested in me because Foster warned him off me."

"Oh wow. Your brother's crazy," Alice said. "I can't believe that he warned Oliver off you. Did your father know that you guys kissed?"

"I don't know if he knows that we kissed. I doubt it, though. Because if he did, there's no way he would've let me stay in the apartment with Oliver without him there."

"That's true," Alice said. "Wow, so your brother warned Oliver to stay away from you..."

"Yeah."

"And so Oliver said something rude about you to make your brother think he wasn't interested."

"Yeah."

"Oh shit. So you stopped talking to him for nothing."

"Well, it wasn't nothing. I was really hurt, and he had kissed me, and he didn't even try to reach out and..."

"True. So then what?"

"So then he said he had kissed me last night because..." I paused. The two men were looking at me again.

"Continue. You can't leave me hanging, girl."

"Sorry, Alice. I'm in the hotel lobby right now."

"Oh shit. He left you there by yourself?"

"No, he's in the other room getting whatever award he's meant to be getting, and I'm pissed off at him, so I'm sitting outside."

"Girl. You're not watching him get his award?"

"He can get the award for biggest jackass of the year for all I care."

"Oh shit, but didn't you work everything out with him?"

"No, I did not! It gets worse, girl."

"Oh shit. Okay. Tell me more, Rosalie."

"Okay. So he thought I stopped talking to him because I thought he kissed horribly."

"Aw, poor Oliver."

"Not poor Oliver. Anyway, he kissed me last night because he wanted to show me he was an amazing kisser or whatever. Anyway, I thought,

'Okay, we're finally telling each other the truth. You're attracted to me. I'm attracted to you. Let's see where this might go,' right?"

"Yeah. Sounds good to me. So are you guys going to go on a date or...?"

"No, Alice. I have not told you the biggest bombshell yet."

"Oh shit. What is it?"

"Well, Oliver."

"Oh my God. Don't tell me he had a sex change."

"What are you talking about?"

"You said that the biggest bombshell hasn't been dropped yet. And I'm just reading between the lines. Do you mean he dropped his penis?"

"What are you talking about? How can he drop his penis?"

"If he cut his penis up, it would drop to the ground, and that would be because..."

"Oh my God, Alice, really?"

"Sorry," she said. "I guess I've been watching too much TV recently."

"Yeah, you have. And no, that's not what the bombshell is. The bombshell is, Oliver is partnered up."

"Oh fuck! He's married?" Alice screamed into the phone.

"No, Alice. He's not married. Don't you think we

would've known if he was married? I mean, I'm sure I would've gotten an invitation to the wedding. You forget, my brother is his best friend."

"Oh yeah. So he's got a fiancée?"

"No, he doesn't have a fiancée. He has a girlfriend."

"Oh shit. He kissed you last night, and he has a girlfriend."

"Well, it's his ex-girlfriend, but I guess they're still friends with benefits, and they're going to get back together maybe, or... I don't know, but she was this blond bitch, and when I tell you that if daggers could have flown out of her eyes, they would have. She looked at me like she wanted to kill me."

"Girl, she was jealous of you because you're young, and hot, and gorgeous."

"I don't think so." I sighed. "Anyway, I'm pissed. I cannot stand Oliver. I'm not giving him another chance. I'm not kissing him. I'm not letting him deflower me. To think I was going to let him take my virginity."

"Um, excuse me, ma'am," one of the men who was sitting a couple of couches away from me gave me an awkward smile.

"Yes," I said, glaring at him.

"Could you keep your voice down just a little bit, please?"

"Excuse me?"

"Well, my colleague and I are trying to have a conversation, and..."

"And what?"

"Hey, Rosalie, is everything okay? What's going on?"

"It's fine," I said as I jumped up. "Two very rude gentlemen, actually, wannabe gentlemen, just trying to tell me that I was being loud."

"You are being kind of loud," Alice said. "I had to put the phone away for my ear, and I could still hear you."

"That's because I'm enraged, Alice. I'm absolutely pissed off!"

"And you have every right to be. I would be pissed off too," she said. "So what are you going to do?"

"I'm going to find me a man, and I'm going to bring him back to the apartment tonight, and I'm going to flirt with him."

"Oh God, Rosalie. Please don't tell me you're going to have sex with him."

"No, I'm not going to have sex with him. I'm just going to make out. Maybe. If he's hot and smells good, and..."

"Oh, Rosalie"—Alice giggled—"I wish I was there with you."

"You know what, Alice?"

"Yeah?"

"Come."

"What do you mean?"

"Come to New York."

"I can't come to New York. I have nowhere to stay in..."

"You can stay with me at Foster and Oliver's apartment."

"What? Did you ask them? Is that okay?"

"I don't care if it's okay. Oliver owes me, and so does Foster."

"Oh no. What did your brother do?"

"He's just a jackass." I laughed. "He hasn't done anything recently, but what's he going to do? Throw you into the street?"

"I would hope not," she said. "But I don't even have a ticket, and I don't have much money."

"Look, girl, my parents gave me a thousand dollars. I have nine hundred and ninety left. I'll buy you a ticket."

"No, I cannot let you use your hard-earned money to buy me a ticket."

I started giggling then. "Come on now, Alice, I didn't earn that money. Please come. I don't want to be here without you. I miss you. I just can't keep calling you twenty-three hours a day."

"I mean, you can," Alice said. "I mean, are you sure you really want me to come? You're not just saying that because Oliver pissed you off?"

"I'm totally saying it because Oliver pissed me off, but I really want you to come. And I don't know why I thought I could start this new adventure and journey without you. You're my best friend. We do everything together. We went through high school together, we went to college together, and we moved back home together. We should start this next part of our life together."

"I mean, I've always wanted to live in New York. If you're serious and you don't mind getting me the ticket, I'll get a job as soon as I get there. I don't care if I have to work at Chipotle, or the grocery store, or whatever."

"Girl, we might both be working at the grocery store," I said with a giggle. "But when I get home, I'm going to look for tickets, okay? And I'll get you one."

"Yay. Awesome. Thanks, Rosalie. You really don't have to."

"Of course I do. We're best friends."

"Is there space on the couch for me to sleep?" she asked curiously.

I chewed on my lower lip. The couch was spacious, but it wouldn't be that comfortable with us both sleeping on it. "Not really, but we'll figure something out. I mean, maybe you could sleep in Foster's bedroom," I said with a laugh.

"Yeah, that would be nice," she said wistfully, and I frowned.

"What do you mean that would be nice?"

"I mean, when he's not there," she said quickly.

"Oh, okay. I was about to say, you know Foster's a dickhead. If Oliver is a playboy, then Foster is the king of the playboys."

"I know," she said. "You forget, I grew up with you and him. I saw all the different girls he had coming in and out of the house."

"Yeah. He's such a douchebag. I thought Oliver was a douchebag, but they're both douchebags. Down with men!" I said, laughing, but all of a sudden, I felt better. "I'm so excited that you're going to come, Alice. Thanks."

"But where am I going to sleep?"

"If anything, we'll get an air mattress and put it in the middle of the living room."

"Oh Lord. Rosalie, Foster and Oliver are going to regret letting you stay."

"I don't care," I said with a giggle. "They deserve what they get." I heard the sound of music coming from the room Oliver had gone into and loud cheering. "You know, I'm starting to feel a little bit bad about Oliver getting an award and me not being there."

"Yeah, girl. You should go and support him. I

know everything's kind of a mess, but at the end of the day, he is still your friend."

"Yeah, I guess. He's just a loser, but he's still a friend, and he did pick me up at the airport yesterday. Fine. I'll call you later tonight when I get in. Okay?"

"Okay. And tell Oliver I said congratulations. And thank you."

"Thank you for what, girl?"

"For letting me stay."

"Alice, he doesn't even know you're coming yet."

"Oh yeah." She giggled. "Oh man. I don't know if I should come."

"You're coming. That's settled. I'll speak to you later. Okay."

"Okay. Bye."

I hung up with Alice and then hurried toward the door and opened it. The room was filled with attorneys sitting at tables, drinking wine, and eating little canapes. So these were the hors d'oeuvres that Oliver had been talking about. I stepped inside and was about to take a seat when a lady at the front of the room says, "And Oliver James, please come up to the stage and collect your award." The crowd went wild, and I watched as Oliver stood from a table on the far right and headed toward the front of the stage. He looked so handsome and so debonair even in just a pair of slacks and a shirt.

When he got to the stage, I saw his eyes looking around the room, and then they found mine. He smiled at me, and for a moment, I felt like I was the only person in the room. I smiled back at him and gave him a little wave. He cleared his throat and started his speech.

"Thank you, ladies and gentlemen. I really appreciate the applause, though I don't think I deserve it," he said, and everyone laughed. I looked around to see if anyone was paying attention to me. And then I felt eyes on me coming from the other side of the room. When I looked to the left, there was Diana with her cat-like blue eyes glaring at me. I gave her my widest smile and waved slightly. I was about to head back out of the room when Oliver... The voice made me jump.

"Rosalie," he had said to the entire room. I paused and looked back at the stage. "Come up here. I saved a seat for you at the front. Ladies and gentlemen, this is my best friend's sister, Rosalie. We grew up together, and I'm happy she's here to witness me getting this award tonight." I blushed as everyone turned to gaze at me and made my way toward the front. I felt like I was a muddle on a catwalk as I strode in my tall heels to the front of the room. I couldn't believe that Oliver was embarrassing me like this, though I was kind of happy that he'd called me out and didn't want me to leave. Someone whistled at me as I walked by, and Oliver chuckled on the stage.

"Yes. This is how all the youngsters are dressing today." I glared at him and rolled my eyes. It was his fault that I was dressed like a hoochie. It was his fault that I was dressed to seduce and not to impress. If he'd told me... I sighed. There was no point getting angry about it again. The moment was done. I squared my shoulders and held my head up high. I looked hot, and I wasn't going to be ashamed of the fact. If men wanted to ogle me and women wanted to be jealous of me, so be it. Maybe, just maybe, I'd find a guy to make Oliver jealous, and then he'd feel like shit.

Chapter 14

Rosalie

I listened to Oliver speak, and I was surprised at how different he sounded when he was in a professional setting. Gone was the teasing, funny guy I knew at home, and in his place was a businessman talking about precedent and the blue letter of the law. I looked around to see if Diana was still glaring at me when I realized that the guy next to me was staring at me.

"Hi," he said, reaching his arm out.

"Hi." I looked at him in confusion.

"I'm Chad," he said, wiggling his fingers, "and it's nice to meet you."

"Oh, I'm Rosalie," I said, reaching out and shaking his hand. "Nice to meet you too."

"I'm a first-year associate at the firm where

Oliver works. He's amazing. He's probably going to make partner next year. Super fast."

"Oh cool," I said. That didn't mean anything to me, but it was obviously a big deal because this guy was impressed.

"So you're his friend's sister."

"Yeah. I grew up with Oliver. He's been best friends with my brother, Foster, for years. I just moved to the city, and they're letting me stay with them for a little bit."

"Oh, cool." He smiled. "So are you single?"

"Maybe," I said. "Why are you asking?" He chuckled and blushed slightly.

"Sorry. I'm not usually this awkward, but..."

"But what?"

"But you're so pretty."

"Oh, thanks," I said, wondering if he meant sexy as opposed to pretty. I knew that my dress was showing off a lot.

"So... Are you having a fun time?"

"Ummm... I don't want to lie. Not really," I said, laughing.

"Oh, it's because it's a law thing. These legal events are usually boring, and I'm a lawyer."

"Yeah. I mean, I think there's a reason I didn't go into the law."

"So you said you just graduated?"

"Yeah, from college. I have a degree in English literature."

"Oh cool. Shakespeare, aye?"

"Yeah, I did study Shakespeare."

"I like Shakespeare," he said and then made a face. "Sorry, I can't lie. I've only read one of Shakespeare's works."

"Oh, and which one was that?"

"*Macbeth*," he said, laughing.

"Oh, you read *Macbeth*?" I was surprised. That's not normally the first Shakespeare piece people read.

"I didn't have a choice. We studied it in English in high school." He smiled. "Busted, I guess."

"No, it's okay. So..." I was about to ask him another question when he made a face.

"Oops. I guess we should talk after he's finished his speech." I nodded and looked up. I could see that Oliver was staring at me as he spoke. His eyes were narrowed, and he didn't look happy. It had been kind of rude to have a conversation with a brand-new guy, especially as I was sitting at the front of the room. I pressed my lips together and smiled at him. He didn't smile back.

He finished his talk in about five minutes, and I watched as Kramer and two other older men walked up to him and handed him a plaque. They all stood on the stage and posed for photographs, and then everyone started clapping again, and people stood.

"So would you like a drink, Rosalie?" Chad asked me as we both stood.

"I think I need one," I said with a small nod.

"Come, there's wine over here." He led me to the side of the room with a table full of glasses. "Prefer white or red?"

"I'll have some red, please."

"And here you go," he said, handing me a glass. "So do you have a job yet, or..." I shook my head.

"Not yet. I'm hoping to find one soon, though. Then I'll have enough money to get my own place and..."

"Yeah, I feel you. It's hard when you've just graduated. Unless you have parents who are billionaires and want to buy you a place."

"Yeah, I wish," I said, laughing. "My parents barely got me the plane ticket to come here."

"Aw," he said. "I mean, I make a good salary, but I also have a lot of debt from law school, you know?"

"Cool."

"I went to Yale."

"Oh," I said, smiling.

"Yeah, it's the number one law school."

"Oh cool. Congratulations."

"Doesn't really matter now. But it did help me get this job, and I figured it might impress you..." He paused. "But you don't really know anything about law school, so I guess that didn't really work."

"It's okay. You don't have to impress me."

"Well, I was hoping that I could..."

"Rosalie." Oliver's deep voice sounded from behind me. I turned around with a small smile.

"Hey, Oliver. Good speech. Congratulations."

"Hmm. Are you sure you heard it? You seemed to be busy talking." He looked past me at Chad. "Chad."

"Hi, Mr. James. I was just getting Rosalie some wine and..."

"I see." Oliver looked at the glass in my hand. "Should you be drinking?"

"Um, I'm over twenty-one. I can drink."

"Yes, but you haven't had dinner yet."

"So?" I rolled my eyes.

"So I don't want the alcohol to go to your brain and for you to make rash and stupid decisions."

"I think I can handle one glass of alcohol. Thanks, though." I looked at Chad, who looked slightly uncomfortable.

"So Oliver, I just wanted to say that..."

"Not right now, Chad." Oliver shook his head. "Rosalie, can I speak to you over here?"

"What?"

"I'd like to speak to you in private, please."

"Okay." I looked over at Chad. "I'll be right back."

"Okay," he said, clutching the glass in his hand

tightly. Oliver and I walked about ten feet away and stopped.

"What do you think you're doing," he said angrily.

"What are you talking about?"

"You came here to pick up a guy who works with me."

"What?" My jaw dropped. "What are you talking about, Oliver?"

"You're flirting with Chad. You know he's a first-year associate. He needs to concentrate on his work to make a bonus and not on—"

"Um, number one, Oliver, if you'll recall, I didn't even know I was coming to your work event. So no, I didn't come to pick up a guy who you work with. Number two, Chad started speaking to me. And number three, if I do want to flirt with him, and date him, and whatever else, that's up to me. I can do whatever I want. I'm a big girl."

"So you admit you're interested in him."

"Oliver, I don't know what your problem is, but I think you need to do something else right now."

"Excuse me?"

"I'm sure Little Miss Diana must be looking for you. Like you're her little puppy dog."

"I don't give a shit about Diana."

"Well, tell Diana that. Because if looks could kill, I'd be dead right now."

"I already told you..."

"Oliver, I'm not playing these games with you. Is there anything else you have to say?"

"Yes, we're leaving in five minutes."

"What do you mean we're leaving in five minutes? Isn't this, like, meant to be the good part of the whole evening?"

"We're going to get something to eat."

"I'm fine. I'll have some hors d'oeuvres and some wine."

"You said you wanted dinner."

"Well, you didn't take me to dinner, did you?"

"I'm going to take you to dinner now."

"I don't want you to take me to dinner now." He pressed his lips together.

"Rosalie, do not get me started."

"What do you mean do not get me started?"

"I mean, do not make me..."

"Do not make you what?"

"Do not make me take you into one of these side rooms and give you a spanking." I stared at him for a couple of seconds and started laughing. I laughed so hard that I almost spilled my wine.

"You think that's funny," he said, his lips twitching.

"Oliver, who the hell do you think you are? You're going to spank me, like to tell me off, like I was disobedient or something?"

"Spanking is not just done for disobedience, you know."

"Yeah, it's also done, I guess, in kinky sex, but we've already established that we're not going to have sex."

"So you're saying you don't want my hand on your ass?"

"I'm saying I don't want your hand anywhere. I don't know if you think you're Christian Grey or some other hot romance book hero, but you're not. And I'm certainly not some innocent little damsel in distress who will let you do whatever you want after being a jackass."

"So you'd let me do what I wanted if I hadn't been a jackass?" he asked, raising an eyebrow. I stared at him for a couple of seconds. His blue-gray eyes looked really gray tonight, smoldering as if a thunderstorm were about to erupt inside him. I certainly didn't want to be on the receiving end of that wrath.

"Oliver, let's get one thing straight. We kissed five years ago, and it was good. We kissed last night, and it was good, but we're not going to kiss again. I'm not interested in being with a guy who plays games. I'm not interested in being with a guy who has a maybe girlfriend, bitchy girlfriend, whatever. And I'm certainly not interested in a guy who's trying to be possessive over me when I talk to a handsome, young, promising attorney for five minutes and have two sips of wine. You're not my dad. You're not my brother. You're not my husband. You're not even my boyfriend. You are my brother's best friend. And you need to remember that." His lips were trembling now, and I couldn't tell if he was angry or about to laugh.

"Well, well, well, Rosalie Sloane. You certainly have matured, haven't you?"

"Yes, I have. I'm not the little girl you knew back in the day."

"Rosalie, you may be more mature than a teenager, but you're still only twenty-two. Trust me, you're not the most mature person on this planet."

"I didn't say I was the most mature person on this planet, Oliver James. I just said I'm mature enough not to have to deal with your bullshit."

"Okay then. So you're not hungry?"

"I am hungry, but as I said, I'm going to have some hors d'oeuvres." At that very moment, a server walked past. "Excuse me," I called out to him, and he stopped. "Any canapes there?"

"Yes, ma'am." He presented the tray to me, and I took two small quiches and a sausage roll.

"Thank you." I ate them greedily. "Mmm, good. Yummy." I rubbed my stomach. Oliver shook his head.

"Really, Rosalie?"

"What?"

"That's going to fill you up."

"I mean, I don't know if it's going to fill me up, but maybe Chad will want to take me to dinner for a nice juicy steak. And maybe after dinner, we'll go back to his place, and we'll bang." I said the word deliberately. This time, Oliver's eyes narrowed, and his lips thinned. I knew he wasn't about to start laughing.

"That's not funny, Rosalie."

"What's not funny?"

"You are not—"

"I can do whatever I want, thank you very much." I gave him a sweet smile and chugged down the rest of my wine. After handing him the glass, I leaned forward and gave him a kiss on the cheek. "You have a good night with your bimbo, Diana, and I'll have a good night with Chad. Ciao," I said and turned around and headed back to Chad. Chad was standing there holding his wine. He looked at me with a worried expression on his face.

"Is he mad at me?"

"No, he was just upset at me because he doesn't like me drinking."

"Are you sure? Because..."

"I'm sure, Chad. It's fine. He's my brother's best friend, so he's a little overprotective, but he just needs to know that I'm a grown woman. I can do what I want."

"If you say so, because he was looking at you like you were more than..."

"It's fine. So what are we going to do now?"

"What," he said, looking surprised. "You want to do something?"

"Yeah, let's have fun. Let's go paint the town red."

"I do know this little club..."

"Rosalie." I groaned as I saw that Oliver was back.

"Yes."

"I need to speak to Chad for a second."

"What?" I said.

"Give me two minutes, and then you guys can continue whatever you wanted to do."

"Fine," I said, rolling my eyes.

"Chad, will you speak with me over here, please?"

"Yes, sir." Chad nodded and followed Oliver to the same spot where I'd been standing. I watched Oliver say something to Chad very quietly. Chad nodded a couple of times, and Oliver smiled. I frowned. I had no idea what was going on, but I didn't like the fact that Oliver was smiling. It didn't seem like that was good for me. And then I watched as Chad walked away. He didn't even look back at me. He didn't even say goodbye as he walked to the other side of the room. I headed over to Oliver.

"What the hell?" I said. "What did you say to him?"

"Wouldn't you like to know?" he said with a smile. "Now, are you hungry? Should we get something to eat?"

Chapter 15

OLIVER

"*W*hat the hell do you think you're doing, Oliver?" Rosalie's voice sounded angry, and her lips were trembling. I just wanted to pull her into my arms and kiss her, but I knew this wasn't the time or the place for many reasons.

"I told Chad this was a work event, and he wouldn't like his managing partner to be told that he—"

"You what?" She grabbed my arm and tugged. "You did what, Oliver James?"

"I just told you what I did."

"How dare you? So you scared him off."

"I didn't scare him off. I told him the truth. You really want this boy to lose his job because you're trying to hurt me?"

"What do you mean trying to hurt you, Oliver? How am I trying to hurt you?"

"Well, hurt might be the wrong word, but you're trying to upset me by flirting with that imbecile."

"He's not an imbecile. He seemed like a really nice guy."

"He's a first-year associate. All he cares about is getting laid."

"That's not true," she said. "You don't even know him."

"What, and you do?" I chuckled then. "Rosalie, come on now." I knew what I'd done was wrong, and I'd reacted in the moment. Normally, I never would've done such a thing, but the thought of Rosalie going to dinner with that man and possibly kissing him, well, it made my blood boil. There was no way I was going to let her go on a date while she was still living under my roof. I mean, what would Foster say? He'd kill me if he knew she was already going on dates. A little voice in my head said he'd kill me if he knew I'd kissed her, but I ignored that.

"Oliver, you're really overstepping here."

"Are you hungry, Rosalie? Let's go get something to eat."

"I don't want to eat anything with you. You can

take me home, and I'll find something to eat in the fridge."

"And waste your makeup and that pretty dress?"

"I don't care about my makeup, and I don't care about this dress. In fact, I want to go home and take it off as quickly as possible."

"Ah," I said. "Well, I'm not opposed to that."

"And I'm going to put on pajamas."

"Oh, you don't have to," I said with a slight smile. "You could—"

"I could what?" she said, glaring at me.

"Nothing." I winked at her, and she just shook her head.

"You're too much. You know that?"

"How am I too much?"

"Because I feel like you're playing games with me."

"I'm not playing games with you. We both know we want each other. And you thought you were coming to the hotel tonight to have fun, so why don't we? I can always get a room. It might not be the penthouse. I don't have a couple of thousand dollars just to waste."

"Just to waste?" she said, glaring at me. "So you think getting a penthouse room for the two of us would be a waste?"

"No. I mean, if you really want me to get the penthouse, I will, but—"

"No, Oliver, it doesn't work like that. You already said it was a waste. If that was something you were actually willing to do, you would've done it. You know what? I am hungry."

"Okay."

"And shall we get something to eat?"

"Yeah."

"And I don't want tacos either. I want steak and lobster, and I don't know, French onion soup and cheesecake and—"

"You want all of that?" I raised an eyebrow. "Right now?"

"Yeah. I'm hungry. I want you to take me to the most expensive restaurant you can get reservations to right now."

"Okay? Because you want to spend all my money or because you want a really memorable first date?" She started laughing.

"Oliver, I don't want a first or a last date with you. I want zero dates with you. I just want food. Good food."

"Okay. So I'm just to take you to an expensive restaurant for you to stuff your face, then we go home, and you watch another crappy rom-com?"

"I told you that movie wasn't crappy. Adam Sandler is a genius actor."

"Uh-huh. Said you and exactly zero other people."

"That's not true. He wouldn't be a multimillion-aire if people didn't think he was funny."

"I'll give him funny. What I won't give him is leading man." She rolled her eyes.

"Oliver, you think guys need to be hot to get women? That's not what us women want. We want a good guy. We want a funny guy. We want a loyal guy. We want a guy we can count on, not an asshole."

"I'm taking it that I am the asshole?" I said, smiling smugly at her. "Or should I say, I'm the handsome hunk?"

"You're so full of yourself. This is what I mean." She rolled her eyes and looked me up and down. I stifled a chuckle. I didn't want to get her even more riled up. Though that wasn't exactly true. I'd love to see her more riled up.

"What can I say, Rosalie? It's been a while since you've seen me. And it's been a while since I've seen you. So maybe I'm just..." I shrugged. "Not used to being around you."

"Or maybe you've changed, and you're just a dickhead."

"But you thought I was a dickhead anyway, right? So..."

"Yeah, I thought you were a dickhead for reasons that weren't correct. I thought you were a dickhead because I thought you were saying rude things about me, but you were only saying that because you didn't want Foster to know that you were into me."

"Well, I didn't even say all of that," I say to her.

"Oh, so which part of it was wrong?"

"I mean, I don't want to say I was into you."

"So you weren't into me. You were just making out with me and touching me for fun?"

"I mean, obviously, it was more than that, but..." I sighed. I didn't want to acknowledge the depth of my feelings for her because I didn't know that they could go anywhere. I didn't know that we would ever be able to really be together successfully. Rosalie was beautiful and feisty and fun, but I wasn't sure that our personalities were compatible. I wasn't sure she'd forgive me for not telling her about Diana. I wasn't sure that an actual relationship between the two of us would work. And if it wouldn't work, then there was no point risking the friendship with her or her brother. So as far as she was concerned, I was just going to pretend that it had just been a one-time innocent dalliance.

I wasn't going to tell her that I'd spent months thinking about asking her on a date and trying to muster up the courage to speak to Foster. I wasn't going to tell her that her smile made my heart race and that her eyes did things to me that no other woman had before. I wasn't going to tell her that her voice was like a symphony I never wanted to end.

No, none of those things mattered because I didn't see us going anywhere. They didn't seem to be something solid we could build upon. Rosalie was mad at me, and she was immature. I wasn't sure she was ready for a relationship, not a real serious one. And why should she be? She just graduated from college. She didn't even know what she wanted to do for a living. And yes, I could tell she was attracted to me. Yes, I could tell she wanted to be with me sexually, but I didn't want to hurt her.

I didn't want us to just have a sexual relationship. And then everything went crazy, and she stopped talking to me because I knew that if something like that happened, I would lose Foster as well. No way could he and I stay friends if I broke his sister's heart. And even worse than that, if she broke mine, I wouldn't be able to see him again because I knew the pain would be too strong.

"Oliver, so are we going or not?" Rosalie poked me in the chest.

"I mean, if you really want to go to an expensive restaurant, we can." I gave her a small smile. "But if you really would prefer to hang out with Chad, I can go get him and—"

"What?" She looked confused. "You're the one who just sent him away."

"I know. But after thinking about it, that wasn't right of me. If you and he have a connection and—"

"Oh my gosh, Oliver, you're going to give me whiplash." She sighed. "Do you want to take me to dinner or not?"

"I do," I said with a small smile.

"Then come on, let's go."

"Are you sure?"

"Yeah, I'm hungry."

"But what about Chad?"

"What about him?" she asked, rolling her eyes. "I barely spoke to the guy for ten minutes."

"Okay. So you don't want to bang him tonight?"

"No, I don't want to bang him tonight."

"You want to bang me tonight?" I laughed.

"No, Oliver," she said. But her eyes dart to my lips. Taking a step forward, I grabbed her hands and pulled her against me.

"I want you as well, Rosalie. But you're right. We shouldn't go any further than we already have. It would be a mistake. I'm sorry for kissing you yesterday. I'm sorry for leading you on. I'm sorry if I ever gave you—"

"Oliver," she said, "did I say I wanted to sleep with you?"

"No, but the way your heart is racing right now and the way you're breathing heavily, the way your eyes keep darting to my lips." I smiled at her. "I'm a man. I can tell when a woman's into me."

"Yeah?" she said.

I felt her press her body up against mine, and she smiled.

"And I can tell when a man is into me as well."

Her hand reached down and rubbed the front of my pants. And I stared at her in shock. I knew she could feel my hard-on. She gave me a small little smile.

"Oh, and by the way..."

"Yes?" I said, not sure if she was going to blow my mind yet again.

"I have something to tell you."

"Yes?" I said, licking my lips, grabbing her hand as she squeezed me. "You can't do that here, Rosalie."

"Why not?" She giggled.

"Because we're in a room full of my contemporaries, and I do not need them to see a hot young thing grabbing my cock."

"Okay. Well..."

"Yes?" I said.

"I just wanted to tell you one thing."

"Tell me, Rosalie. What is it?"

"Well," she said coquettishly. " I think that tonight we can have a lot of fun."

"Oh yeah?"

"Because..."

"Because why?"

"It won't just be the two of us soon," she said, giggling.

"Yeah, that's true. Your brother will be back. I mean, I don't mind doing some things." I looked into her eyes, and I could see that she was laughing at me. "I mean, we can fool around if you really want to, but no sex. I don't want to complicate anything."

"Okay." She pulled away from me slightly.

"But there's one other thing I want to say to you, Oliver."

"Yeah?"

"There are going to be four of us in the apartment soon."

"What?" I stared at her in confusion. "What are you talking about?"

"I'm getting Alice a ticket tonight. She's going to move in with us." She bit down on her lower lip and gave me the most innocent look I'd seen in a long time. "Because if you say no, I might just have to tell Foster that you told me you want to ruin me."

"I what?" My jaw dropped as she gave me a sweet little smile. So she had heard me that night.

"We both know that when you said you'd ruin me, it had to do with little Oliver." She nodded down toward my cock, and I groaned as I grabbed her hands and pulled her into me hard. I leaned down and whispered in her ear.

"Trust me, Rosalie Sloane. There's nothing little

about my cock. One fuck from me and you would be ruined for life." She gasped as I moved back and gave her a charming smile. "And don't forget, when you complain to Foster about me, remember to tell him about the fact that you want to be ruined by me in every way possible." I winked at her as she blushed. "Now, let's go and get that food."

Chapter 16

I trailed Oliver as he made his way to Contour, the restaurant in the hotel. Oliver stopped suddenly and looked back at me.

"Are you going to sulk for the rest of the night?"

"Are you going to be a jerk for the rest of the night?"

He grabbed my hand and started laughing then. "A jerk would have told you that Alice can't come and stay."

"Wait, what?" I looked at him in surprise. "You're okay with her coming?"

"Sure." He nodded. "You're like Batman and Robin. Can't have one without the other. Just let me

166

know when her flight arrives, and we can go pick her up."

"You'd pick her up?" I chewed on my lower lip and pressed my arms to my side so I wouldn't hug him.

"Well, you don't have a car or money." He shrugged nonchalantly.

"True, and I'm really going to have no money after paying for her flight."

"Wait, what?" He frowned. "You're paying for her flight?"

"Yup, her parents won't help at all." I sighed. "But she'll pay me back as soon as she gets a job."

"You can't spend your last dollars on her ticket." He shook his head.

"If I don't, then she can't come." I looked down at the floor, knowing I sounded like a loser. I was going to hit the ground running first thing in the morning and look for a job. I didn't care what it was. I just needed to do something before I figured out what I wanted to do in my life. I needed a paycheck coming in. My self-respect wouldn't allow me to live off my brother and Oliver. No matter how badly I wanted to.

"Let me get the ticket—"

"No." I was adamant in my response. I didn't want Oliver to pay for Alice's ticket. That was not his responsibility.

"I have miles." He held his hand up. "Neither one of you would have to pay me back. I'm more than happy to use my miles to have your best friend come."

"Are you sure?" I stared at him gratefully. This was such a generous gift, especially given our eventful evening.

"I'm sure." He smiled at me warmly and held his hand out. "Can we start over as friends?"

"Sure." I shook his hand, slightly disappointed at his words. I didn't want to be just friends. "Friends, it is."

"Great." He looked at me for a couple of seconds and then froze when we both heard the familiar tinkle of Diana. "Oh no," he mumbled under his breath as she approached.

"Oliver, there you are." She hurried over and embraced him. I flinched as she pressed her lips against his. "Congratulations on the award. I've always known you were—"

"Diana, Rosalie and I are about to grab a bite to eat. Can we talk later?"

"I'm quite peckish as well." She touched the side of his arm. "Maybe we can have dessert back at my place. I have whipped cream." She looked at me and smiled. "He does love his whipped cream." I smiled back at her, though I wanted to scream.

"That's enough, Diana." Oliver sounded

annoyed. "Rosalie and I have some business to discuss tonight, so no, we won't need you to join us."

"Want to come back to mine after, then?" She then leaned forward and whispered something in his ear that made him blush.

"I don't think so, Diana." He shook his head.

"Think about it before you make up your mind. The tunnel has been missing your train," she said with a wink. She then looked me up and down and laughed as if something about my appearance was funny. "And Oliver, next time you want to bring your playthings to a work event, please take them out shopping first. Kramer was asking me if your friend here was a high-class escort. I said I doubted it. She looks far too cheap for that line of work."

I gasped at her comment and looked over at Oliver. His face looked furious.

"Diana." His voice was low, and I could see his body was rigid.

"What? She's dressed like she's gone to a party in Panama City on spring break with her sorority sisters." She looked me up and down dismissively. "There are no frat guys here, darling."

"Diana, you do not talk to my guest that way." Oliver's voice was steely. "Rosalie is a longtime friend and has more class in her little finger than you have in your entire body. Do not call me again. Do not email me. We are done. I want nothing to do with you."

"That's not what you said when—"

"Enough." He pressed his lips together. "Maybe you should go back to screwing Kramer because I want nothing else to do with you." He smiled as Diana gasped. "Yes, dear. I knew that you were fucking Kramer to get ahead. We all do. And no, I didn't care because you mean nothing to me." He grabbed my hand and then dropped it quickly. "Ready to go, Rosalie?"

"Yes, please." I nodded, grinning like a fool. I was ecstatic that Oliver had stood up for me and put Little Miss Diana in her place. "But can we go home and order a pizza? I don't think I want to eat here."

"Sure," he said, smiling. "Let's do that."

Diana stood there huffing and puffing, and I couldn't stop myself from getting one last dig in.

"Have a nice evening, Diana. I would say it was nice meeting you, but then I don't want to lie. I hope you enjoy Kramer's wrinkly dick. Don't worry about Oliver's because I'll take good care of it." I grabbed Oliver's hand and started walking away quickly. I looked up, and his face and eyes were laughing at me.

"That was wicked," he said as we exited the hotel. "I can't believe you said that."

"She deserved it." I giggled as Oliver walked to

the curb to hail a taxi. "She doesn't have to know that we haven't had sex."

"Yeah." He nodded as he looked back at me. "Or that we never will." His voice trailed off as he looked me up and down. I smiled at him in response. I knew Oliver thought it was better for our friendship if we never hooked up, but I wasn't sure if I agreed with him. Tonight had been such a crazy night that I didn't know how I felt.

Chapter 17

"So what do you want on your pizza?" Oliver asked me as we sat on the couch. He was on the phone with what he said was the best pizza restaurant in Manhattan, and I was excited to see if the pizza would be the best I'd ever had.

"I don't know. Pepperoni, ham, onions, extra cheese." I grinned at the look on his face. "Any of those toppings will do."

"I thought you just said you didn't know," he said, shaking his head, his hand pressed against the mouthpiece. "That's a lot of toppings for someone who hasn't got a clue." There was a teasing glint in his eyes as he spoke to me, and I could feel my body heating. Oliver had a way of making me feel hot and bothered when I was close to him.

"Well, I mean, I don't want to be greedy."

"Anything else?" he asked.

"Um, maybe red peppers. Actually, no red peppers."

"Okay." Oliver grinned and held the phone back up to his ear. "Hi. No worries," he said. "Yes. I do know what I'd like to order. Can I get one large pizza with ham, pepperoni, onions, and extra cheese? Anything else, Rosalie?"

He looked at me, and I shook my head, then grabbed his arm. "Wait, see if they have cheese sticks."

"Cheese sticks as well?" he asked.

"Yes."

"Do you have cheese sticks, please? Okay. They have small and large."

"Large," I said quickly.

"Large?" He raised another eyebrow, and I started laughing.

"You forget, I like to eat."

"I guess I did forget. Um, soda?" He looked at me. "You don't want soda, do you?"

"See if they have 7UP."

"Do you have 7UP?" He paused and nodded.

"Okay. Get a two liter of 7UP."

"Can I also have a two liter of 7UP, please?"

"Ooh, and see if they have any brownies or anything."

He gave me a small smile as I kept adding items. "Do you have brownies? No. Sorry, Rosalie. They don't have brownies."

I sighed. "Well, do they have any dessert stuff or wings or—"

"Do you have anything sweet? Okay. They have cinnamon sticks with icing."

"Oh yeah. Get one of them," I said, grinning. "Do they have chicken wings?"

"Chicken wings along with pizza and cheese sticks?"

"Yes, please."

"Do you have any chicken wings, sir? Okay. They have plain, barbecue, and honey mustard."

"Barbecue." I smiled at him, happy.

"And some barbecue wings. No, that will be all. Thank you. Let me just get my credit card."

I watched as he jumped up and walked over to grab his wallet from the table. I sat back on the couch, happy as I slipped off my high heels. The night had been kind of crazy. It had started off exciting and then plummeted like someone falling off a cliff, but then it had gotten better, and now I felt like I was living my dream. I was sitting here on a couch with Oliver, someone I considered to be the most gorgeous man in the world. Not that I would ever tell him that. I was wearing a sexy dress. I felt pretty. And he was ordering delicious food. "Oh, man. I want french fries as well," I mumbled to myself.

"What did you say, Rosalie?" he said, frowning from the table.

"Nothing."

"Are you sure?"

"Yeah."

"Okay." I sat back and watched him read the credit card number to the guy on the phone. He put the phone down and came to sit next to me. "So we're going to watch a movie?"

"Yeah, but let me order the ticket first, or rather, you get the ticket. I was going to call Alice so we could get her information."

"Um, you want to do that right now?" He seemed surprised.

"Yeah, because I don't want you to change your mind."

"I'm not going to change my mind."

"I just want to make sure." I smiled at him.

"Fine," he said. "You want to call Alice while I go get my laptop?"

"Sounds good." I grabbed my phone and called Alice.

"Hey, what's going on?"

"Guess what?"

"Um, I have no idea. And I can't even guess. You've already had a crazy evening."

"I know," I said, laughing, "but everything's better now. Well, kind of. I spoke to Oliver, and he's going to get your ticket."

"He what? No, Rosalie. I can't have him buy my ticket."

"It's fine. He's not using cash or anything. He's going to use credit card points, and you know credit card points are like free money."

"I don't know about that, but he doesn't mind?" She sounded surprised.

"Yeah, right?"

"So what happened tonight? Are you—?"

"I can't really say anything right now," I whispered into the phone, "but I'll tell you more tomorrow. Okay?"

"Okay. So what are you doing?"

"We're going to get your ticket. Then we're going to watch a movie, and we ordered some food."

"Ooh, what did you get?"

"Pizza and chicken wings." I sighed.

"Why are you sighing?" Oliver was standing next to me. He had his laptop in his hands.

"Well, I kind of wanted french fries as well, and I wish I would have asked you to see if they had any."

He looked at me with wide eyes. "Seriously? We got pizza, cheese sticks, chicken wings, cinnamon sticks, and the 7UP. And you want french fries as well?"

"Hey, what can I say? I love me some fries."

"You really want them?" he said.

"I mean, I did, but it's too late now."

"It's never too late." He picked up his phone and called the number again. "Hi. I just placed an order for Oliver James. Yeah. I'd like to order some french fries as well, if you have them."

I stared at him in surprise. Alice gasped into the phone. "Is he ordering french fries for you? No way."

"I'm shook right now," I said in shock.

"You're shook?" Alice said. "I'm shook. How sweet is that of him?"

"I know. I can't believe it."

He hung up the phone. "Done. Please don't say you wanted to order garlic bread or something else."

"I'm okay. Thanks. I really appreciate it, Oliver."

"You're welcome. You've had a crazy evening, and well, this is my way of saying sorry."

"It's okay." I grinned at him. We just stared at each other for a couple of seconds, and I wondered if he was going to lean down and kiss me.

"Are you still there, Rosalie?" Alice said into my ear, and I laughed.

"Oh yeah. Sorry. I almost forgot I was on the phone with you. Oliver's bringing up his laptop now.

I just wanted to make sure we had all your information correct for when we get the flight."

"You're getting the flight now?" She sounded as surprised as Oliver had.

"Yeah. There's no time like the present."

"I guess," she said.

"So when can you come?"

"I guess in a couple of days. Is that okay?"

"Of course. Oliver said he's also going to pick you up. So—"

"Oh my gosh. He really doesn't have to do that." She paused. "So what did Foster say?"

"What do you mean, what did Foster say?"

"About me coming. Is he happy or…"

I frowned as I made a face. "I don't know. Foster doesn't even know." I looked at Oliver, slightly concerned. "Should we tell Foster about this?"

"It's fine. I'll call him tomorrow."

"Okay. Sounds good."

Alice sighed. "Oh, so he doesn't even know."

"No, but who cares? By the time he gets back from his work trip, we'll probably already have jobs, so we can find our own place, and—"

"You two can stay here as long as you want," Oliver said quickly. "You don't have to rush out and get your own place."

"I mean, we'll need a place of our own at some point. This apartment isn't really big enough for four people. Plus, I don't know how Foster will feel about both Alice and me being here."

"Do you think he'll be mad?" Alice asked.

"I don't know," I said. "Why?"

"Just wondering," she said quickly.

"Oh, okay." I looked at Oliver as he opened his laptop. "See if you can find any flights coming up, maybe next weekend."

"Okay. Saturday?"

"Sure. That work for you, Alice?"

"Yeah, that sounds good."

"Do you prefer to fly in the morning or the evening?"

"Whatever works best for you guys."

"Um, I guess whatever works best for you, Oliver. She's flexible."

"Sounds good," he said. "Okay. Well, there are a couple of flights on Saturday that I can get with my points, one leaving at six o'clock in the morning."

"No way. That means she'd have to be there at like five o'clock."

"Thanks for looking out for me," Alice said into the phone. "No way I want to get up that early."

I laughed. "Don't worry, girl. I've got your back. What else do they have, Oliver?"

"There's another one leaving at one o'clock and one leaving at five in the evening. How about the one o'clock flight? That way, she gets in early enough so we can all go out on Saturday night."

"Oh my gosh. That would be so fun," Alice said.

"Want to get that flight, Oliver?"

"I can. Where are you guys planning on going?"

"I don't know. Somewhere fun where we can meet some hot men."

He frowned as he looked at me. "This is New York City. You're not in college anymore. You can't just go and pick up men."

"I'm joking, Oliver." I rolled my eyes. "Don't worry about it. And you can come as well, if you want."

"I just might," he said. "Okay. I just need her date of birth, phone number, and email address."

"Okay. I'll hand you the phone. I'm going to change. Okay?"

"Sounds good."

"Here, Alice. I'm going to give you to Oliver. He just needs some information. I'll talk to you later. Okay?"

"Okay. Thanks, girl."

"Bye." I handed Oliver the phone and headed to the bathroom. I slipped off my dress and stared at my reflection in the mirror. I giggled to myself as I wondered what Oliver would do if I walked out in just my panties. He would probably go crazy. I kind of wanted to see that, but I was too embarrassed to walk out topless. I mean, yeah, I kind of wanted to seduce him, and I wanted to see lust in his eyes, but I certainly didn't want to parade myself around like some sort of bimbo.

I grabbed the T-shirt I'd left in the bathroom that morning and pulled it on. It reached just past my ass, and I knew it was too short, but I didn't have any shorts in here. I'd have to grab a pair from my bag. I washed my face, brushed my hair, and then headed back into the living room. Oliver was sitting on the couch. He turned to face me, and his eyes widened slightly as he took in my appearance. "So ready for bed, eh?"

"Well, ready for eating and relaxing." I smiled.

"You're not going to wear any pants?" He looked at my long legs.

I cocked my head to the side and smiled at him. "What do you mean? I've got on a T-shirt."

"But it's not very long."

"I have on panties, so it's not like you'd see anything." I grinned at him, and at that moment, I decided not to put on any shorts. I walked over to the couch and sat next to him. My T-shirt rode up, and I realized he was seeing all the way up my bare legs. His eyes hovered on my face before falling to my legs. He shifted in his seat slightly, and I gazed into his eyes. They were dark and smoldering.

He spoke huskily. "I don't think this is a good idea, Rosalie."

"You don't think what's a good idea?" I said innocently.

"You sitting on the couch wearing barely anything."

"What are you talking about? I've got on a T-shirt. I've got on panties."

"Yeah, but the food's going to be hot, and if you spill it, you'll burn yourself."

"Is that why you're worried, Oliver?" I laughed, throwing my head back. I watched as he stared at my throat, and I swallowed hard as he pressed his lips together.

"Rosalie, I really don't want you to get burned."

"I don't think I'll get burned. I'll be careful."

"You just can't be careful enough in these situations," he said.

"I think I can. And I've got a pillow that I can put on my legs to protect me."

"That pillow's not going to protect you from anything," he said. And that's when I realized he wasn't talking about the food burning me at all.

"So you really think I'll get burned, Oliver?"

"I have a bad feeling that you might." He let out a deep sigh. "And I already realized—"

"You already realized what?"

"Nothing." He sighed. "Look, here's your phone. Let me give it to you before I forget."

"Thanks," I said, taking it and putting it next to me. "So what were you going to say?"

"It doesn't matter. Shall we see what we want to watch?"

"Hmm, I guess we can." I sat back for a couple of seconds, then turned back toward him. "Oh yeah. Oliver, by the way."

"Yes, Rosalie?"

"I just wanted to say thank you for getting the ticket."

"It's okay. You're welcome."

"No, I mean, thank you."

Chapter 18

"*I* said I want to thank you, Oliver."

He frowned slightly. "And how would you like to do that?"

"Well, how would you like me to do that?" I pressed my hand against his shirt and undid the top button. He grabbed my hand and pulled it away.

"Rosalie, I don't..."

"You don't what?" I grinned at him. I ran my hand all the way down the front of his shirt toward his pants and shifted slightly so that I was pressing myself against him.

"Rosalie."

"Yes, Oliver? That's my name. Don't wear it

184

out." I pressed my lips against the side of his face and rubbed lightly over his cock. I could feel that he was slightly hard, and I grinned to myself, happy.

"Oh my gosh, what are you doing?" He grabbed my hand and then jumped off the couch. "I don't think this is a good idea."

"I don't think it's a bad idea. Plus, didn't I tell Diana that your cock would be well taken care of?"

"You were joking. We both know you were joking."

"Yeah? And so?" I stepped forward and wrapped my arms around his shoulders. "Kiss me, Oliver. Kiss me." I looked up at him with imploring eyes, and I knew I would absolutely faint to the ground if he told me no. He looked down at me, his eyes dark with lust. He groaned, and then I saw his face heading toward mine. I grinned as I leaned up on tippy-toes to kiss him.

He wrapped his arms around my waist, and I felt his hand squeezing my ass as he brought me into him, and I pressed myself against his body. His tongue slipped into my mouth, and I kissed him passionately, loving the warmth of his body against mine and the feel of his cock swelling against my stomach.

"Ah shit," he said, pulling away slightly and shaking his head. "What are we doing?"

"I told you what I'm doing. I'm thanking you."

"And I said..."

"You don't need to talk anymore," I said, pressing a finger against his lips. I reached up and undid the buttons of his shirt and then tugged the sleeves. He stepped back, and I thought he was going to walk away from me, but then I watched gleefully as he pulled his shirt off and threw it onto the ground. He then undid his belt buckle and his zipper, then pulled his pants down. I stared at him in his white boxer shorts and swallowed hard. I licked my lips as I grinned at him.

"So now we're both almost naked," I said, laughing.

"You are something else," he said, grabbing my hand and pulling me into his arms. "Come."

"Well, where are we going?" I said.

"Let's go to my room." I realized I hadn't even seen his room yet, so I followed him excitedly. He opened his door, and I stepped inside, gasping in awe as I saw the floor-to-ceiling windows that looked out at the city. He had a king-sized bed in the middle of the room, and everything was so neat. I looked over at him in surprise.

"This is really nice."

"I'm glad you like it. But there's one thing I should tell you."

"And what's that?" I said.

"I only have on boxers."

"Yeah."

"And you have on a T-shirt and panties."

"Yeah, so?"

"So I think you need to get down to my level of undress."

"Oh really?" I said, licking my lips seductively.

"Yeah, I think so." He stepped toward me, and I giggled as I jumped onto his bed.

"I think you'll have to take it off for me then, Oliver." He growled as he got onto the bed next to me, reached over, and pulled my T-shirt up. He threw it to the floor and then stared into my eyes before looking down at my breasts.

"Wow, you're amazing," he said as he brought me toward him and kissed me. I felt his hands on my waist sliding up, and I gasped as I felt his fingers on my nipples, rubbing and teasing and tugging.

"Oh," I said, feeling hot and bothered.

"Oh yeah? You like that?" he said as his lips pressed against my neck and moved toward the valley between my breasts. I felt his mouth on my right nipple, sucking, and I closed my eyes as my fingers ran up and down his back. I moved them toward his front and rubbed the front of his boxers to get him even harder. He groaned as his hands slid down my stomach toward my panties. I gasped slightly as I felt his fingers rubbing against the silkiness of the material between my legs, and then I felt him slip a finger inside my panties, and I froze slightly.

"Shit, you're already wet," he whispered into my ear, and I looked at him with wide eyes.

"And you, sir, are already hard." He chuckled then as his lips kissed down my stomach.

"Yes, I am," he said. I felt his tongue in my belly button, and I gripped the sheets. I'd never felt this hot and wet before in my life. And then his teeth gripped the top of my panties and pulled them down. I stared at him in shock and awe, and I couldn't wait to find out what would happen next.

He kissed along my legs toward my thighs, and I felt him parting my legs. He looked up at me with a big grin, and before I knew what was happening, his face was between my legs, and his tongue was on my clit, licking and sucking. I'd never felt such immense pleasure before in my life.

"Oh, fuck. Fuck, fuck, fuck, Oliver," I said as I gripped the top of his hair. He grinned as he sucked on my clit. And then, just as I thought I was about to explode, he stopped and kissed back up my body. I pouted as I stared at him.

"Why did you stop?"

"Because," he said, "I wanted to kiss you again." He kissed me softly and ran his fingers up and down the side of my body, and I felt myself shivering. Reaching over, I slipped my hand inside his boxers and rubbed his hard cock. He groaned, and I watched as he quickly pulled his boxers off and threw them onto the floor. I stared at his cock, large and magnificent, and my eyes widened.

"Wow," I said, licking my lips.

He smiled down at me. "Now you know how to make a man feel good."

"Well, you should," I said as I pushed him down onto the mattress. It was my turn to kiss his chest. I licked his nipples, and he groaned, and then I kissed down his abdomen toward his cock. I stared up at him before I took him in my mouth, and he grunted as I deep-throated him, taking him as far as I could. I reached down and gently rubbed his balls as I sucked him, and I felt his body trembling underneath me.

"Fuck," he said. "Oh shit. Oh yeah. Oh, Rosalie." And then I stopped and kissed back up his chest. He growled as he looked at me.

"What the fuck? I was..."

"Well, now you know how it feels," I said with a small smile.

"You little..." He laughed as he reached over to the side table and grabbed something. I realized it was a condom wrapper, and I watched as he opened it up and slipped the condom onto his cock. This was it. I was about to have sex for the first time, and I was so excited.

He positioned himself over me, leaned down, and kissed me.

"Are you sure, Rosalie? Fuck, I can't believe how..."

"I'm sure," I said. "I want you." I reached up and pulled his head down to kiss me, and I felt his hands parting my legs as he positioned his cock between them. I felt his cock rubbing up and down on my clit, and I could feel myself coming slightly. "Oh yeah, baby." I felt the tip of him inside me, and I froze slightly.

"Hey, what is it?" He blinked as he pulled up slightly.

"I'm just"—I bit down on my lower lip—"I'm just a little nervous."

"Nervous about what?" he said. "Do you not want to do this? It's fine if you've changed your mind."

"No, I want to," I said breathlessly, "but there's something you should know."

"What?" he said.

"I'm a virgin," I spoke softly, and his eyes widened.

"What?" His jaw dropped.

"I'm a virgin, but it's okay. I..."

"Oh, hell no." He jumped off the bed and looked down at me. "Rosalie, we can't do this."

"What? What do you mean? I..."

"I'm sorry, but..."

"Oliver, is it really a big deal?"

"Yes, it is. You need to put some clothes on, and I need to go shower. We'll talk about this later." And then he hurried out of the room.

Chapter 19

OLIVER

I walked out of the bedroom, grabbed a T-shirt and a pair of shorts, and headed to the balcony.

"Oh shit," I said to myself. I could not believe what had just happened. I'd literally been moments away from taking Rosalie's virginity, and I didn't even know when. I was still hard as hell and turned on, but there was no way I could deflower her. She was Foster's sister. She was someone who deserved the love of her life to take her virginity, to give her everything that she'd ever wanted, and I didn't know if I was that person. Tonight was just meant to be fun. Tonight was just meant to be a little dalliance.

When she'd pressed herself against me on the couch, telling me she wanted to thank me, I thought she'd been joking. I hadn't expected it to go this far until we hit my bedroom. And then when I'd seen her beautiful naked breasts and her mouth sucked on my cock, I'd known she was serious, and I'd known I wouldn't be able to stop. I'd known I'd wanted her too badly. It had felt amazing how her fingers touched my skin, how she kissed me eagerly, how she reacted, how her back arched, when I'd almost made her come. And then when I'd been on top of her, about to thrust inside her, the way her eyes had widened in shock and glee and surprise.

"Fuck," I said as I ran my hands through my hair. I didn't know what I was going to do. If Foster knew what we'd almost done, he'd kill me. He would absolutely kill me.

"Oliver, can we talk about this?"

Rosalie stepped out onto the balcony wearing just the T-shirt. I looked down at her naked feet and shook my head.

"Um, what do you have on underneath that T-shirt?"

"Nothing," she said, giving me a sweet little smile. Actually, it was far more sexy than sweet.

"Rosalie, go and put on some proper clothes."

"I don't want to. In fact, I don't even want to have this T-shirt on right now." Stepping forward, she pressed her hand against my arm, and I glared at her.

"What do you think you're doing?"

"What do you mean what do I think I'm doing? I'm touching you, and I want you to touch me. I want us to——"

"No," I said firmly and gave her a stern look. "I am your brother's best friend. I am not going to take your virginity."

"Oh, but you were just about to sleep with me."

"Yes, but I wasn't about to deflower you."

"So it's okay to sleep with me if I've already had sex, but it's not okay to sleep with me if I haven't."

"Well, you're a very smart young lady."

"Stop it. Oliver. Why are you treating me like this? I want it as much as you do, and I know you want it. You practically came in my mouth just now."

"You shouldn't have been sucking on my cock just now," I growled. "Oh, my gosh. I cannot believe these words are coming out of my mouth."

"What? I sucked your cock, and it was hard, and you were licking my——"

"Rosalie." I pressed my finger against her lips. "Please, no."

"What? Are you afraid to hear the words or something? What if I tell you that I want to feel your big, hard cock in my pussy right now? My very wet pussy."

I groaned at her words as I pulled her against me. I grabbed her ass and moaned as I felt the warmth of her skin. My fingers slipped between her ass cheeks and slipped between her legs. She was still wet. I rubbed a finger against her clit, and her feet buckled.

"Oh, yes. Don't stop, Oliver," she moaned out loud. Her hands ran down the front of my shorts and rubbed my cock. Her lips pressed against my neck.

"Please, Oliver. Don't say no. I really want this. I want you to be my first."

For a couple of seconds, I nearly lost myself. I nearly took her. But then I thought about how she stopped speaking to me just because she thought I said a mean comment about her, and I couldn't risk something like that happening again. Not now. Not when there was nothing that I could promise her. Not when I didn't know if we would even work in any way other than physically.

"I can't," I shook my head. "I'm sorry."

"But why not?" She looked upset. "Do you not want me?"

"You know I want you. You just said that you know that."

"Well, then, why won't you?"

"Because it's not right, Rosalie. You want a boyfriend. You want a partner. You've obviously been saving yourself for someone special. We haven't even spoken in years. I don't want to take your virginity and then-"

"And then what?" she said, pointing at me, poking me in the chest.

"I don't want to break your heart."

"You what?" She looks up into my eyes, dazed and confused. "What are you talking about?"

"Sex is a very intimate act. It's the most physical intimacy you can have with another person. Some say you create soul ties with every person you sleep with. I don't want to do that with you."

"Yet you were fine doing it with Diana?" She raised an eyebrow. "You could have a soul tie with her, but not with me?"

"Diana meant nothing to me. We created no soul ties, trust me."

"But you still slept with her."

I sighed. "I don't expect you to understand, Rosalie, but I'm not sleeping with you because I value you. I care about you."

"Oh, shut the fuck up, Oliver." She shook her head. "You know what? I'm done with these games. If you don't want me, I'm sure I can find a man who does." As soon as she said those words, I froze.

"Rosalie, listen to me. Don't just go-"

"Don't tell me what to do," she said, glaring. "I'm about to go and have a shower, and then I'll come out when I'm ready, and we can eat the food. Where is the pizza, by the way?"

"Really, Rosalie? Pizza?"

"What? You don't want to sleep with me, so I might as well look forward to the next best thing."

"So sex with me was number one, and pizza is number two?"

"Yeah. Actually, tell a lie. Pizza is number one. Sex with you was good for being number two. But that was only because the pizza wasn't there yet."

I shook my head and stifled a laugh. "I know I've hurt you, Rosalie, but…"

"You haven't hurt me, Oliver. You've got a big head. You think that you rule the world and just because you don't want to sleep with me, that hurts? Whatever. There are a billion other men who want to be with me."

"I'm sure there are, but-"

"Maybe I'll try to figure out Chad's number. Do you have it?"

I glared at her. "Really?"

"What? You don't think he wants me?"

"We both know he wants you, but he's not the right guy for you."

"Oh, why not?"

I pressed my lips together. I didn't really have a

good reason. I didn't really know Chad whatsoever. He actually seemed like a pretty nice guy. I sighed. "Rosalie, you just got to New York. Shouldn't your focus be on finding a job? And Alice is coming soon. Don't you guys want to find jobs and get a place, and then you can start thinking about dating and hooking up."

She stared at me for a couple of seconds and then turned around and walked back into the apartment. She walked into the bathroom, and I heard doors slamming. I let out a deep sigh. Fuck, fuck, fuck. I had no idea what I was doing, but I knew my intentions were good. I knew she was hurt because I could see it in her eyes. But everything I said was true. Women, especially young women, tended to fall in love after they'd had sex. And, well, I didn't want that for Rosalie. I didn't want her to have expectations of our time together that I couldn't fulfill. Even though a part of me knew that if we did make love, it would be more than sex. It would be meaningful. I just didn't know how meaningful or where it could take us, and I wasn't willing to risk it.

I walked into the apartment and closed the sliding door. I sat on the couch and listened to the water running in the bathroom. "Oh man," I mumbled to myself. If I hadn't been such an idiot, perhaps I could have been in the shower with her right now, fucking her against the marble walls. That would have been amazing. But no, here I was sitting on the couch alone, my dick harder than it had been in a long time. But at least my conscience didn't feel like I was a complete and utter bastard that only thought with his small head. At least I had that.

Chapter 20

Rosalie

So it turns out I'm really good at ignoring people once I feel rejected. It had been three days since I'd talked to Oliver. I was still angry at how he'd turned me down. It was humiliating to be buck naked on a bed, begging for a man to take you and for him to then jump up off the bed and go running. Like what the actual fuck? Thanks for nothing, dickhead. I kept my eyes closed as I heard Oliver walking toward the couch to speak to me, as he did every morning and night.

"Hey Rosalie, not sure if you're awake or not..." His voice trailed off, and I kept my body as still as possible. "I could tickle you and find out." I knew that if he attempted to tickle me, I'd kick him in the balls so hard that one would fall off. "Anyway, I'm headed to work now. I'm leaving early today, so maybe we can grab lunch...Alice arrives tomorrow, so you'll need to talk to me before then." He let out a huge sigh. "You know I'm sorry, and I didn't say no because I don't think you're attractive..." I wanted to roll my eyes so badly at his comments. I wasn't sure what was more offensive. Him not finding me attractive or him not thinking I was girlfriend material. Because I'd read between the lines. This was about more than me being Foster's sister or a virgin. This was about him not seeing any future relationship for the two of us.

"Well, I guess I will just let you continue sleeping," Oliver said.

I kept my eyes closed and tried not to move. I heard his footsteps as he walked toward the door, and then, about thirty seconds later, I heard the door open and slam shut. I counted to ten and then slowly opened my eyes. He was gone. Sitting up, I stretched and looked around the apartment.

Today will be a new day. I jumped up off the couch. That was my new mantra. It was from a post I'd seen on Instagram that inspired me, and I knew I couldn't let myself commiserate over Oliver's rejection forever.

I headed toward the kitchen to make myself

some breakfast. I opened the fridge and looked for some orange juice. I poured myself a tall cup of orange juice, chugged it down, and then walked back to my bed.

I stared at the couch, and the sheets strewed across it and the two pillows and decided to fold them and put them into Foster's room for the day. I knew that if I left the sheets on the couch, I'd just want to lie down and watch TV all day, and I couldn't do that again. I grabbed my phone to call Alice.

"Hey, morning," she said, immediately answering.

"Hey girl, you know what I love about you?"

"No, what?"

"I love that whenever I call, you answer immediately."

"I mean, why wouldn't I?"

"I don't know. You know some people play games and let the phone ring on and on and on to pretend that they're doing something or have a life."

"What are you trying to say, Rosalie?" Alice laughed. "That I don't have a life?"

"No, but you don't play games with me."

"Of course not. You're my best friend. How are things, by the way?"

"Fine. I'm still not talking to him if that's what you're asking."

"So how long are you going to ignore him?"

"Forever," I said simply. "I'm folding my sheets now and taking them into Foster's room."

"Oh? Why?"

"Because I realized that leaving the sheets on the couch was making me lazy, and I need to start looking for a job and who knows, maybe I'll find something online that will fit me or you or both of us."

"That sounds cool. I've been looking too. There are so many jobs in New York, but not many that pay well that we're qualified for."

"Well, I was looking at apartments as well."

"You were?" Alice sounded surprised. "But... we're both broke asses."

"I know we're both broke asses, but we need a goal, right?"

"I guess. So you were looking at apartments and...?"

"Well, there are some cheap ones really far down in Brooklyn and in Queens and in the Bronx."

"But didn't we move to New York to be in Manhattan?"

"Alice, beggars can't be choosers. We're broke asses, remember?"

"Yeah, but right now, you're staying in your brother's bomb-ass apartment, right?"

"Yeah, and...?"

"And it's free, right?"

"Yeah, and...?"

"So why would we leave that to go to some crappy apartment that's not even in the city?"

"I know what you're saying, but I can't stay here forever with Oliver and his smarmy voice and laughing, mocking eyes."

"Oh, Rosalie. I know you're upset, but I'm actually kind of proud of him."

"What?!" I shrieked in shock. "What do you mean you're proud of him?"

"I know you don't want to hear this because you feel rejected. I would feel the same way, but wouldn't it have been so much worse if you gave him your virginity and then he acted like it was nothing?"

"No, I would have felt amazing because I would have been deflowered by the hottest guy I've ever met in my life."

"Rosalie, yeah, you would have been elated for five seconds, and then you would have been like, 'What the fuck? Why isn't he proposing to me, and why aren't we getting our own place on Fifth Avenue?'"

"I don't talk like that, Alice."

"I know, but look, he's a man, and obviously, he wanted you because you were about to do it. The fact that he could walk away says a lot about his character."

"Alice, are you my best friend or his best friend?"

"Sorry," she said. "He's a dick. End of story."

"Exactly. That's all I want to hear."

"Fine," she said. "But can we not move to the Bronx? I really don't want to move there."

"You love J-Lo, though."

"So?"

"J-Lo's from the Bronx."

"Yeah, but she doesn't live there now, does she?"

"Touche." I laughed. "Well, I'm really excited to see you tomorrow."

"I'm excited to see you, too. So you and Oliver still coming to pick me up or?"

"Yeah, we're coming."

"But if you're not talking to him."

"It's fine, Alice. He booked your flights and knows what airport we're going to and at what time."

"True, but I don't want it to be awkward when I get there. I mean, am I allowed to talk to him, or...?"

I frowned slightly as I realized the conundrum I was putting her in. It wasn't like Alice could arrive and ignore him too. He had bought her ticket, and he was picking her up at the airport. Even I wasn't that immature to think I could expect my best friend to ignore him just because I was.

"It's fine. You can talk to him too."

"Can I be friendly with him?"

"I mean, if you want to."

She sighed.

"This sounds like it's going to be uncomfortable."

I thought about it for a few moments.

"I know, but…"

"But nothing. I mean, I totally understand where you're coming from, and I support you 100 percent. And we will get jobs, and we will save money, and we will look for our own place. In Manhattan, though, or the nicer parts of Brooklyn."

"Yeah, so I saw a couple of places, and they were two grand."

"Two grand? Okay, that's doable-ish if we split the rent."

"Yeah, I think so. We just have to get jobs."

"Yeah, and I guess we could do anything."

She didn't sound that happy about that.

"Don't worry, Alice. I'm not going to make you work at McDonald's or something."

"I mean, I don't mind if that's what we have to do to…"

"No! I did not make you leave your parents' beautiful home on Midnight Pass near the beach in Sarasota to come and sleep on a couch or an air mattress and work at McDonald's."

She giggled.

"Well, when you put it like that. That does sound kind of shitty."

"I know, but I think we have a real shot at some of the jobs I circled."

"Oh yeah? What are the jobs?"

"Well, one of the jobs I've seen is for an assistant."

"Okay, I guess I could be an assistant."

"Another one I've seen is to be a hostess at an exclusive club."

"Ooo. That sounds cool, and it doesn't sound like it'd be too much work. I mean, when you're a hostess, all you have to do is greet people, right?"

Alice sounded enthusiastic.

"That's exactly what I was thinking! And it said it starts at a hundred grand a year."

"What?!" She sounded doubtful.

"How does a hostess job start at a hundred grand a year?"

"We're in New York, Alice. Or at least, I'm in New York, and you'll be here soon. They make huge money here. It's probably some fancy-dancy steak restaurant where people pay like a thousand dollars for a rib eye."

"People pay a thousand dollars for a rib eye? It's like twenty-two dollars at Publix."

"How do you know exactly how much a rib eye costs at Publix?" I laughed.

"Because I went with my parents yesterday, and we bought steaks. And my dad was complaining about how 'steaks were now twenty-two dollars a pop.'"

"Well, tell him not to complain." I giggled. "If he came to New York, he'd be paying a thousand dollars."

"Oh, Rosalie!" Alice started laughing. "No way I'm going to tell my dad that. My parents are still very uncomfortable with me moving to New York, but I told them I'm an adult and will do what I want."

"Wow. What did your mom and dad say to that?"

"They actually looked kind of proud. They're giving me a thousand dollars because I told them that's what your parents gave you."

"Oh, cool."

"Yeah, I was surprised because I didn't think they'd give me anything."

"I knew they wouldn't be that cheap," I said.

"Yeah, but they told me it's time to grow up and figure out my path, and they hoped that…"

She paused.

"They hoped that what?" I asked curiously.

"Well, they said they hoped that both of us grew up."

"What?! What is that supposed to mean?"

"Well, my mom and dad think we're spoiled and impulsive and dreamers and, as they say, 'Dreaming doesn't pay the bills unless your dad is

Bill Gates.' And, well, neither of our dads is Bill Gates."

"I don't think there's anything wrong with being a dreamer," I said, sighing.

"Yeah. We don't have jobs yet, but it's not because we're stupid."

"Yeah, but we graduated from college and... We moved back home." Alice sighed. "It made me feel kind of like a loser."

"I know. I felt the same way. But you know what?"

"What?"

"We got this. We are going to be women of the city. We are going to... We're going to dominate, right?"

"Yeah, we are!"

I heard the door opening, and I froze.

"Oh shit. I think Oliver's back."

"What?" Alice said. "What are you gonna do?"

"Well, I can't pretend I'm asleep now because I folded up the sheets." I stood there and watched as the door opened. I wanted to close my eyes, but I couldn't.

"Who is it?" Alice said.

And then, my jaw dropped when I saw my brother walking in.

"Foster?!" I said, standing up in surprise.

He broke into a wide grin as soon as he saw me.

"Hey, sis. How's it going?"

"But I thought you would be gone for much longer?"

"I was, but I told my boss that my sister had just moved to New York, and I felt bad being away. So he let me leave early. Come on, give me a hug."

I walked over to him, phone by my side, and gave my brother a big hug. He kissed me on the cheek, and he looked me over.

"Looking good, sis. I've missed you."

"Really? It seemed like you didn't want me to move here."

"I was just teasing. I'm your big brother. I'm always here for you. So... are you on the phone with someone?" He looked down at the phone in my hand.

"Oh my gosh! Yes! It's Alice."

"Oh." His eyes lit up. "How is she?"

"You can speak to her," I said. "Hey, Alice," I spoke into the phone.

"Hey, what's going on?"

"It's just Foster, not Oliver." I looked at Foster. He looked at me curiously, and I pressed my lips together. And I didn't want to tell my brother that I was ignoring his best friend because he didn't fuck me when I begged him.

"Anyway, Alice. Say hello to Foster."

"Okay. Sure." She sounded girlish, and I frowned slightly.

"Here you go, Foster."

"Hey Alice, how's it going?" He spoke into the phone.

I watched my brother, smiling.

"When are we going to see you? I feel like it's been such a long time." He paused.

Oh shit, I thought to myself. I hoped that Alice didn't tell him that she was arriving tomorrow because then I knew I would be in deep shit and the huge smile that Foster had given me would soon turn into a frown.

"You what?" he said, turning to me. "Ha! No, I didn't know." He pointed his fingers at me, and he frowned. "Well, okay then. Yeah, I'll speak to my sister about this, and I guess I'll see you tomorrow. I won't hand you back to Rosalie right now because she and I need to chat. But you have a good day, Alice." He hung up the phone, folded his arms, and glared at me.

"Alice is moving to New York, and she's moving in?"

"Yeah, and...?" I said, giving him my best smile. "I thought that..."

"You thought what, Rosalie? You didn't even ask me."

"Oliver said it was okay. Oliver got the ticket. He—"

Foster let out a deep sigh. "You've got to be joking." He shook his head. "I go away for less than a week, and my sister and her best friend are now living with me?"

"What? Don't you like Alice?"

He looked at me for a couple of seconds, and his eyes narrowed.

"This has nothing to do with whether or not I like Alice. This is going to complicate everything."

"What do you mean? It's going to complicate what? It's fine. Once we get jobs and save enough money, we'll get our own place."

"Uh-huh," he said. He handed me my phone. "Oh, Rosalie. I've missed you, but what a whirlwind you've already brought with you."

"What are you talking about? What confusion?"

"Nothing," he said. "Come on, give me another hug."

I hugged my brother, and he kissed my forehead.

"I have missed you, you know."

"I missed you too."

"How's the job search going?" he asked as he stepped back.

"Um... I've seen some promising leads that I hope will lead to something else." I gave him my most winning smile.

"Okay, and how are you doing for cash?"

"I'm fine. Mom and Dad gave me a thousand dollars, and I have nine hundred and something of it left."

"Okay. That's good. Well, you let me know if you need anything before you get a job."

"Really?" I asked him in surprise. "You'd help me out?"

"Of course, I would. You don't think I'd just leave you hanging, did you?"

"Well, when I called you on the phone and emailed you, you didn't seem that excited about me coming to stay."

"Yeah, well..." He gave me a lazy grin. "I can't let you have a life too easy, right?"

"Oh, Foster," I said, love in my heart for my big brother. "You're such a goof."

"And how have you and Oliver been getting along?" he asked, staring at me casually.

"Um, fine. Why? What did he say?"

"Nothing," he said, shaking his head. "Actually, I haven't even spoken to him."

"Oh, that's good."

"Why? Is there something I should know?" He raised an eyebrow.

"Of course not."

"You're not making life difficult for him, are you? You know he splits the rent with me here, so it's really a lot for him to expect my sister and her best friend to stay. So you need to be on your best behavior."

"It's fine. I would never do anything to upset Oliver. He's the most wonderful man I've ever met," I said sarcastically.

Foster looked at me with clear, light-brown eyes.

"Hmm. That doesn't exactly ring true, but I'll take you at your word."

"It's fine. Oliver's amazing."

"Okay. Well, if you say so. I'm going to go into my room and take a shower. It's been a long day, but you want me to take you to breakfast later? Maybe a late brunch?"

"Yes, please! I was just about to make something, but O... I hadn't decided what I wanted yet."

"Okay. Well, give me twenty minutes, and I'll be out."

"Sounds good," I said. "Thanks, Foster."

"You're welcome, sis."

I watched as he walked into his bedroom, and then I went and sat down on the couch and leaned back. Well, I had a decision to make. I was going to have to be friendly to Oliver now because there was no way I could act like a bitch now that Foster was back, or he would know something was up.

Chapter 21

Rosalie

Foster and I were watching TV after our late breakfast, discussing my plans for the future. When I heard the door opening, I bit down on my lower lip, knowing that I would have to put on a show so that Foster didn't question what was happening. The door opened slowly, and Oliver walked in. Immediately, he looked over at the couch. His eyes widened when he saw Foster. "Dude, you didn't tell me you were coming back early."

Foster jumped off the couch. "Yeah, I figured my little sister is here. It's not right to leave you to suffer."

"Very funny, Foster," I said, rolling my eyes. "Hey, Oliver. How was work today?" I said, offering him a huge smile.

His lips twisted slightly, and he raised a single eyebrow as he looked at me. "It was pretty good. Thank you. How was your day?"

"Oh, great. I was so excited to see Foster, and we went to breakfast, and we've just been discussing what jobs I should look for." I smiled at him winningly. "I'm so excited for us to pick up Alice tomorrow. Foster knows she's coming. I gather you didn't tell him, after all."

"I didn't tell him." Oliver shook his head. "No, I didn't tell him. Was I supposed to?"

"I thought you said you were going to. That's why I didn't call him."

"Uh-huh," Oliver said. "I think I'm going to need a beer."

"Really? This early?" I asked him.

"Yeah. So you're talking to—"

"Oh, Oliver. You're so funny. Beer in the afternoon," I said, interrupting him quickly.

Foster looked at me. "You okay, Sis?"

"I'm fine. Why?"

"Because you're suddenly acting like someone on a game show."

"What do you mean?"

"You're acting all chirpy and shit. And just ten minutes ago, you were bitching and moaning about not knowing what you wanted to do with your life."

"Oh, well, you know how it is. I'm just happy

we're all home, and we can get the place ready for Alice's arrival tomorrow."

"So we need to figure out how this will work," Foster said, frowning. "I think I'll have a beer with you, Oliver."

"Sure thing, man. You want a pale ale?"

"Yeah, I'll have one."

"What about you, Rosalie?" Oliver asked me as he opened the fridge door.

"Sure. Why not feel like part of the group?"

"Well, you are part of the group," Oliver said with a smile. He took three bottles out of the fridge, and I watched as he popped the caps off each. He walked over to me and handed me a bottle. His fingers brushed mine, and I almost jumped back. "Here you go, Rosalie, my darling."

"Shut up," I hissed at him. "I'm still mad at you."

"Yet you're talking to me," he said softly.

"Only because Foster's here."

"Oh, so you don't want him to know that you're pissed off at me."

"I don't want him to know that we almost had sex. Do you?"

Oliver shrugged slightly. "I mean, I didn't do anything wrong. I walked away when you came on to me."

"You asshole," I said, glaring at him.

"Sorry. What did you say?" Foster said, staring at

us with a confused expression on his face. "I couldn't hear you properly."

"Oh, nothing. I was just telling Oliver that he should give me his bedroom." I laughed. "And he should take the couch."

"Yeah, right. Like that's going to happen," Foster said, laughing as he walked over and grabbed his beer from Oliver. "So where exactly is Alice going to sleep? I mean, she can sleep in my bed, but I don't think she'd like that. I mean, if she wouldn't mind if it was with me."

I stared at Foster. "Are you offering us your bedroom?"

"No, that's not what I was offering."

"Then what?" My jaw dropped. "Oh, my gosh, Foster. You were not saying that you could sleep with Alice."

"Not going to sleep sleep with her. I was just saying she could share the bed." He shrugged. "I mean, she's your best friend. She's a friend of mine, you know?"

"So you'd be okay if I shared the bed with Oliver?"

"What would I care?" he said, laughing. And then his eyes narrowed. "Though don't go thinking about it. Do you hear?"

"Why would I ever want to share a bed with Oliver?"

"Yeah. And why would I want to share a bed with Rosalie? She snores like crazy."

"No, I don't," I shouted.

"Yeah, you do. This morning you were snoring your ass off when I left for work."

"No, I wasn't." I glared at him.

"Yeah, you were. I thought that I was going to have to get some earplugs."

"Really," I said. "I was snoring when you left for work this morning."

"Yeah. Why do you think you weren't?" he said with his eyes on mine, a devilish glint in them.

"Oh, I don't know. I was asleep when you left. So maybe." I shrugged. I turned back to Foster. "And no, Alice is not sleeping in your bed. I thought we could get her an air mattress."

"Okay, that's going to take up practically the entire living room," Foster said.

"I mean, what else are we going to do? I'm on the couch, and it's not big enough for us. Neither one of you is offering your bedrooms."

Oliver sighed. "I mean, if you really want a bedroom, I can—"

"No," I said quickly. "You can't offer your bedroom to Alice and me." I didn't want his kindness. And also, there was no way I could sleep in his room, smelling his scent and seeing his possessions. It would drive me crazy and make me feel worse than I already did. Because even though I hated him, and even though he got on my last nerve, standing here next to Oliver, looking into his blue-gray eyes and staring at his slightly too long, dark hair, I just wanted to kiss him. I just wanted to touch him. He was so fucking sexy. I hated it.

"Yeah, you can't do that, Oliver," Foster said. "If anyone's going to give up their room, it should be me." He sighed. "And I don't really want to give up my room, but I guess let's see what happens when Alice gets here."

"You're seriously considering giving up your room?" I stare at him in shock. "No way."

"I mean, we'll see. So what's the plan for tonight?"

"I don't know," I said. "What do you guys normally do on a Friday night?"

"We go to a bar, or one of us has a date, or both of us have dates," Foster said with a laugh. "Speaking of, Diana called me the other day."

"Oh?" Oliver looked at him, though nothing in his expression gave anything away.

"Yeah. I was in a meeting, so I didn't answer. She didn't leave a voicemail or anything, and I didn't call her back. I was wondering what was going on."

"Don't know." Oliver shook his head. "She and I are over."

"Really? Like over over or just kind of over?"

"We're done. She and I are not looking for the same things. And I realized that her personality wasn't really…"

"Dude, her personality's always sucked," Foster laughed. "But you said she…" He paused and looked at me. "Well, I guess I don't want to have this conversation in front of my sister."

"Why not, Foster? Is this how you normally talk about women?"

"Have I said anything bad about women?" he said, looking at me with his light-brown eyes laughing slightly. "So shall we get dinner tonight? Maybe we can go to a comedy show."

"That sounds fun," I said. "Are you paying?"

"Didn't you say Mom and Dad gave you some money?"

"Yeah, but I don't want to spend all of it, especially not on a comedy show. I don't know how long it's going to have to last me."

"Oh my gosh. I'm going to be supporting you through everything?"

"And I'm kind of hoping you'll get dinner, too."

Foster stared at me. "Rosalie Sloane, you are lucky that you're my sister, and I love you."

"Hey, I'm sure Oliver would pay for me if you didn't want to. Right, Oliver?"

Oliver stared at me for a few seconds, a glint in his eyes as he looked at me, and then he looked at

Foster. "Yeah. I probably would," he said with a small smile.

"And you know what, guys?"

"What?" they said in unison.

"You don't have to worry about supporting me for too long because I'm going to find me a boyfriend, and he's going to want to spoil me. And—"

"Really?" Foster said, laughing. "You think you're going to find a boyfriend who's rich enough to spoil you?"

"Yes. You don't think I can?"

"I'm just saying."

"You're okay with that?" Oliver said sharply, looking at Foster.

"I mean, if she can find him, go right ahead," Foster said, shrugging.

"Really, Foster, you want your sister to..."

"To what?" Foster stared at him, a puzzled expression on his face.

"To pimp herself out?"

"How is she pimping herself out if she gets a boyfriend who wants to spoil her?" He shrugged. "Shit, I've dated many women I've spent thousands of dollars on." He shrugged. "That's just how it is in relationships. If Rosalie can find a man who wants to treat her, who am I to say no?"

"Thank you, big bro." I leaned over and gave him a kiss on the cheek. "You're amazing."

"Yeah. Well, I try. So shall we do steak or—"

"Sounds good to me," Oliver said, nodding. "Well, let me finish up some work emails, and then we can figure out the plans. Or do you want to choose a comedy show and just let me know?"

"I'll choose," I said. "I know Foster's sense of humor, and I don't want to go to some crappy redneck show."

"What do you mean?" Foster said, raising an eyebrow.

"You love those redneck comics. I don't want to hear any redneck jokes."

"What's a redneck joke?" Oliver said, laughing.

"You know, like, 'What did two rednecks take on a date?'"

"I don't know," Foster said, shaking his head.

"A gun and a fishing rod," I said, laughing.

Oliver and Foster exchanged glances and then looked at me. "You okay, Sis? That wasn't funny."

"Exactly. Redneck jokes aren't funny."

"Um, they're hilarious. Just because you're not hilarious... Oliver, did you think that joke was funny?"

"Um, can I plead the Fifth?"

"Well, I'm choosing the comic show. Okay?"

"Fine. I don't care," Foster said.

"Just please don't make it like *Legally Blonde* something or *The Vagina Monologues*," Oliver said, groaning.

"*The Vagina Monologues*? What do you know about *The Vagina Monologues*?"

"Well, Foster went on a date with this girl. She wanted to double-date with her friend, so he made me come, and we went to see *The Vagina Monologues*."

"It sucked," Foster said, laughing.

"It more than sucked," Oliver said. "So please, no *Vagina Monologues*."

"Fine," I said, but secretly, I now wanted to book *The Vagina Monologues* or something like that just to get on their nerves and, more specifically, Oliver's.

"Okay. Well, let me go to my room," Foster said. "I need to call someone."

"Okay. And Foster?"

"Yeah?" he asked.

"Can I ask why you were so upset earlier about me inviting Alice over, and now you're okay with it?"

"I mean, it's already done. It's not like I have any say, right?" He shrugged and looked away. "We'll figure it out." He walked to his bedroom and closed the door.

Oliver stood there, staring at me. "So Rosalie, it's nice to hear your voice again."

"I'm not friendly with you, Oliver."

"What do you mean, you're not friendly with me?"

"I mean, we're not friends, and I'm not going to be friendly."

"But you are being friendly."

"Only in front of my brother. When my brother's not here—"

"Ah, you're going to go back to being immature."

"I'm not immature. I'm just—"

"You're just what?"

"I'm just pissed, okay? I feel like you led me on, and I feel like—"

He sighed. He grabbed my hands, and he pulled me into him. "I've missed you, Rosalie."

"Missed what?"

"This," he said. And then he leaned down and gave me a long, deep kiss. I pressed my hands against his shoulders and kissed him back. He tasted like candy.

When he finally pulled back, I frowned. "Were you eating Skittles or something?"

"Yeah," he said. "How could you tell?"

"Your breath tasted like strawberries," I said.

"Ah. I thought it might have been your lips."

"What do you mean?" I asked him, confused.

"You're always wearing that strawberry lip gloss."

"Oh, yeah. I didn't realize you'd noticed."

"I notice everything, Rosalie," he said.

"Well, good for you. But don't do that again."

"Don't do what? Don't notice you?"

"No, don't kiss me."

"But why not? You seem to enjoy it."

"I thought it was okay, but I'm not going to just let you kiss me when you want to. Remember, we're nothing."

"We're friends."

"Yeah. And friends don't kiss."

"We could be kissing friends."

"Yeah, I don't think so. I'm not going to be kissing friends if I can't be a fucking friend."

"So you want to be friends with benefits." He raised an eyebrow.

"Excuse me?" I said, licking my lips.

"You want to be friends with benefits. Is that what you're telling me?"

"What? No, that's not what I said."

"Well, you want to sleep with me."

"Not anymore. I used to."

"Liar," he said. "I still want to sleep with you. Yeah, okay, I didn't because it wasn't a good decision. But..."

"But what?"

"But if you're going to sleep with someone, why shouldn't it be me?"

"Oliver, it's not going to be you because you're a jackass." I smiled at him. "And now I'm going to go and sit on the couch, and I'm going to play a game on my laptop. You can go and finish your work email because this conversation is over." I walked over to the couch and sat down, then I grabbed my laptop and opened my emails.

"Really, Rosalie?" he said, but I didn't look up. I couldn't. My heart was racing, and I knew he was playing games and that there was no way I could win. I didn't even know what he really wanted from me. That kiss had lit me on fire, and my panties were wet. I'd go into the bedroom with him right then and there if he asked. I wanted him so badly, yet he didn't deserve me. Yeah, I liked him, and yeah, I thought he was the sexiest man I'd ever seen in my life, but I wasn't going to play these games. I wasn't lying about that. He had really hurt me when he dissed me and rejected me, and I wasn't going to just let him go in and out of my life, making me have ups and downs beyond my control. He'd have to pay the price for dissing me. And that meant not getting me again.

Chapter 22

I knew I was fucking with Rosalie's head because I was fucking with my own head. When I saw her standing there giving me sexy glances, I couldn't stop but pull her into my arms and kiss her. And the kiss was amazing. And the way she squeezed my shoulders made me think about what it would be like to fuck her. I was in deep shit. I couldn't believe that Foster was back already. And I couldn't believe he was giving his blessing for her to find a boyfriend. I'd hoped that he would ban her from dating. Though I knew how ridiculous that sounded. She was twenty-two, soon to be twenty-three, and an adult. And even though she didn't have a job, she was capable of making her own decisions. She wasn't someone who could be told what to do. And I knew she was serious when she told me she wasn't entertaining the thought of sleeping with me again.

I knew I'd hurt her. I'd been shocked when she hadn't spoken to me for days. It had aggravated the shit out of me. I wanted to do nothing more than grab her by the hand and apologize and tell her that I would do whatever she wanted, but I knew that was stupid. Sexual attraction wasn't anything to base any sort of relationship on. And while we'd always been attracted to each other, I wasn't sure that we had anything strong enough to risk me losing Foster's friendship. It was starting to sound like a broken record. I sat down on the edge of my bed and sighed as I leaned back. Everything was getting so complicated. When Foster told me that Rosalie was coming to stay, I wasn't sure how I would feel.

It had been so long since I'd seen her since I'd spoken to her, I'd almost convinced myself that the old feelings were gone. But as soon as I saw her sitting in the airport, beautiful and vibrant, every feeling came rushing back. And the feelings had intensified when we bantered, and she'd flashed her beautiful brown eyes at me. What had been a young puppy crush had developed, and the chemistry between us was potent. And I could cut the tension with a knife. I wanted Rosalie so badly. I'd barely been able to concentrate all week. I kept replaying in my mind that night on my bed, the way she'd kissed me, the way she'd sucked me, the way she tasted. And all I wished was that I didn't have a moral compass. All I wished was that I could have taken her and felt her and know what it was like to be inside her so that I could rid myself of this want and desire. I heard a knock on the door, and I sat up. "Hey, come in."

"Hey, what's up, dude?" Foster walked in. "I just wanted to say sorry."

"Huh?" I looked at him in confusion.

"I know you didn't sign off for my sister and her best friend to move in when we got this place."

"Dude, it's fine. It's a big enough place."

"I mean, it's one thing to have Rosalie on the couch, but it's another thing to have Alice here, sleeping on an air mattress in the living room." He sighed.

I looked at him, nodding, wondering if there was more to the story than he was letting on. "So what are we going to do?"

"I don't know."

"You don't really want to give up your room. I don't want to give up my room. I don't really want to have an ugly-ass air mattress in the middle of the living room. Rosalie can't really stay on the couch forever."

"Yeah, you're right." He sighed. "I think maybe it's time to get a bigger place. I think maybe it's time to buy."

"Oh." I stared at him in surprise. "I thought you were going to wait a couple of years."

"I was going to." He nodded. " But interest rates are pretty low right now. I've got a good deposit saved." He shrugged. "It would just make things easier."

"So I guess we won't be roommates anymore or...?"

"I mean, I'm cool if you still want to be roommates. I was thinking, well, I was thinking we could actually go in on a property together. We could get a brownstone or something. It could be an investment property. And when Rosalie and Alice finally get jobs, they could start paying us rent."

"So they'd live with us full time?" I asked, surprised.

"Well, my parents would prefer Rosalie close to me, and I feel like I should look after Alice as well as she is Rosalie's best friend. Then I want to make sure she doesn't meet any sort of strange guys or..."

"Uh-huh," I said, looking at him suspiciously. Did Foster have a thing for Alice? And if he did, how had I never known this? "I mean, it sounds like a good deal. I got a couple hundred grand saved up as well. And I have been looking at properties recently. So you really want to do this?"

He looked at me and grinned. "I think it would be amazing."

"So we're going to do this," I said, jumping up.

"I think so."

"Awesome. Are we looking in Manhattan or Brooklyn?"

"I guess we should figure out our maximum budget and work from there," he said, "plus I guess we could get some input from the girls."

"Yeah, sounds good. I'd love to get their input. I'm sure Rosalie has many thoughts and ideas," I said with a small smile.

"I'm sure she does," Foster said, frowning.

"Let's not let her think she can make the decision because I know she'll take over." I started laughing.

"Yeah, but maybe this is what she needs. She's been really down recently. And well, I want to make sure she's doing okay."

"Oh, she's been down? Why? I hadn't realized?"

"Oh, well, there's one thing that..." He looked at the door and then closed it. "Sorry, I don't want her listening just in case."

"No worries. What is it?"

"So there's one thing that no one outside the family knows."

"Oh," I stared at him, curious what he was going to say.

He sighed. "So and I guess I shouldn't be saying this, but seeing as you're my best friend and Rosalie's living with us now, I want you to understand that she might be a little bit moody from time to time because of this."

"Dude, just tell me. What is it?"

"So just now, when we were in the living room and you made that comment about Rosalie dating and finding a boyfriend and all that, the reason I was like, 'whatever' was because I know it's not going to happen."

"Oh, sorry. You've got me confused. So you're okay with her finding a sugar daddy, or you're not?"

"Dude, of course not. I don't want my sister banging some random rich dude who's using her."

"Then why did you…?"

"She's not going to get a boyfriend here." He laughed.

"Why not? That's all she keeps talking about."

"Oh, she's just saying it. She has a boyfriend."

"What?" I said, staring at him in shock. "She has a boyfriend?"

"Yeah. That's what I was going to tell you. I guess he moved overseas for some grad program, and she got upset and said she was going to break up with him. And that's why she's here in New York."

"I thought she was here because your parents—"

"No, dude. I'm pretty sure that's an excuse. She's here because she and Graham—"

"Graham?" I said, raising an eyebrow.

"Yeah. She and Graham are on a break because she was pissed that he took the scholarship and fellowship to a school in, I believe it's Germany, as opposed to staying in the States."

"She has a boyfriend? What? I had no clue, dude."

"Yeah. Well, I just wanted to let you know. That's why she might be a little moody. Just ignore whatever she says and does. You know how women are when they're in bad relationships?"

"I guess so. Thanks for telling me."

"No worries, dude. And maybe at dinner, we can tell Rosalie about our plan to buy the brownstone?"

"Yeah, let's do that," I said, "but I've got to send some emails now. Okay?"

"Sounds good, dude. You get back to work." He laughed. "You need to make as much money as possible so we can get big bonuses this year to buy that place."

"Tell me about it." I laughed even though I was pissed as hell. Foster left my room, and I closed the door behind him. I was absolutely furious. Rosalie had a boyfriend. What the fuck? And she'd been begging me to fuck her. She wanted me to take her virginity, but why? Why didn't she just want her boyfriend to do it? Unless she was testing me and playing games with me. I could not believe Rosalie was dating someone. And she had the nerve to get upset about Diana when she hadn't told me about fucking Graham cracker. I pressed my lips together and grabbed my phone. I sent Rosalie a text message. "We need to talk." I was pissed.

She responded immediately, "About what?"

"Your brother just told me something very interesting," I said, typing quickly.

"What?" she responded.

"About someone you forgot to tell me about," I replied. No response came, and I sat there seething. I knew I could go into the living room and have a one-on-one conversation with her. But I didn't want Foster to overhear. Especially if I started raising my voice, so I sent another message. "So were you going to tell me about Graham cracker or not?"

She responded, "Oh."

"Oh? That's it?"

"It's a long story," she answered, "and it's not what you think."

"Really? You're not heartbroken over Graham? You weren't using me to get over him?"

She said a wide-eye emoji and then a laughing emoji. "Think whatever you want to. I don't owe you any explanation."

I pressed my lips together and threw the phone down on the bed. Fuck, I was pissed as hell. And there was no way I was letting this night pass without having a conversation with Rosalie. I don't care where it was. I don't care what she has to say or if she wants to ignore me. She owed me some answers. I needed to know what the make-out session had been all about. Why had she asked me to take her virginity when she was freaking in love with some other dude? I needed to get to the bottom of it fast because I'd never been angrier and more upset. And even though I didn't want to admit it, I could feel the jealousy coursing through my heart.

Chapter 23

The sound of Pink came through my laptop speakers, and I sat on the couch staring at my phone. I couldn't believe that Foster had told Oliver about Graham. I smiled slightly to myself. Foster didn't know exactly what had happened in that relationship, so he hadn't given Oliver the exact truth. And that was why Oliver was so salty. He had no idea that Graham meant absolutely nothing to me.

Yes, Graham and I had dated for a couple of months, but the relationship had ended amicably. We hadn't even really fooled around that much. He'd been someone I'd met in one of my history classes, and I thought he was smart, but we didn't really have any chemistry.

However, I'd played up the breakup to my parents to make them feel sorry for me. Initially, the only option they gave me was to move home. It was only when they thought I was so down and depressed about the relationship that they offered the option of moving to New York and living with Foster. I knew I was old enough to make my own way in life, but I wasn't dumb enough to think I could make it without help.

I was privileged enough not to have had to have worked in college or high school. And I realized that I was lucky in that regard. However, I didn't feel well equipped to enter the real world. It was hard not having money coming in every month. It was hard having to figure out how to pay rent and bills and buy food. And I didn't blame my parents for that because they'd done their best, but I felt lost. And I didn't want to be lost. I didn't want to have to rely upon anyone else. I certainly didn't want to rely upon a man, no matter what I joked about with Foster.

I wanted to go into Foster's room and tell him off for telling Oliver about Graham. But I knew if I did that, he'd ask how I knew. And it wasn't like I could tell him that Oliver had texted me in a bad mood because he was upset that I hadn't told him I had a boyfriend. Not that Graham was my boyfriend.

I let out a deep sigh. I really should tell Foster and Oliver I didn't care that Graham had gone to Germany to study. We had a farewell dinner, and I gave him a big hug right before he left. But I wasn't going to say anything because I wanted Oliver to feel like shit. I wanted him to know that he wasn't the only man out there.

I knew his male ego was wondering why I wanted to sleep with him if I had a man, but let him wonder. Let him think that I was using him. I didn't care.

Foster opened his door and came into the living room. "Rosalie, turn that down."

"What?"

"Your music is way too loud."

"It's fine. Just put some earplugs in if it's bothering you."

"This is my apartment, and I don't think—"

"Oh my gosh. Okay."

I turned the music down a couple of notches.

"So I found a really cool comedy club that looks fun."

"Okay." He shrugged. I could tell he didn't care, but I continued.

"There are going to be ten comics. And then, at the end, we get to vote for the funniest one. And the funniest one will actually have a spot on Comedy Central."

"Good for them."

"So this is really important that we get there on time and we get good seats and—"

"Rosalie, I don't really care. Just tell us what time."

"Well, I need to know where we're eating first."

"Why don't you choose the restaurant?"

"Okay. Awesome." I beamed at him.

"I think I'll call Alice and tell her you're back. So—"

"No," he said.

"What do you mean, no?"

"I mean, no, you can't keep calling her."

"Yes, I can. She's my best friend."

"What are you going to call her about now?"

"I was just going to call her and tell her that we're trying to figure out an option for where we're both going to sleep."

"Uh-huh. You spoke to her earlier and said you would figure it out when she got here, right?"

"Yeah. And we haven't."

"Actually, Oliver and I have come up with a plan."

"Oh yeah? What's the plan?" I asked, narrowing my eyes.

"Well, I figured you can sleep with Oliver, and Alice sleeps with me."

"What?" I said, my jaw dropping. I couldn't believe he just said that. Was Oliver trying to get me into his bed after all? Foster started laughing when he saw the expression on my face.

"Oh my gosh. Of course not, Rosalie. Oliver doesn't want to sleep with you. And I certainly don't want to sleep with Alice."

That stung more than he knew.

"Well, we don't want to sleep with you guys either. So what's the plan?"

"He'll tell you at dinner," he said.

"Okay, I hope it will be good for all this suspense."

"Oh, Rosalie," he said, "Now just keep the music down. Okay? I need to finish up some work. Just because I left early doesn't mean I don't have anything to do."

"Well, bully for you. I'm looking for jobs. So please stop bothering me as well."

"You're looking for jobs while blasting Pink and scrolling on your phone?"

"I'm looking for jobs on my phone. Thank you very much."

"Uh-huh. Sure you are."

"You do know that a smartphone has the internet

on it, right, Foster? Or are you still stuck in the 1700s?"

"I know it's much easier to look for jobs on your laptop. That way, the screen is bigger, and you can read the qualifications needed for the positions."

"Blah, blah, blah," I said in return. "You can go back to your room now, Foster."

He stared at me for a couple of seconds and shook his head.

"You know what? You're lucky I just got to town because I'm going to go easy on you right now, Rosalie. But if you still have that attitude in a week—"

"Whatever, Foster. Please don't go all daddy on me. You're my big brother. You're not Dad."

"Yeah. Dad told me I'm in charge while you're living with me. And I want to make sure that you—"

"Foster, really? Listen to yourself. Also, never have kids because you would be the most annoying father ever."

He smiled at me then.

"I can't say what sort of mother you would be because I don't even think there are words in the dictionary."

"You're so juvenile, Foster."

"I'm juvenile?" He shook his head. "Look in the mirror, kid."

I pressed my lips together and sat back down on

the couch. I was not dealing with my brother and his arrogant, bigheaded attitude. He thought just because he was older that he always knew best. And he always treated me like a little kid. He was so freaking annoying. I'd probably be seventy years old, and he'd still call me kid. No, that wouldn't fly, and I had to let him know.

I grabbed my phone and called Alice.

"Hey girl, what's going on?"

"Is Foster there?"

"Why do you keep asking about Foster?" I asked her curiously.

"I was just wondering because I wasn't sure if he was mad I was coming."

"He's fine. He said he has some solution."

"Oh, what's the solution?" she asked eagerly.

"I don't know. He said you sleep in his bed, and I sleep in Oliver's."

"Really? She sounded happy. "He wants me in his bed?"

"He was joking, Alice. Oh my gosh. Is there something you're not telling me?"

"No. Why? What do you mean?"

"Are you interested in my brother?"

"No, of course not," she said too sharply and quickly.

Suddenly, it dawned on me.

"Alice," I said softly.

"Yes, Rosalie?"

"Do you have a crush on Foster?"

"What are you talking about?" she squeaked out.

"Oh my gosh, you do. You have a crush on my brother. Are you crazy?"

"No, I don't. I…"

"Alice, do not lie to me. I'm your best friend."

"I know," she whined. "I'm sorry."

"Oh no, no, no. Alice, how can you have a crush on my brother? He's such a dickhead."

"But he's so cute. He's always been so cute."

What? How long have you had this crush?"

"Since we were fifteen."

"And you never told me?"

"Rosalie, you are always arguing with Foster. Could you imagine if I told you I had a crush on him? You'd kill me."

"I want to kill you now." I sighed.

"So what the fuck does that mean? What do you mean, Rosalie? "

"I mean, are you going to try to make a move on him? Are you-

"No, of course not. I wouldn't do that. That would be way too awkward and weird.

"I mean, it would be very weird." I sighed. "Oh my God. I can't believe you like my brother."

"Don't tell him. Okay?"

"Of course, I'm not going to tell him. I don't want him to get a big head."

"Oh, Rosalie." She giggled. "So what's going on?"

"Frigging Foster, the love of your life."

"He's not the love of my life," she said quickly.

"Well," I continued, "he told Oliver about Graham and me."

"What? What do you mean?"

"I don't know exactly what he said, but Oliver seems to think that Graham is the love of my life, and that I'm still dating him, and that I was really sad." I started giggling. "And he got all pissed off and was like, 'Why would you try to sleep with me? Is it because you're trying to get over Graham'?"

"But you couldn't give two shits about Graham."

"I know, but he doesn't know that. It's perfect."

"Oh, Rosalie. You're not going to let him think that you still like Graham, are you?"

"I don't know. I mean, he deserves to feel a little bit of pain and worry and concern after what he put me through."

"Oh, Rosalie. We really need to find a place. I guess maybe the Bronx doesn't sound so bad after all."

"Girl, we're not moving to the Bronx. If we play our cards right, we'll have the guys in the living room, and we'll each have our own bedroom." I started laughing. "I mean, maybe. Don't count on it."

"Trust me, I'm not," she said. "But hey, I'll call you later. Okay? I need to finish packing. And then my parents are taking me out for a goodbye dinner, which I'm sure is going to be to lecture me on what I should and shouldn't do and all the things to look out for while I'm in the city."

"Oh, yay. Lucky you. My parents had that talk with me. So annoying."

"I know. So I'll speak to you later?"

"Yeah, girl."

"Bye."

I hung up the phone with her, feeling happy and disgusted at the same time. Freaking Alice had a crush on Foster.

On the one hand, it was kind of cool. If they got together, she'd be my sister, and we would be family, like real legit family. But then eww, I couldn't imagine her kissing Foster or doing anything else. Frankly. I didn't think he was good enough for her.

Yeah, he was handsome in his own way. I mean, he was my brother. I didn't look at him like that. And he had a good job and made good money, but he was a player. I knew for a fact that he hooked up with more women than I knew. And I didn't want that for Alice. I wanted her to be with a nice regular guy just looking for one woman. And I was pretty sure Foster didn't even know what monogamy meant.

My phone started beeping, and I looked down. I grinned when I saw it was a message from Oliver. I opened it and read it.

"So why exactly did you want to sleep with me if you have a boyfriend? Please do tell."

I turned my phone off, then sat back and smiled. Oh, Oliver, I'm going to let you stew on that for a long, long time.

Chapter 24

"Wow. Dinner is amazing," I said, beaming at Oliver and Foster. "Do we have time to get dessert?"

"I don't know, Rosalie." Foster stared at his watch. "You're the one who booked the tickets for the comedy show. What time does it start?"

"Nine o'clock, but I don't know how far away it is from here."

"Didn't you check to make sure that the restaurant was close to the comedy show?" Foster sounded annoyed.

I pressed my lips together. He was really trying to

248

ruin my buzz. "So Oliver," I said sweetly, "you've been quiet all evening."

"Have I?" he said, raising a single eyebrow. "I thought you were the queen of quiet."

"Huh?" Foster said, looking at Oliver. "Since when has Rosalie been quiet? She knows how to talk a mile a minute."

"Very funny, Foster. Hold on. Let me check my phone and see. I entered the address to the comedy show into Google Maps. Oh, it's only a seven-minute walk from here. We're fine. I'm going to get the cheesecake. Or should I get the creme brulée?"

"I don't know. Get whatever you want," Foster said.

"Why are you in such a bad mood?"

"I don't know," he said, frowning. "Maybe because—"

"Maybe because what? Is it Amelia?" Oliver asked him curiously.

"Who's Amelia?" I said, looking at Oliver and then looking at my brother. "You never told me about any Amelia."

"That's because she's not important," Oliver said, sighing.

"Um, but who is she if she's not important." I looked at Oliver. "You brought her up, so tell me who she is."

"It's really not for me to tell," he said, shaking his head. "It's your brother's friend."

"Your friend or your friend with benefits?"

Foster looked at me and rolled his eyes. "Oh my gosh. Really, Rosalie?"

"What? I want to know who Amelia is and why she's got you in such a bad mood."

"Fine. Amelia was a lady I was dating, and we have not gone out in a while."

"But?"

"But what?"

"She's back in town tomorrow," Oliver said, shrugging as he looked at Foster. "Sorry, bro. But you know she would get it out of you eventually, and we didn't want this to drag on all night."

"It's fine. Yep. She's a lady I've kind of seen, and she's back in town tomorrow."

"So who cares? New York's a really big place."

"She lives in the building," Oliver said, his lips twitching.

"Ah," I said. "And what? She doesn't get the hint that you're not interested."

"Maybe because Foster didn't exactly tell her," Oliver said, laughing.

"What?" I stared at him. "What do you mean you didn't tell her?"

"Look, it was casual," he said, shrugging. "I didn't think it was any big thing. We met in the elevator one day. We hooked up a couple of times, but then she got a little bit clingy. I wasn't interested, so I stopped answering her calls. But then she saw Oliver and asked Oliver how I was doing. Oliver told her that I was away on business, so now she thinks I haven't been calling or answering her messages because I was at a very important work meeting."

"How do you know this?" I asked curiously.

"Because she's texted me a billion times saying, 'Oh, I forgive you. Don't worry about it. I went away on a long cruise, and I'm coming back tomorrow. So when you get back...'" Foster paused. "Well, you get the gist of it."

"Ah, so she's back tomorrow, and she wants to resume things with you, hey?"

"Well, just be a man about it and tell her you're not interested."

"She's crazy," Oliver said, grinning. "Like really crazy."

"She can't be any crazier than Diana," I said, staring at him.

Oliver groaned. "Well, Diana is also crazy but in a different way."

"Diana was a bitch," I said. "I'm sorry, but how you slept with that—"

Foster held his hand up. "Hold on a minute. You met Diana and you know the situation? You didn't tell me this."

"I met her when we went to Oliver's work event the other day at The Ritz-Carlton."

"I didn't know you went to The Ritz-Carlton with Oliver for his work event." He frowned. "What else are you guys not telling me?"

"Nothing," I said as I quickly picked up my wine-glass and chugged. Oliver looked around for the server.

"I think we should be ordering desserts soon so we can get it quickly."

Foster didn't seem to realize something was up. "So anyway, Amelia is in town tomorrow, and Alice is in town tomorrow. I just don't want there to be any complications."

"What complications?" I stared at my brother. "You're not planning on making a move on Alice, are you?"

"What? No. Of course not. Why would you think that? I would never make a move on your friend. She's young and immature, just like you."

"Uh-huh." I stared at my brother through narrowed eyes. "I think you're being way too defensive. But just in case you're trying to play mind games with me, Alice is off-limits to you."

"Excuse me?" he said, lifting up his glass of wine and finishing it. "What do you mean, Alice is off-limits to me?"

"Alice is my best friend, and she deserves the

world. She deserves a man who will treat her like a princess, just like I do." I gave Oliver a pointed look. "And, well, Foster, you can't even communicate with women. I definitely don't want you playing around with Alice."

"I'm not interested in playing around with Alice, so don't worry about it in the meantime," he said.

"Well, why are you so concerned that Alice is coming tomorrow and Amelia is coming back to town tomorrow?"

"I just don't want Amelia thinking that Alice and I have something."

"Hmm, okay. And why would Amelia think that?"

"You don't know Amelia." Oliver interrupted. "There you are."

"Hello? How can I help you? You called me over, sir?" The server stopped next to the table.

"Yes. Rosalie here would like to order some dessert."

"Yes, please." I beamed up at the handsome server. "Do you recommend the creme brulée, strawberry cheesecake, chocolate tort, or... I have an idea." I paused and looked at my brother and Oliver. "What if each of us orders one, and then we can try a piece of each other's?"

"I don't want to have dessert," Foster said. "What

a waste of calories and way too much sugar and carbs."

"Oh, you're a bore, Foster." I rolled my eyes. I looked at Oliver. "What do you think?"

"I don't really do dessert," he said, shrugging.

"Okay." I was disappointed. "So then, what do you recommend?"

The server gave me a conspiratorial grin. "Well, you can always get all three desserts yourself and try each of them. There's nothing that says you have to finish all of them."

"Ah, that's true," I said, beaming at him. "Thank you, Carlos."

"No worries. Your name was Rosalie?"

"Yeah. I'm new to town. I'm living with my brother and his best friend until I find my place and a job."

"Oh, well, if you're looking for a job, we're hiring here."

"You are? For what positions?"

"Serving, hosting, bussing." He grinned at me. "But I have a feeling that you would like to be a host-ess. You've got such a beautiful smile. All of our guests would be more than happy to be greeted by you."

"Oh my gosh. Thank you so much. That is so sweet of you to say." I beamed at him.

"No worries. If you want—"

"We'll get all three desserts. Thank you." Oliver cut him off. "And the check. We have a comedy show to get to, and we don't want to be late."

Carlos looked over at Oliver, who was frowning at him, and he nodded. "Yes, sir. Of course." He turned back to me. "I'll give you my number, and you can call or text if you have any questions about the job."

"Will do. Thank you," I said, smiling at him. I looked over at Oliver. "That was so rude of you."

"What was rude? I was just being honest. You want to get to the comedy show on time, right?"

"Of course I do, but..." I looked at Foster. "Come on, Foster. Wasn't Oliver being rude?"

"I think Oliver was being very nice to you. You're lucky that he ordered you all three desserts. Frankly, I was gonna tell you not to get any dessert."

"Excuse me? You're rude."

"Well, I'm just saying, do you really need dessert after you had an appetizer, a main course, and two glasses of wine?"

"Oh my gosh, Foster. You're such a bore. Definitely don't date Alice. She would dump you in a heartbeat."

"Why would she dump me? She'd be lucky to date someone like me."

I started laughing then. "Oh my gosh. You're just

as obnoxious as Oliver is. Both of you think you're God's gift to women, but you're not."

Foster frowned then. "Why do you think Oliver thinks he's God's gift to women?"

"Because he does, the way he... Well..." I mumbled, not knowing what to say. I didn't want to play my hand. Oliver's eyes twinkled as he laughed at me.

"Yeah, Rosalie. Why am I obnoxious? I thought I was a sweet gentleman, you know? Protecting the virtue of all innocent women."

I glared at him for a couple of seconds. "Ha ha, very funny, Oliver."

"I'm glad I could make you laugh."

"Did you hear me laughing?" I said.

"No, but I could tell you wanted to." He smirked, then I felt someone's hand on my knee.

"Oh," I said loudly as it slid up my thigh.

"What is going on, Rosalie?" Foster looked irritated.

"Oh my gosh. You should just go home. You're being so mean and rude to me."

He let out a deep sigh. "I'm sorry. I'm just not looking forward to the confrontation I know I'll have with Amelia tomorrow. Because she can't take a hint. And she'll show up at the apartment and demand answers."

"I just hope she's not wearing a negligee again,"

Oliver said, shaking his head. "The last time I had to see her titties shaking, well, it almost gave me a fright."

"You what?" I said, staring at him.

"Hey," he said, shrugging. "It wasn't me. It was her."

Foster rolled his eyes. "She wanted to seduce me, so she came over wearing a negligee. She was standing in the living room doing what she thought was a sexy dance, and Oliver came out of his room and basically—"

"Basically, I saw her titties popping about," Oliver said. "She's got a nice body, but, yeah, she's crazy."

"Oh my gosh," I said. "You two are hot messes."

Chapter 25

Oliver

"And that's how babies are made, folks!" The comedian took a bow, and the crowd started laughing. I watched as Rosalie couldn't contain her giggles. She threw her head back and laughed out loud. Her long dark hair was shaking against her back. She looked over at me with warm crinkled eyes.

"Oh my gosh. He's so funny. He's absolutely the best."

"Yeah, he's pretty funny." I nodded in agreement. I looked over at Foster. "What'd you think?"

"Yeah, he's pretty good. I'd see him again."

Foster smiled congenially. "Good job, Rosalie. You picked a great comedy show."

"Wow! Praise from my big bro. I'm shocked."

"Hey, I give praise when praise is due," he said.

"Well, I'm glad you're in a better mood," she said, smiling at him. I guess all he needed was a good couple of laughs. We stood with the rest of the crowd and headed out of the comedy club. I looked at my watch. It was midnight.

"So do you guys want to get one last drink or..." I looked at Foster and Rosalie. Rosalie nodded eagerly.

"Yeah, let's do it."

Foster sighed. "I hate to say this, but I'm feeling a little bit beat up right now. Probably with the time change and all. And we have to be up early to get stuff ready tomorrow."

"Yeah," Rosalie said, "I guess, but it's Friday night. I thought we could have some fun."

"But aren't we taking Alice out tomorrow?" Foster said.

"Yeah, but can't you have two nights of fun?"

"Rosalie, I'll go for that drink with you if you want. Foster can go home." Rosalie looked at me with a small smile.

"I mean, you don't have to do that, Oliver."

"It's fine," I said, "Hey, we're friends, right?" She stared at me and nodded.

"Fine. Okay. We'll meet you back later."

"Okay," Foster said with a nod.

"Don't do anything I wouldn't do."

"Now would I?" I beamed at Foster, and he laughed. He gave Rosalie a hug and a kiss on the cheek.

"See you later, chica. Don't drink too much. You know you don't do well if you have too much alcohol."

"I'm not going to drink too much. Thank you, Foster."

"I just don't want you throwing up like that time when..."

"Oh my God, Foster, really?" She glared at him.

"Sorry. You're my kid sister. What can I say? I'm always going to see you as..."

"I know, a little girl," she said. "La dee da. Come on, Oliver, let's go. Bye, Bro." Rosalie grabbed my arm, and I welcomed the touch. We made our way down the street, and she looked up at me in surprise.

"And before you ask, don't."

"Before I ask what?" I said with an innocent expression.

"Before you ask about Graham."

"You mean Graham crust?"

"His name is not Graham crust."

"You mean Graham cracker?"

"His name is not Graham cracker."

"Sorry, I figured it had to be one of the two." I grinned at her. "And why don't you want to answer?"

"What is there to answer?"

"Why didn't you tell me you had a boyfriend." She pressed her lips together.

"Same reason you didn't tell me about Diana."

"Yeah, but I wasn't using you to get over Diana. I couldn't give two shits about Diana."

"And I wasn't using you to get over Graham either." She sighed.

"Really, you didn't want me to take your virginity because you were upset that your boyfriend took a grad student position in another country and left you. "

"I couldn't care less. I'm the one who helped him choose the universities to apply to for grad school." She rolled her eyes, and then she pressed her lips together. "Not that it's any of your business." I stared down at her curiously.

"So you're really not upset that he broke up with you?"

"It was a mutual breakup, and no, I couldn't care less."

"So why does Foster feel like you're absolutely beside yourself with grief?"

"Because I kind of pretended to my parents that I was really upset when we broke up so that they would have sympathy on me and allow me to come to New York."

"Oh," I said, staring at her, suddenly feeling light and happy.

"So you are really not heartbroken over Graham."

"Yeah, that's what I said."

"And then you really did want me to take your virginity."

"That was pretty obvious."

"And so you really are into me for me."

"I'm not into you for anything, Oliver. Actually, I'm not even into you anymore."

"Liar," I said, grabbing her hands and pressing her against the wall.

"What are you doing?" she asked, blinking up at me in shock.

"I think I'm about to give you the kiss you've been asking for all evening."

"I haven't been asking for anything," she said. But I could tell from the way her lips were trembling and the way she was staring at my lips that she was lying.

"Really?" I said in a deep, throaty voice as I lowered my face toward her. I blew into her ear slightly and felt her body tremble against mine.

"Oh, Rosalie, what am I going to do to you?"

"Oliver, I don't want to play these games. Either

you're interested in something with me, or you're not."

"I mean, I think it's very clear that I have been interested in something with you."

"Well, then, why did you turn me down?"

"Because I didn't think it was a good idea for me to take your virginity."

"But you're okay with kissing me?"

"I think that's already been proven."

"So what, we're just going to kiss and pretend we don't want it to go further?" I looked down at her.

"Perhaps."

"No, I'm not interested in that. And I'm also not interested in someone who would tell me that they didn't think I was good enough for them."

"When did I tell you I didn't think you were good enough for me?"

"When you said you couldn't really see us in a relationship."

"I didn't mean it like that," I said, shaking my head. "I didn't mean that I didn't want to date you because you weren't good enough for me."

"So then what did you mean?" she asked, an attitude in her voice.

"I meant that I don't know if our personalities are compatible. You're still quite young. You're trying to find yourself. I found myself, and I have a career. I'm an adult."

"I'm an adult too."

"Yeah, you are, but sometimes you act like a little kid."

"Sometimes you act like a little kid as well, Oliver."

"Really, when?"

"How about the fact that you didn't want me until you thought I still had the hots for my ex-boyfriend? And then, all of a sudden, you wanted me, and are willing to talk and try to make something happen." I stared at her for a few seconds and nodded. She had a point. Hearing about Graham had made me hella jealous and upset.

"I will admit that thinking you were using me to get over your ex-boyfriend did piss me off. See, and I will admit that it has made me reconsider what we could possibly have."

"But you don't want to date me, and you don't want to fuck me."

"Well, that's not true, Rosalie. I want to fuck you very badly. I just don't want to fuck you and then break your heart."

"You think so highly of yourself that just because you fucked me, it would hurt me?"

"I think, as I said before, that it could get complicated really quickly, and I don't want your brother to be pissed off and kill me if things go badly."

"Well, then, maybe he doesn't have to know." I stared at her for a few seconds.

"So what are you saying?"

"I'm saying we could sneak around." She gave me an innocent smile and batted her eyelashes at me. "I'm sure you've snuck around before."

"Perhaps I have." I nodded. "And you'd be okay with that?"

"Yeah. I mean, you're not the only one who wonders if anything between us could work." She stared at me, and her words hurt me a little bit.

"So you don't think we could work if we got into a relationship?" I asked her.

"Yeah. I'm not sure if we could. You might be hot, but..."

"But what?"

"You have a bad attitude, and you're temperamental, and you think it's your way or the highway and—"

"Okay," I said, cutting her off. "So there are several things you don't like about me."

"There are several things that I think are lacking in your personality, yes. Just because you're an attorney, and you're older than me and making money doesn't mean you're better than me. And it really doesn't mean that you're that much more mature than me." She pressed her hand against my chest. "I like you, Oliver. I fancy you, at least. I've got the hots for you. I always have, and yeah, I would like you to be my first because that's something I've wanted for a long time. Seeing you again just reminded me of how much chemistry we have, and you make me laugh. And well, I still want you," She looked up at me. "But I'm not going to play these games with you. So you have a choice to make."

"I do?" I asked, staring at her in surprise. "I have the choice, or you have the choice?"

"You have the choice, Oliver. We either have some fun, keep it a secret from my brother…"

"Are we also going to keep it a secret from Alice?" I stared down at her. "Because you know, as much as I love her, she can't really keep a secret."

"Who is she going to tell?"

"I don't know, but what if she let something slip in front of Foster, and then we have to explain why we've been lying to him."

"Fine. I won't tell Alice, but you know what that means?"

"No. What does that mean?"

"It means she's going to want to go out clubbing at night. It means she's going to want us to date other people."

"What do you mean?"

"It means I'm going to have to see other guys, or she and Foster will get suspicious."

"I don't like the sound of that." I frowned,

staring at her. "I don't want you seeing other guys. I don't want you kissing other guys."

"So that would make you jealous?" she asked, her lip twitching. There was a laugh in her eyes.

"I mean, yeah, I mean, weren't you jealous when you heard about Diana?" She glared at me.

"I was pissed off more than jealous."

"Uh-huh," I said, staring at her. "So then my choice is..."

"What? Your choice is..."

"You'll be cool about everything I do, and we'll have fun. And then we'll see how we feel about the situation in a couple of months." I licked my lips and stared down at her.

"Okay,"

"And you're fine with this?"

"Why wouldn't I be?"

"Well, I'm not sure how you'll feel if I'm going on dates with other women." She froze, so she stared up at me.

"Why would you be going on dates with other women?"

"Well, wouldn't Foster and Alice get suspicious of me if I, all of a sudden, am a loser at home every night?" She bit down on her lower lip and sighed.

"Fine, but..."

"But what?" I said.

"You can't sleep with them."

"Okay, that's a deal. You can't sleep with any guys you go on a date with."

"Well, I've never even had sex before, so I don't think that will be an issue."

"Yeah, but once we consummate this arrangement," I said, "I don't know what you might feel recklessly inclined to do."

"I'm not going to sleep with anyone else."

"Okay, good. And no making out either."

"What?" she said. "Are you not going to make out either?" I stared at her for a few seconds and realized I didn't want to make out with anyone else. And as that thought hit me, I suddenly realized that I was venturing into dangerous territory because I hadn't even slept with Rosalie yet. All we'd done was kiss. And while we had amazing chemistry, I had never fallen for someone from just a blow job and a couple of kisses. If I was already feeling this attracted to her and this attached, how would I feel playing this game? "Oliver?" She said, "Are you having second thoughts?"

"No." I said, "I was just thinking to myself that we should be really sure that this is something we want to do."

"This is something I want to do." She said softly. She held out her hand. "So we're going to have a secret relationship."

"I guess so," I said. Holding out my hand, I waited for her to shake it.

"Okay, awesome."

"Awesome," I said, nodding. And then I grabbed her hands and pulled them up above her head. I pressed them against the wall and pressed my body against hers. Her eyes widened as I gave her a seductive smile. "Now that we have that sorted, I can get to business," I said. I pressed my hardness up against her stomach, and she gasped. I pressed my lips against her cheek and then moved them toward her lips and kissed her passionately. My tongue moved into her mouth, and she sucked on it eagerly. I ran my right hand down the length of her arm toward the top of her shoulders. And then my fingers caressed her breast, and she murmured against my lips inside. I felt her hand rubbing down my back. She groaned as she reached up and pulled my hair. I sucked on her lower lip and tugged on it gently before pulling back. "Fuck, I'm so hard right now."

"Well," she said, "what are we going to do about it?" She reached her hand down and rubbed the front of my pants. I closed my eyes at the feel of her fingers against my cock, which was growing harder and harder.

"I don't know," I said, "What should we do?"

"I have an idea," she said softly.

"And that is?"

"I think that we should," she looked at me and licked her lips nervously. "Well, you know."

"But your brother's back."

"So? Do we have to do it there?" I stared at her for a few seconds, then grinned wickedly.

"You're a really bad girl, you know that, Rosalie?"

"Hey, what can I say? I know what I want, and I'm going after it." She squeezed my cock gently and then pulled her hand away. She moved her fingers up to her mouth, and I watched as she sucked on her index finger. My eyes narrowed as I stared at her. Shit, she was hot. And then she grabbed my hand and sucked on my finger. And I growled as I stared at her.

"Come on, Rosalie. The night is not ending now. I know exactly where we're going."

Chapter 26

R OSALIE

"So I need you to keep your eyes closed, Rosalie." Oliver's voice was soft and warm as he held my hand.

"But I want to see where I'm going," I said excitedly.

"You'll see soon enough. Now, I want you to sit here." He stepped forward and tapped me on the shoulder.

"Where? I can't see." I laughed.

"Don't worry, I got you. Just sit down."

"But what if I fall onto the ground?"

"You won't. There's a chair there. It's an armchair."

"Okay." I sat back and found myself in a really comfortable leather chair.

"This feels nice," I said. "I'm glad. I want the entire evening to feel nice, but why can't I see?"

"Because if you could see, then it would ruin the surprise."

"But it doesn't need to be a surprise," I said.

I couldn't quite believe that I'd finally come out and given Oliver an ultimatum. The evening had been fun; dinner and the comedy show, and we'd flirted undercover all night long. I knew I wanted him, but we would keep playing this game unless I said something. And so, I had to find out either way —he wanted me and was going to have me, or he didn't. I was proud he had gone along with what I had hoped. I just hope it didn't get complicated. When I told him we could keep it a secret from Foster, I truly believed it. But the more I thought about it, I worried that it wouldn't be possible. Though, I wasn't going to bring up my concern now, not when I was in such a precarious and exciting position.

Music came from the room, and my ears perked up. "What's that?" I said.

"You don't recognize it?"

"No."

"Listen carefully."

"Okay," I said and listened as carefully as I could.

"Is that Savage Garden?" I said, laughing.

"Yeah, it is. Remember how much you used to love them?"

"Yeah, I really did. Wow. I can't believe you remember that."

"There are many things I remember about you, Rosalie. How could I forget?"

"True. I remember a lot about you."

"Oh yeah? Like what?"

"I remember that your favorite movie is *Scarface*."

"Isn't that every guy's favorite movie?"

"No." I laughed. "Most of the guys I meet love *The Matrix*."

"Okay, then. So you remember my favorite movie as *Scarface*. What else do you remember?"

"I remember how disappointed you were when you were a junior in high school and broke your arm right before the big baseball game of the season."

"Yeah, I was devastated. I really thought I was going to go pro and that ruined my chances."

"Do you regret that?" I asked if he wished he could have been a baseball player instead of an attorney.

"Not really." I heard him chuckling. "I wasn't really that good. Hold on a second," he said.

"Why? What's going on?"

"Just hold on." I heard him walk over to the door and open it.

"Oliver, are you leaving?"

"No, just wait." He whispered slowly to someone and then closed the door.

"Okay, mainly ready."

"Who was at the door?" I asked him curiously.

"Don't worry about it, Rosalie."

"Did you get condoms delivered or something? Did you not have protection and..."

"Rosalie, I'm a man. A virile man. I always have condoms on me."

"Oh, well, bully for you."

"Why? Do you carry condoms as well?"

"No. Why would I?"

"I mean, I don't know. I've met plenty of women who do."

"No need to remind me that you've had plenty of sex with random crazies," I said, trying to keep the jealousy out of my voice.

"Who said they were random and who said they were crazy?"

"Okay. Then just bitchy?"

"Oh, Rosalie, your jealousy is showing."

"No, it's not," I said. "Can we take this blindfold off yet?"

"Not yet. I will tell you when it's coming off."

"I mean, I already know what hotel we're in," I said, laughing. "I walked with you into the hotel and stood next to you when you got the room."

"Yes, but you don't know what the room looks like yet, do you?"

"No, but..."

"But nothing. Patience, my dear Rosalie."

"I'm trying to be patient, but my panties are wet, and I'm..."

"Are you trying to turn me on?" he said in a deep husky voice, and I laughed.

I heard footsteps, and then he leaned down and pressed his lips against mine. I kissed him back eagerly, loving the feel of him against me.

"Now, wait. I'm not done yet."

"This better be good, Oliver," I said.

"It will be. Trust me," he said. He stepped back, and the next song that played was Eminem. I started laughing.

"This is so romantic."

"Hey, I just was playing some music," he said. "Don't worry. It will get better."

"I sure hope so because listening to Eminem try to rap is not my idea of romance." He chuckled then.

"Okay. I'm nearly done."

"So I can take the blindfold off?"

"No, Rosalie."

He started laughing. The music stopped, and my breathing stopped, too. I was feeling slightly nervous. I bit down on my lower lip. I had no idea what he was doing. I trusted him. I knew he wasn't going to kill me, but what if he was setting up some sort of dungeon or some sort of sex swing? I mean, I was adventurous and didn't mind trying new things, but I hadn't even had sex yet. I didn't know that I wanted to be on a sex swing or something crazy my first time.

"Okay, Rosalie." I felt his hands on mine, and he pulled me up.

"Can I take it off now?"

"I'll take it off," he said, taking off my blindfold.

I blinked and looked out around the room and gasped. There were at least fifty different candles lit up. Their lights flickered across the room. I stared in surprise and then looked into his face.

"Do you like it?" he said.

"Wow, it's really beautiful," I said. And then, I noticed the rose petals all over the bed.

"You got roses?"

"I did." He nodded.

"But how? When?"

"I have a phone." He laughed. "I got them delivered."

"That's who was at the door?"

"Yeah. Actually, two delivery men came at the same time. Got the candles, the lighter, the rose petals, and a bottle of champagne." He nodded toward the side table.

"Wow. You did all this for me?"

"It's your first time," he said softly. "I wanted it to be special. I want you to remember it."

"I didn't think you were so romantic, Oliver."

"I'm not, but I know you and I know you live for romance, and well, I wanted to give that to you tonight. And..." he said.

"Yeah?" I gazed at him, wanting to pull him close to me so I could kiss him.

"Before anything happens..."

"Yeah?" I said curiously.

"I thought we could dance."

"Dance? You hate dancing."

"I do, but I remembered a long time ago, you said your perfect date would include dancing in the rain and then going to your boyfriend's room. And there would be candles everywhere and rose petals on the bed."

"Oh my gosh, you remember that? That was me talking late one night, mumbling stupidness."

"I remember so much. I told you that, Rosalie." He pressed his lips against mine and tugged on my lower lip slightly.

"And well, it's not raining, and I don't feel like dancing in the street, but we can dance here."

"Okay. That sounds good."

He grabbed his phone and pressed pause, and

Eminem stopped screeching. I laughed as I stared at him.

"Can we dance with slightly less clothes?" I said, softly wanting to take off his shirt so badly.

"Patience, Rosalie," he said. "The clothes will come off soon enough."

And then, I heard the familiar crooning of Frank Sinatra and I beamed.

"Strangers in the Night, you really did remember.

"I did. And while I'm not a stranger, and we're not dancing in the rain, I thought I'd like to give you this dance."

He grabbed my hand and spun me around, and I giggled as he pulled me to him, and we waltzed around the room.

"You're beautiful, Rosalie."

"Thank you, Oliver," I said, my heart racing fast.

The mood in the room had changed, and all of a sudden, I was looking into the face of a man I'd loved secretly for years. I swallowed hard as I gazed into his blue-gray eyes staring at me so intently.

"I think there's magic in the air tonight," he said, pulling me toward him.

He leaned down and kissed me, and I felt his hands on my ass. I ran my fingers up to his hair and down his neck and squeezed his muscles, and he groaned as he bent down and kissed my neck. I eagerly unbuttoned his shirt and ripped the last few buttons open. He started laughing.

"Wow, you really do want me badly."

"I do," I said, almost whispering. I gazed at his chest and pressed my lips against his golden skin. He was absolutely gorgeous. He took his shirt off and threw it to the ground, and I squeezed his biceps and laughed as he pulled me toward him and pulled off my top.

I stared at his pants and reached forward, and undid his belt slowly. And then unbuckled the top of his pants and pulled them down. He gazed at me as he stepped out of them, and I licked my lips nervously as I stared down at his large cock pushing against the thinness of his gray boxes. His thighs were thick and golden, and he had the most beautiful body I'd ever seen in my life. He stepped forward and undid the button on my jeans. Then he pulled the zipper down, and I stepped out of my jeans and stood there in my panties and bra. His eyes looked at me from head to toe, and he whistled as he just stared.

"Absolutely gorgeous," he said.

I laughed as he ran his fingers down my arm and my stomach because he was tickling me and his eyes gazed at me in amusement.

"So you're still ticklish then."

"I am, and I'm sure you are, too."

I reached forward, pretending I was going to tickle under his arms, and he grabbed my hands and pulled me toward the bed. We fell back into the bed laughing, and he leaned down and kissed the side of my neck. I felt his hands on my stomach, his fingers trailing down toward my panties, and I felt like I was going to stop breathing from the excitement of it all. Reaching up, I touched the side of his arm and squeezed his muscles. He grinned down at me.

"You like my big guns, huh?"

"Oliver," I chuckled. "That's so..."

"I know. Not modest of me at all," he grinned. He pulled me over so I was lying on top of him.

And I felt his hands on my back, undoing my bra and slipping my bra off. He threw it to the ground, and I sat on top of him. His cock nestled between my legs, and I rubbed back and forth slightly. He groaned as I ground on him, and I felt his fingers reach up and play with my breasts. I looked down at him, loving how his handsome face stared back at me. He pulled me down to him and then rolled over so he was on top of me. I felt his lips against mine as he slipped his finger into my panties. And I moaned as I felt him rubbing my clit gently.

"Oh, Oliver," I simpered as he slid a finger inside me.

He grunted as he continued to kiss my neck and finger me at the same time. I moved my body back and forth slightly, and my breasts rubbed against his chest. I was so horny and wanted him so badly. I reached up and pulled on his briefs, and he laughed as he jumped up, pulled them off, and threw them to the ground. He then bent down, pulled my panties off, and stared at me.

"I will never forget tonight," he said.

He leaned down and gave me a kiss on the lips. And I stared up at him.

"If you dare walk away from me tonight, I will never speak to you again," I said, only half teasing.

"There's no way in hell I could walk away from you a second time, Rosalie. It's just not possible," he said.

He reached to the side and grabbed his wallet to pull out three condoms. And I laughed as he threw them on the bed next to me.

"Hey, a man's got to be prepared," he said, winking before putting his wallet back on the side.

He got onto the bed, pressed his lips against my collarbone, then kissed down toward my nipples. I felt his mouth sucking on my nipple, and I cried out as he tugged. I reached up and pulled his hair and dug my fingers into his skull, not wanting this feeling to end. It felt absolutely amazing. His body was warm, hard, and sexual, and I couldn't believe I had lived all my life without being in a situation like this with him. And then, he spread my legs and kissed down, and I felt his tongue on my clit. He was sucking, licking, and doing things to me that made my mind want to explode. I closed my eyes and grabbed the sheets as he slid his tongue inside me. I cried out loud. And this time, he let me fall over the ledge. I screamed as I felt his tongue flicking against my clit. And then, I heard him laughing as I orgasmed.

"Oh, Rosalie, you make the most wonderful sounds. I'm so fucking hard," he said. "Fuck me, please."

"Oliver, I need you right now. I need this. I need to feel you inside me."

"I'm going to fuck you so hard," he groaned, "but I can't. I want to, but I can't."

"You can," I said, nodding. "I want that."

"Trust me," he said as he positioned himself on top of me. I felt the tip of his dick rubbing against my clit.

"I can't fuck you hard the first time. You're a virgin. You're going to be very sore tomorrow as it is. I don't want you not to be able to walk tomorrow."

"Very funny, Oliver," I said, giggling.

"Trust me, you'll see what I mean."

He reached over and ripped open one of the condom wrappers, and I watched as he slid it on. I closed my eyes and spread my legs, waiting.

"Open your eyes," he said. "I want to see every emotion on your face and in your eyes as we do this."

He pressed his lips against mine and positioned himself on top of me again.

"Don't be scared, Rosalie."

"I'm not," I said, smiling at him. "I've waited for this moment all my life."

"Fuck," he said as he reached down and grabbed my ass to shift me slightly on the bed. He rubbed his fingers against my clit for a couple more seconds, and I felt my wetness oozing. He positioned his dick at the entrance of my pussy, and he slid in slowly.

"Just let me know if it hurts, okay?"

"I will," I said, nodding.

And then, he thrust into me, gazing into my eyes.

"Ow," I said slightly. He moved back and forth slowly until the pain turned to pleasure.

"Oh yes, Oliver."

"Oh," he groaned as he thrust faster inside me, and my fingernails dug into his back. He started moving even faster, and I wasn't sure I was going to be able to take it. I couldn't believe how deep he was inside me. I couldn't believe how it felt to finally be making love with him.

"Wrap your legs around my waist," he said. "That way, I can get in even deeper."

"Okay," I moaned into his ear.

"Oh fuck," he said, thrusting faster and faster.

"Oh yes. Oh yes," he groaned.

"Oh, Oliver," I screamed and bit his shoulder. I felt myself coming harder and faster than before.

"Oh fuck, Rosalie. You are so tight. Oh shit."

And then, he slammed into me one last time, and I felt his body shuddering before he collapsed on top of me. He kissed me and stared into my eyes.

"You okay?" he whispered.

I nodded. "That was amazing."

"I'm glad."

He lightly touched the side of my face and just stared into my eyes for a couple of seconds.

"That was probably the best sex I've ever had in my life."

"It was the best sex I've ever had in mine," I said, laughing, and he chuckled.

I felt him slowly sliding out of me, and he pulled the condom off. I saw blood on the latex, and he looked down at me.

"You'll be okay. Let me know if you want to go and wash up," he said.

He jumped off the bed, and I watched as he threw the condom and wrapper into a waste basket. I stood gingerly and stared at him.

"I feel okay, but maybe I should wash off. I don't know if I have blood on me or..."

I looked down at the sheets and gasped. "Oops, we got blood on the bed."

"It's okay," he said. "Don't worry about it."

He pulled me into his arms and kissed me for a few more minutes, and I wrapped my arms around his neck, pressing my body against his.

"You okay?" he said, gazing at me with concern in his eyes.

"I'm more than okay, Oliver. That was amazing. In fact, I want to do it again."

"We will," he said, laughing. "Come on, let's take a shower, and I will clean you off. Make sure that there's no dried blood left on you or anything."

"Okay," I said, "And maybe I'll clean you, too?"

"You bet you will," he said, winking at me.

And as I stared at him, I realized that this was probably the best moment of my life.

Chapter 27

Rosalie

"*I* wish we could spend the night together," Oliver said, looking at me with sweet eyes and a soft expression on his face.

"Me, too." I nodded. We lay in bed, still wrapped in our towels from the shower. "You are quite sweet when you want to be, aren't you?" I stared at him in surprise as I stroked the side of his face.

"I thought I was always sweet," he said, laughing. He leaned forward and kissed me. "But we should probably get going soon because Foster will be wondering where we are."

"He will be," I said, nodding and feeling slightly upset.

"Hey, what's wrong?" Oliver said to me immediately, and I blinked at him.

"What do you mean?"

"Your eyes just fluttered, and then you got a sad little expression on your face for a couple of seconds. Why are you upset?"

"I don't know." I shrugged.

"Do you regret us making love?" he said softly, and I stared at him, surprised at his terminology. At least he was trying to be nice. I'm not sure how I would've felt if he'd said something like, "Are you upset that we fucked?" or "Are you upset that we banged?" Not that I considered what we'd done as making love. Yes, it had been amazing, and, yes, I was pretty sure I was in love with him. But he wasn't in love with me, and I didn't even want to fool myself for a moment that he was.

"No, I'm not regretting it at all," I said. "It's probably the single most amazing night of my life."

He grinned and nodded. "That's what I like to hear."

"It's just, I always imagined that the first night that I…" I paused and bit down on my little lip. "Made love," I whispered.

"Yeah, what about it?" he said.

"Well, I just always imagined that the guy would cuddle me and hold me close, and well, you know."

"Oh," he said. He stared at me for a couple of

seconds. I could see a light in his eyes that hadn't been there before. "I understand." He sighed and ran his hand through his hair. "I mean, I do have one idea."

"What's that?" I said.

"We could stay the night."

"But we can't, Foster."

"We could stay the night and go back late tomorrow morning and say we woke up early and had breakfast."

"What?" I said. "Foster wouldn't believe that."

"He'd have no reason to think that we lied if we were convincing about it." He gave me a short smile. "I mean, it's risky, of course. He could come out in the middle of the night. He could wake up super duper early." He shrugged. "But if you really want to spend the night together, that's an option."

"But what if he found out? He would—"

"Hey," he said, "let's worry about that if it happens."

I smiled at him happily. "So you don't mind spending the night with me?"

"Of course not," he said. "I've always wanted to spend the night with you, the whole night. I've always wanted to hold you in my arms and kiss you, and who knows? Maybe you'll be lucky enough to wake up to some morning sex."

"Maybe I'll be lucky enough?" I started laughing. "Really, Oliver? Maybe you'll be lucky enough."

"Hey, I would be the lucky recipient, yes. I do agree with that."

"Dude, it would be like you won the lottery."

"It would be like I won ten million dollars in the lottery," he said. "I mean, I already feel like I won a million."

"Oh?" I said.

"Yeah, just this moment, right here, being with you, talking and not arguing." He gave me a look.

"Well, you know, the argument can come later."

He shook his head and kissed me. "You are the most..." He paused then.

"What were you going to say?" I asked him curiously.

"Nothing." He shook his head quickly. "Do you want to order some room service? I imagine you might be a little bit hungry now."

"I'm okay. I mean, I'm peckish for sure, but I'm not starving. Why, are you hungry?"

"I mean, I could eat some chicken wings and pizza." He grinned, and I laughed.

"Well, this is a fancy nancy hotel, so let's see what they have for room service."

"Okay." He reached over and picked up the phone. "Let me check and make sure they have room service still going."

"Okay." I nodded. "Fingers crossed."

"Hi, this is Oliver James in Room 1234. I was wondering if room service was still available? Oh great. It's all day? Perfect. And how do I find the menu? Ah, okay. Sounds good. Yes, I will place my order in a little bit. Thank you." He hung up the phone and looked at me with glittering eyes. "All we have to do is turn on the TV. We can scroll through to the menu and place an order on the TV."

"Now that's amazing. Why can't we have this at home?"

"That would be kind of cool, but who would be fetching the food? Me? I don't think so. However, if you want to volunteer..."

I stared at him for a couple of seconds. "So just because I don't have a job, and I have no money, and I'm sleeping with you, I'm your maid now?"

"No, I didn't mean that," he said quickly, flustered, and I started laughing.

"Got you, Oliver."

"Oh my gosh, Rosalie. Don't do that."

"What? I can tease you. You tease me all the time."

"You do. That is true. Shall we turn the TV on and place an order?"

"Sure," I said. I watched as he reached for the remote and turned the TV on and scrolled through the different menus.

"Do you see anything you fancy?"

"Yeah. I wouldn't mind the crab cakes," I said.

"And let me guess, you want to try the cheesecake?"

"How did you know?"

"I don't know how many times you're going to ask me a question about how I know something about you, Rosalie. I know you almost better than I know myself."

"Okay, sure you do. So what are you getting?"

"I think I'm going to get the shrimp cocktail, a Waldorf salad, and some garlic bread."

"Garlic bread?" I raised an eyebrow.

He thought for a second and chuckled. "True. Maybe not garlic bread. I don't want you to repel me when I try to kiss you again."

"Well, I mean, if you don't want to kiss anymore tonight…"

"Oh, I want to kiss more tonight." He pressed the buttons to place the order, then turned the TV off.

"Oh, I thought we were going to watch a movie or a TV show or something."

"No," he said, turning to look at me. "I thought we could just chat."

"Oh?" I stared at him. "Chat about what?" I stared into his beautiful eyes and felt my heart melting at the gaze he was giving me.

"Have you seen any jobs you'd like to look up?"

"There was one job I saw that I think Alice and I could both do. It was hostess at some exclusive restaurant club, and they're paying like a thousand dollars a year."

"A thousand dollars a year? That's nothing."

"Oops," I said. "I mean, a hundred thousand dollars."

"A hundred thousand dollars a year to be a hostess?" He raised an eyebrow. "Um, really?"

"I figure it must be some sort of exclusive steak restaurant."

"I guess that must be very exclusive or..." he said, pressing his finger against my lips.

"What?"

"Or you're trying to work at a gentleman's club."

"A what?"

"Oh, you're so naïve, Rosalie. A gentleman's club."

"You mean like a strip club?"

"Well, no, it's not exactly a strip club. It's not tacky like that. It's a private club for rich men who have a lot of money and want to have some fun without their wives knowing."

"Oh, you think?"

He nodded. "Yeah, I've been in a few a couple of times."

"Oh my gosh. Really, Oliver?"

"It's not like I was a member. I went with some partners at work."

"Let me guess, Kramer."

"I will neither confirm nor deny," he said, his eyes twinkling. "But let's just say one of the hostesses that night was thrilled with the five thousand dollar tip she got for her panties."

"What?" My jaw dropped.

"Yeah. Let's just say a certain partner wanted a certain hostess's panties and some feet pics."

"Wow. Five grand for panties and feet pics? Maybe I should take the job."

"Oh no, you don't," he said, shaking his head at me, his eyes narrowing. "Very funny, Rosalie."

"What? Five grand would get me my own place really quickly."

"You're not moving out, and you're not taking a job at a gentleman's club."

"I can do what I want," I said, giggling.

He pulled me close to him, and my towel came apart slightly. He stared at my naked breasts, and I heard him inhale deeply. "Fuck, you're so gorgeous." He leaned forward and kissed my collarbone, and I felt his hands on my breasts, cupping and squeezing. "And I shouldn't be telling you this because Foster wanted us to tell you later once Alice got here, but—"

"But what?" I said, closing my eyes and moaning as I felt his fingers pinching my nipples.

"We're going to buy a place."

"You what?" My eyes flew open, and I stared at him in surprise.

"We're going to invest together and buy like a brownstone or something so you and Alice both have your own rooms and somewhere to stay."

"Wow. Oh my gosh, you guys can't do that. You—"

"We want to," he said. "It's important to us that you and Alice both feel comfortable. It's important that you both have your own rooms, and we don't want you to rush into jobs that you hate. It will be good."

"You just want to be able to sneak into my room to fuck me whenever you want," I said, laughing.

"Well, when I told your brother I was down with the idea, I didn't even know that I would be fucking you," he said, smirking. "However, that does sound like a very interesting proposition."

"We'd have to be careful, though, or Foster or Alice could find out."

"Oh, I think we can be cautious, Rosalie."

I felt his tongue against my skin, and I closed my eyes. "If you say so." I breathed deeply. "Oh yeah. Oh, Oliver," I moaned as I felt his lips kissing down my body. "What, what are you doing?"

"I want to pleasure you again before the food comes."

I stared at him with wide eyes. "But I thought we were talking about what jobs I wanted."

"We'll talk about them in a little bit," he said, winking at me. "Don't worry. It won't take long for me to make you come."

"Is that a promise?" I said.

"Yes." He nodded, and then I felt his lips on me, sucking and licking, and I knew he was correct. He grabbed my hips and lifted me slightly, and I felt his tongue sliding inside me.

"Oh my gosh. Oh." I almost screamed as I gripped the sheets. How was it possible for his tongue to feel almost as good as his cock?

"Oh shit," he said, pulling his tongue out and kissing up my body. "Fuck, Rosalie."

"What?" I said, laughing.

"You are like my kryptonite." He reached over and grabbed another condom and slipped it on. "I think it's time for round three," he said.

"Come on, Big Daddy." I winked at him, and he just groaned before he thrust into me. I screamed out loud this time, and he grunted in my ear. I had never felt more pleasure before in my life.

Chapter 28

"What exactly did you guys have for breakfast?" Foster asked me as we drove to the airport to pick up Alice.

"Blueberry pancakes and bacon," I said with a small smile. "I promised Rosalie last night when we came home that I'd wake up early and take her to breakfast."

"Okay." Foster nodded and looked back at his sister. "You're lucky that Oliver did that for you."

"Yeah, I'm so lucky. Thanks, Oliver." She glared at me. And I stifled a smile. Rosalie was really trying to play the part of being pissed at me, but I didn't mind. I'd had such a wonderful evening with her.

And it was really special. I was glad we'd spent the night together. I couldn't believe I'd almost been such a doofus to rush home and let her sleep alone on the first night after she'd made love for the first time. She had been absolutely amazing. And it had felt like the most special experience. I wasn't sure exactly how we were going to make the sneaking around work. Foster seemed like he was already getting slightly suspicious, and I had a feeling that Alice would be even more cynical. I knew I would do whatever I could to make it work.

When Rosalie came up with the idea for us to sneak around together, I'd been shocked and thrilled. It wasn't that I wanted to sneak around with her, and it wasn't that I didn't want to try dating her. It was just that I didn't know what dating her meant. And I didn't know if Foster would be down with that. I mean, I was pretty confident he wouldn't be happy if he knew that I'd taken his sister's virginity.

"Hey, dude," Foster said. "What airline again?"

"Oh, sorry. United."

"I asked you like five times."

"Maybe I'm still a little sleep-deprived. And you know, the carb load from the pancakes." Foster groaned.

"Oh, don't even talk to me about pancakes. I haven't had pancakes since I was a little kid."

"Oh, my gosh. You're so health conscious," Rosalie said from the back seat.

"I'm not health conscious."

"Exactly."

"But I do like to watch what I eat."

"So what would you call that then, big bro?"

"I don't know. Caring how long I lived till?" Rosalie groaned.

"Well, thank you very much, Oliver. Last night and this morning were very special. I think I'd love to do it again."

I looked back at her with a glint in my eyes. "Yeah, I think we will."

"Me too," she said with a wink. And I just shook my head.

"Oh my gosh. You guys are like the pancake king and queens," Foster said. And Rosalie burst out laughing. I watched as he frowned. "I don't really think that's funny."

"You don't think anything's funny."

"So I don't want to be late," Foster said. "What time does Alice arrive again?"

"It's fine," Rosalie said. "She's my best friend. And if I'm not worried about us being late, you shouldn't be worried."

"Well, I want us to give her a warm welcome."

"Not too warm, I hope," Rosalie said, waggling her tongue at her brother.

"What's that supposed to mean?"

"Nothing. I just don't want you getting any thoughts."

"I have no thoughts about Alice. Don't worry about it."

"Good," she said. "Because I don't want Alice being confused by you. And I don't want her upset when Amelia comes over, flashing her titties to everyone." Foster groaned.

"Yeah. I'm going to have to speak to Amelia. I really don't want her showing up again." I listened to Foster and Rosalie bantering back and forth. And it brought a huge smile to my face. It reminded me of my childhood and how they always argued about random little things. It was funny how siblings did that. It was something I'd missed growing up, having a brother or a sister. Someone to always talk to. Someone to scrabble with. Someone I knew who would always have my back. Though Foster was like my brother, even if he wasn't blood.

"Okay, let's park here," I said. "I think this will be the fastest way to meet Alice near her luggage."

"Oh my gosh. I hope she didn't bring a lot of stuff," Foster said. "She does know we don't have a big place right now."

"Right now," Rosalie said. I quickly looked at her and glared. I really didn't need her to spoil the surprise. Foster would kill me.

"Yeah. Right now. Okay." Foster parked in the slot and jumped out of the car. "Come on, guys. We don't want to be late to pick up Alice."

"That should be my line," Rosalie said. We trailed Foster, who was walking a million miles a minute.

"Dude, is my brother into Alice?" Rosalie asked me softly, and I shrugged.

"I don't know. I mean, he's never said that to me, but…"

"But what?" she asked.

"I guess I never told him I was into you either."

"Yeah. True. But I'm his sister. Alice is not your sister."

"True. But maybe he figured I would tease him in front of you. I don't know."

"He certainly is acting kind of funky, though. I mean, he's practically racing toward the airport. Her plane just landed three minutes ago. I doubt she's even off it yet. She hasn't even texted me."

"You know Foster likes to be punctual and on time."

"He wasn't rushing to come and pick me up at the airport."

"That's because he wasn't in the country."

"Yeah. Well, I mean." She stared at me for a couple of seconds.

"Anyway. Not really important. So do you want to try to have a quickie in the airport?"

"What?" I said in shock. "Rosalie. No, we can't."

"We can. I'm sure they have those family bathrooms. We could sneak into one of those and..."

"Rosalie. Oh my gosh. I'm not fucking you in a family bathroom in the airport with your brother waiting outside."

"He doesn't have to be waiting outside. He can wait by baggage claim for Alice. And we can sneak off. It doesn't even have to be fast."

"So you're asking me to be a five-minute man," I said, staring at her. She giggled.

"I mean, I don't mind. I think it will be fun and exciting. Plus, I already know you can go much faster than that."

"Rosalie. No, I can't."

"Please. Oliver," she said. And she slipped her hand on my ass and squeezed.

"Rosalie, you can't. What if Foster sees?"

"Foster is not looking at us." And then her hand moved to the front, rubbing my crotch. I grabbed it and pushed her away.

"Rosalie, this is craziness. You can't." And even though I was super scared that Foster would see, I was thrilled and excited about the possibility of fucking her in a public place. I mean, I was a man. What man wouldn't be slightly turned on by the fact that the woman they were sleeping with wanted to experience lovemaking everywhere they could? "What have I done, Rosalie? I've turned you into some sort of nymph."

"Maybe, but how do I turn you into one as well? You're such a bore, Oliver."

"I'm a bore?" I stared at her.

"Really. I mean, if you don't fuck me in this airport, I'm going to definitely think so."

"Really?" I could feel my heart racing as I stared at her. "So you're trying to egg me on, huh?"

"Hey. I mean, if you want me and if you're a man, you'll figure out a way to make it happen."

"So if I don't fuck you in the airport, I'm no longer a man?"

"I don't know. Maybe not an alpha man."

"Maybe you want me to boss you around?" I chuckled then.

"Oh, Rosalie. You can try. But trust me, I'm not a man who can be bossed around."

"Then take me somewhere in this airport. If you don't want to do it in the family bathroom, then we don't have to. You choose the spot."

"I don't want to get arrested for having public sex in the airport."

"Okay. Be a scaredy-cat," she said, "Hey, Foster. Wait up." She went running after her brother, and I watched her. She turned and gave me an impish smile. And I shook my head. She was pure dynamite. And I knew I wouldn't let her get away with that. I wasn't the sort of person to risk getting arrested. I was an attorney, after all, but I never back down from a challenge or a dare. And I knew that Rosalie needed to be fucked. And I knew that I needed to be inside her.

"Hey, Foster," I said as I caught up with them. "Can you wait by the baggage claim? Rosalie asked me if I'll get her a drink. Do you mind?"

"That's fine," he said. "Just don't be long."

"Oh, I'll try not to be," I said and laughed. Rosalie licked her lips and pouted behind her brother's back, and I stifled a groan as she started sucking on her finger to tease and torment me. She knew just how to turn me on, and I wasn't sure that I'd ever be able to resist her.

Chapter 29

Rosalie

"Well, that sucked," Oliver said, giving me a look. "You're not disappointed, are you?"

"No." I laughed. "We tried." And we had. We'd gone to the family restroom and waited outside, but it turned out there was a mother with two babies who had dirty diapers. And, well, it took her a long time to change one. We didn't know how long it would take for the other one.

"I appreciate that you were going to try," I said softly. "I mean, I know you were scared of getting caught and all."

"You know what? If we weren't in a public place right now, I totally do you, Rosalie."

"Oh really? Is that a promise?"

"Well, what am I supposed to be promising?" Oliver said.

"I don't know," I said, wrinkling my nose. "I just realized that doesn't really make sense."

"Yeah, it doesn't. But I'm glad we have some time to just talk, you and me, without Foster around."

"Yeah. What do you want to talk about?" I said as we made our way back to baggage claim.

"I don't know. I just wanted to see how the job search is going and how you're feeling about ..." He paused and waved his hands back and forth between us.

"How I feel about what?"

"You know," he said, giving me a look.

"You can clarify, please, Oliver."

"How you feel about us, and what's going on, and ...?"

"I mean, it's fun, and it's sexy. And I like you, and we haven't argued too much."

"We argue all the time, Rosalie."

"I know, but that's our thing."

"I guess so. And how do you feel about keeping it a secret from Foster?"

"It's not ideal, but you don't want my brother to kill you. And I don't want my brother to kill me. And the last thing I want is for him to call my parents and tell them, and then they get all crazy and ... Well, I don't need it to be a big thing."

"Yeah," he said, "me neither. Your parents love and respect me. And I would hate for them to think that I betrayed them."

"Oh my gosh. Really, Oliver? Betrayed them? What is this? Are we in the mafia, or ..."

"No, I'm just saying." He chuckled. "They trust me. And well, I kind of ..."

"Don't even say it. If you're going to say you feel bad for taking my virginity…"

"Now, don't remind me that I did that," he said.

"What? Most guys would be over the moon to take a woman's virginity."

He stared at me for a couple of seconds. "I'm not going to lie. I love knowing that I'm your first. And maybe that's selfish of me, but it's not because I took your virginity. It's because I get to share something with you that no other man has."

"Aw, look at you being so sweet and sensitive." I laughed. Then my phone started beeping. "Oh my gosh, I bet it's Alice," I said, pulling my phone out of my handbag. "It is." I read her text message. "She's off the plane and headed toward baggage now. Oh my gosh, I'm so excited to see her."

Oliver smiled at me. "Yeah. I haven't seen her in

a while, either. It will be good to have her here in town."

"You're sure you're not mad? I know I kind of forced the situation on you."

"Hey, I'm happy that your friend is here in town, and you guys are doing this together. I told you that."

"I know, but—"

"But nothing, Rosalie. Trust me. I don't do anything I don't want to do."

"True that," I said, laughing. "I remember when you came over for dinner, and my parents tried to make you eat Brussels sprouts. And you were like, 'No, thank you.' And my mom was like, 'Come on, just try one.' And you were like, 'I said no, Mrs. Sloane, I don't eat Brussels sprouts."

"Oh my gosh. Really? You remember the weirdest things."

"What? I just thought it was so funny. I could remember my parents looking at you, like, 'What is going on?' But then you ate the broccoli. And my mom was like, 'Well, at least you're eating some greens.'"

"Yeah. I remember that. I think she was mad," he said.

"Why?"

"Because when she served the dessert, which was brownies and ice cream, she gave me a really small piece of brownie and only one scoop of ice cream.

Normally, she always gave me huge amounts of brownies, lots of ice cream, hot fudge, whipped cream, and cherries."

"She did?" I said, laughing.

"Yeah. She always used to call me her favorite son. Foster used to hate it."

"I remember that. My parents absolutely love you." I started laughing.

"Oh man, I've missed this," he said softly.

"What?" I asked him.

"You and me, just laughing like old times."

"Yeah, me too. I forgot how fun it was just to hang out with you."

"Even when we're not making love?" he said, a twinkle in his eyes.

"Hey, I like you for more than your body, Oliver."

"I know," he said, "but I just want to remind you of that. I don't just want this to be a physical thing."

I started laughing then.

"What's so funny?" he said with a serious expression on his face.

"I just think it's funny that you're telling me that you don't want this to be a physical thing, where normally it's the woman telling the man that."

"Yeah, well ... I'm a hot stud, and I know you can't keep your hands off me."

"Oh my God," I groaned, "you're just too much."

"Hey, but you like it, right?"

"I'm not even going to answer that question."

"I would make you," he said, "but I see Foster over there. So ..."

"So I guess we go back to barely standing each other," I said, winking at him.

"Yeah, I guess we do." He nodded with a stern expression on his face. "Foster," he said, "your sister is really getting on my nerves."

I stared at him in surprise. Foster looked over at me and rolled his eyes. "Oh gosh, what did she do now?" I couldn't believe Foster didn't even blink an eye at the comment.

"She told me that she wasn't going to get the smoothie they have available because they—"

"Should we go somewhere specific to see Alice?" Foster cut Oliver off.

"I think we can just stand here," I said.

"Why are you more nervous than me? Actually, I don't even want to know right now."

"Rosalie!"

I heard Alice's familiar voice and looked around in excitement. Then I spied my best friend with her long blond hair and hazel eyes.

"Oh my God! Alice, you look amazing!" I went running and grabbed her. We hugged each other for a couple of seconds, just staring at each other.

"I've missed you," she said.

"I've missed you, too."

"Um, guys?" Foster said, coming out behind us. "It's been, what? A couple of weeks since you've seen each other?"

I turned around and glared at him. "You're so unsentimental, Foster."

"So what?" he said, grinning at me. "Hey, Alice." He gave her a huge smile. "It's so good to see you. It's been what, a couple of years?"

"I think it has," she said with a nod, smiling back at him. "Hey, give me a hug. We're old friends."

He pulled her into his arms, and I watched as they hugged. And then Oliver stepped up.

"Hey, Alice. So good to see you."

"You too, Oliver. Thank you so much for getting the ticket. You really did not have to get me a business class seat."

"Oh my gosh! You flew business class?" I said, pure envy in my voice.

"Hey, maybe if we go somewhere one day, we can fly business class." Oliver smiled at me.

Foster looked at me and shook his head. "Don't go promising her that, Oliver. Because you know who's going to have to pay? Me."

"Excuse me, Foster. I can pay for myself."

"Uh-huh. Get a job, and then I'll believe that."

"I'm looking."

"Well, well, well," Alice said with a small laugh. "I see things are back to normal already."

"Yeah, they are," I said, linking my arm through hers. "Should we go and get your bags?"

"Yeah, let's do it. So what's the plan for today? I'm so excited to see New York. Oh my gosh, I'm so excited to be here. I can't believe it!"

I watched Oliver and Foster exchange glances, and I knew exactly what they were thinking. They were wondering, "What have we gotten ourselves into?"

"So we thought we could grab lunch. Are you hungry?"

"I am starving," she said. "Yay!"

"So we'll grab lunch. Then we'll go home, and then we'll go out tonight. Explore New York City."

"Oh my gosh. That sounds amazing. Like, go out out?" She looked at me hopefully.

"Yeah. I convinced them to take us to a club."

"I mean, we don't have to go to a club," Foster said, "if you would rather go to a bar."

"Oh no, I definitely want to go to a club in New York City. I want to dance," she said. "This is so cool." She wrapped her arms around me. "Oh, thank you so much, Rosalie. This was the best idea you've ever had."

"I know," I said.

"Two best friends in the city. Oh my gosh.

Should we start a blog or a podcast? Or maybe a YouTube channel. We could monetize it and make so much money," she said.

"That sounds like a great idea."

"No, no, and no," Foster said, shaking his head. "I'm sorry. But as someone who works in finance, I can tell you that 0.0000001% of people actually make enough money to live off podcasts and YouTube. And I hate to say it, but I don't think you two will be part of that percent."

"Well, thank you for all your faith and trust, Brother."

"Well, what would your podcast be about, Sister?"

"I don't know. Maybe it would be about Alice and me in the city finding ourselves."

"And having fun and meeting guys and dancing," Alice said.

"Yeah. I wouldn't listen to it," Foster said.

"Would you listen to it?" I looked at Oliver.

"Umm ..." He stared at me for a couple of seconds. "I mean, I'd listen to it for you ... maybe a couple of episodes." He shrugged. "I'm sorry. I'm more into true crime podcasts."

Alice laughed. "Well, thank you for being honest, Oliver and Foster. Thanks for your support. It really means a lot to me. We will remember not to thank you when we win our Academy Award for Best Podcast of the Year."

"Um, Alice? You know there's no Oscar for Best Podcast, right?"

"Okay. Well, when we win our Golden Globe."

"There's no Golden Globe."

"When we win our Emmy."

"Hate to tell you, but there's no Emmy, either."

Alice pressed her lips together. "Well, whatever the podcast award is, when we win it."

"Okay. You won't thank me," he said, laughing.

"Nope, we won't." She stared at me and grinned. "Now, what are we having for lunch? Because I'm super hungry. You know they only had nuts on the plane?"

"Oh my gosh. You only had nuts, too? And you were in business class."

"Well, they did offer me alcohol."

"Lucky," I said. "All they offered me was water. If I wanted a drink, I had to pay five bucks. Can you imagine that?"

"Oh, well, I had a glass of wine," Alice said, "maybe two."

"Oh my gosh. Lucky."

"I mean, but I'm hungry."

"What do you want to eat? We can get whatever you want."

"You know what I really fancy?"

"Tell me."

"It's going to sound really bad."

"No. What is it?"

"I really want some fried chicken." She looked at Oliver and at Foster; they were both laughing.

"Fried chicken! Now, that sounds delicioso," Foster said with a nod. "Welcome to New York City. I think I know just the place."

"You do?"

"You forget. I love me some fried chicken," Foster said. "I know every good fried chicken place in Manhattan, and some in Brooklyn too."

"Oh, well. I guess you live, and you learn."

"Okay. Do you see your bags yet?" Foster asked Alice.

She shook her head. "Oh wait, there's one, that pink one."

Oliver stepped forward and grabbed it.

"And the other pink one that's coming."

"I see we have a theme here," Oliver said, his eyes sparkling. He gave me a quick look, and I smiled warmly at him.

I felt at peace with my life. I felt like everything was coming together, and I was where I was meant to be. I was almost positive that nothing could ruin this moment.

I was young. I was single. I was sleeping with the guy I'd had a crush on for most of my life. And the sex was amazing. Nothing could ruin this moment. I was having the time of my life. All I needed now was to find a job I loved, and everything would be perfect.

I smiled at Alice, and she smiled back at me. I couldn't wait to tell her everything that was going on. I knew I told Oliver that I wasn't going to tell anyone, but Alice was my best friend. There was no way I was not going to share the most important news of my life with her as soon as we had two moments together. Oliver didn't have to know. And I knew Alice. There's no way she would slip up and say anything in front of my brother.

Chapter 30

"*T*his place is absolutely amazing," Alice said as we got ready in Oliver's bathroom. "I can't believe I'm here."

"I know. Isn't it absolutely gorgeous? I was shocked when I got here. I did not think my brother and Oliver had such good taste in furniture."

"Yeah, right? Since when?" She smiled at me. "You look like you're glowing, Rosalie. New York has been really good to you."

"Thank you," I said. I opened the door and looked outside the bathroom to make sure Foster and Oliver weren't standing outside, and then I closed it again. "I have something to tell you," I whispered.

"Oh?" Alice stopped applying her mascara and stared at me. "Tell me now, everything."

"Oh my gosh. You have to promise not to react crazily."

"Of course I won't. What's going on?"

"So," I said, smiling secretively.

"Oh my gosh. Rosalie, tell me. What is going on?"

"Oliver and I made love, not once, not twice, but several times," I squealed.

She looked at me with wide, shocked eyes and slapped her hand against her mouth. "Oh my God. You're right. I want to scream so much right now. How did this happen? When did this happen? Was it good? Oh my God. Tell me everything."

I laughed. "It happened the other night. We went out with Foster. Foster wanted to come home because he was feeling tired. Anyway, we were going to get a drink, and we stopped on the street and were kind of making out and arguing. It was really hot and sexy. I finally said to him, 'Look. You either want to be with me, and we have some fun, and we can keep it secret so Foster doesn't get upset, or don't keep trying to kiss me or whatever because I can't deal with this.'"

"Whoa. What did he say?"

"Hey, what'd you think he said?" I did a little

dance. "He looked at me, and he was like, 'I want you, sexy mama.'"

"He did not say that." Alice's jaw dropped.

"No. He didn't, but that would've been kind of cool. He ended up taking me to this really cool, fancy hotel, and he blindfolded me."

"Whoa. That sounds really hot," she said. "How Christian Grey of him."

"Yeah. It was kind of sexy. Anyway, I opened my eyes and took the blindfold off, and there were hundreds of candles in the room and rose petals on the bed. He starts playing Frank Sinatra, and we do this little dance."

"Wow," Alice said, looking awed. "That's so romantic."

"It was so romantic," I said, remembering it and just smiling. "Then we made love. It hurt a little bit, and there was a little blood, but he was fine. I wasn't self-conscious. Alice, when I tell you it was the single most fantastic thing I've ever done in my life, well, that would be a lie because the other times I've slept with him were just as great, if not better. Sex is amazing. Now I know why people go crazy over it."

"Wow," she said. "So you guys are effing or ..."

"I don't really know what we are. We're just having fun and getting to know each other. It's kind of cool because it's all secret. By the way, he doesn't want anyone to know because he's worried that someone will slip in front of Foster, so you can't tell him that you know, okay?"

"Oh no. Really, Rosalie? What? I'm going to give him a look, and he'll know that I know."

"Just don't give him a look."

"Fine. I'll try. How does it work? Where do you ...?"

"We sneak in kisses here and there. When we go out to eat, under the table, we'll do footsies or rub each other's legs." I smiled at her. "We get it in when we can."

"Foster has no clue?"

"Of course Foster has no clue. If he did, he would've killed us already."

"Oh man. Your brother is so overprotective."

"He's way too overprotective. It's so annoying, but whatever. Tonight, we're going to have so much fun."

"I know. I can't believe we're going to a club in New York City. We have always talked about this."

"I know. We're living our dream, though next week, we really have to start looking for jobs, because I want to buy so many things, and I can't, because I have no income. I know Foster will not be happy if I spend all my money on a new dress or some shoes and then go begging him to pay my cell phone bill."

"I feel you," she's said, laughing. "First thing Monday, we'll start looking for a job."

"Yay. Sounds good to me."

"Guess what," Alice said quickly.

"What?"

"There is this really ..." A knock on the door interrupted her.

"Hey. You guys nearly done?" Foster's voice was loud and annoying.

"We're still getting ready."

"Are you guys dressed?"

"Yes. Why?"

He opened the door. "There's something that Oliver and I wanted to tell you that was a secret. I wanted to tell you at dinner, but I guess we were talking about so many other things that we forgot."

"Okay. What is it?"

"Can you guys come out into the living room? It would be nice for all of us to have this conversation in person at the same time."

"Oh my gosh, Foster. You're so dramatic." I rolled my eyes.

"I'm ready to listen, Foster," Alice said as she walked into the living room. "Is this about me staying here?"

"No, you're good, Alice," he said.

I watched him looking her up and down in her short black dress. His eyes seem to linger for a long time on her legs. As I walked past him, I gave him the eye.

"Don't even think about it," I hissed at him.

He looked at me innocently. "No idea what you're talking about, Rosalie."

"Uh-huh," I said. I stepped out and looked toward Oliver. His eyes widened as he saw me in my slinky red dress. I walked over to him and gave him a sweet, sexy smile. "Hey," I said softly.

"You look fucking hot," he said under his breath. "Fuck. I want to rip that dress off you right now."

"What did you say?" Foster said as he joined us in the living room. "I couldn't hear you."

"I was just mumbling a song to myself." Oliver suddenly turned away.

I withheld a secret smile. I loved turning Oliver on.

"Okay, guys. Oliver and I have decided ..." Foster looked over at Oliver and paused.

"Oh my gosh. Come on. What is it? Are you guys giving us your rooms or what?" I looked over at Alice, who was staring at Foster with a rapt expression on her face.

"No. We're not giving you our rooms, but we do have something even better to tell you," Foster said.

"Oh my gosh. Just tell us, Foster."

"Well, Oliver and I have decided that we're going to buy an investment property together. We both have good jobs and saved a lot of money. We think now is a good time with low interest rates. And well, with you two in town, it just makes sense to have more space."

"Whoa. You're buying a condo?" I said, staring at him in shock. "Really?"

"Well, we were hoping to get a brownstone. We'd need at least four bedrooms. It'd be nice to have a yard, and you know"—he shrugged—"it'll be a good investment."

I stared at Alice in shock.

"Are you guys not going to say anything?" Oliver said, confusion in his voice.

"That is absolutely fantastic." Jumping up, I ran over to Foster and hugged him. "Oh my God. I love you, big brother. Forget everything mean I've ever said about you." I gave him a kiss on the cheek, and then I walked over to Oliver and gave him a big hug too. "You're also amazing, Oliver," I said. I gave him a kiss on the cheek as well.

I felt Oliver's hands on my back, patting me. I stepped back slightly and looked up into his eyes. I could see the lust staring back at me. I really wanted to lean forward and kiss him on the lips, but I didn't want my brother to completely explode.

"You're welcome. I'm glad that makes you happy," Oliver said. "We think it will be the right move."

"You really don't have to do this," Alice said. "I

feel absolutely awful. This is because of me, right? Because there's not enough space here."

"No. It's not just because of you, Alice." Foster shook his head. "It's something I've been thinking about ever since my parents said that Rosalie was going to come. Oliver and I have spoken about it, and we think it's a good decision."

"I know you girls want to get jobs, which we definitely think you need to do, but I don't want you to get something that's not the right fit for you. I want you both to find a career you'll love and enjoy. I don't want the stress of money to be the reason you take the position."

He looked at me. "I know I'm hard on you, and I know you feel lost and you're not sure what to do, but I'm here for you. I have been blessed and am lucky enough to make a lot of money in finance. And well, you're my little sister, my only sister. I want to do this for you. I want you to find a job that you'll love, Rosalie."

"Foster, you're going to make me cry." I stared at my brother, my lips trembling. "Since when did you become so great?"

"I've always been great. You just haven't recognized it," he said, his eyes laughing at me.

"Maybe. Oliver, you don't have to do this. You're not even my brother or Alice's brother."

"Hey. We're all family here," he said. "We all grew up together. We got to look out for each other."

"Yeah," I said. "I will definitely repay you when I get my job. It might only be ten cents or ten dollars, but if you're lucky, it'll be a hundred."

"Yeah. Well, you don't owe us anything," Foster said. "We're going to start looking at places tomorrow. See what's on the market and figure out what we want. You guys are welcome to give some input."

"Oh my God. I love looking for houses. That would be amazing."

"Well, I didn't say you can choose the place," Foster said quickly. "I'm just saying we will look forward to your input."

"Okay. I get it," I said, smiling. "Oh my gosh. We need to party tonight. We need to celebrate."

"Well, we didn't get the place yet," Foster said.

"Yeah. We didn't get the place yet, but Alice is here. We're all together in New York City. We're all young. We're all single. We're all having fun." I paused. "Well, hopefully Amelia doesn't show up tonight."

Foster glared at me. "Really, Sis?"

"Who's Amelia?" Alice said. Blinking, she looked around, confused.

"She's just my brother's crazy ex who doesn't know they're exes."

"Really, Rosalie? After everything?"

"What? It's possible she could show up, right? Shouldn't everyone know who she is?"

He rolled his eyes, and Oliver chuckled.

"That is true, but it's maybe not the right time to have that conversation. Are you guys ready? Shall we hit the club?"

"I'm ready to get my dance on," I said. "Let's go."

We all headed to the door. Alice walked right behind Foster. I stayed behind with Oliver next to me.

"You really shouldn't have called out Amelia then and there. That was so cold of you, Rosalie," he said quietly.

"Look. I saw the way my brother was looking at Alice just now. I want Alice to know that just because Foster is giving her the eye, and might be attractive and rich, he is not the guy for her."

"He's your brother."

"Yeah. He's my brother, and I know he's a player. She's my best friend. The last thing I need is for her heart to get broken, and then she wants to move, and then I never see her again."

"Isn't that the situation with you and me and Foster?" he said, his eyes narrowing.

"Yeah, but we are mature enough to handle a breakup or whatever, the dissolution of our relationship, or whatever we have is."

"Well, are we? You stopped talking to me for five years because you thought I called you a pig," he said.

I sighed. "I was younger then. I was immature. I didn't know why you said it. Now I know."

"I just don't think you should interfere like that, Rosalie."

"I'm not interfering," I said. "Alice deserves someone amazing. Foster is amazing, but he's not ready for a real relationship yet. I don't know that my brother will ever be one to settle down. I haven't seen any sign that he would make a good husband or boyfriend."

"What about me?" he said.

"What about you, Oliver?"

"Do you think I would make a good boyfriend or a good husband?"

"I don't know," I shrugged, wondering why he was asking me. "Do you think he would?"

He stared at me for a couple of seconds and shook his head. "I guess I don't know either."

"Come on, guys. What's taking you two so long?" Foster said as he stood next to the elevator. "Let's go. I don't want to be at this club all night. I would like to do some stuff tomorrow morning."

"Oh my gosh, Foster. Can we go and have fun without you complaining?"

"Yeah. It will be fun," Alice said. "We can dance and ..."

"Oliver and I are not really big dancers," Foster said.

"You're not going to come on the dance floor with us?" I looked at my brother. I grabbed Alice's hands and twirled her around. "I guess we got to find two hot young men to dance with tonight."

"I will dance on the dance floor," Foster said grumpily.

Oliver stood next to him. "I will dance too. This is Alice's first night in New York. I wouldn't want to disappoint her."

"Uh-huh," she said, laughing. "I'm sure that's why you want to come on the dance floor."

The club was popping. There were strobe lights everywhere, and silver mirror balls on the ceiling. It was packed. Usher was blasting through the speakers. Someone thought they saw Chris Brown. I was officially having the best time of my life.

I danced to the beat of the music, grabbing Alice's hand. We swung our heads around, flipped our hair, and shook our booties. I could see Foster and Oliver staring at us with looks of amusement on their faces, but I didn't care. I was having the time of my life.

"I'd like another drink, please." I looked at Oliver. He raised an eyebrow.

"Haven't you already had three vodkas?" he said. I stared at him. "You sure you want another one?"

"Please don't pull a Foster on me."

"I'm not trying to," he said with a laugh.

"Dance with me." I grabbed his hand, not caring who saw or what they thought.

Oliver looked at Foster, but Foster was too busy dancing with Alice to pay attention to me. "Fine," he said. I grabbed his arms and put them around my waist, and we started dancing. The music changed to Rihanna, and I screamed out loud as I recognized one of my favorite songs.

"Oh my God. I love this song." I leaned forward slightly and moved my hips back and forth to rub my ass in Oliver's crotch. I could feel him growing hard behind me. I smiled to myself. He pulled me up and turned me toward him.

"What do you think you're doing?" he whispered in my ear.

"What do you mean?" I said. Laughing, I pressed my body against his, whispering back into his ear.

"Rosalie, your brother is standing right there. You cannot be grinding on my cock."

"Why not?" I said, laughing. "Don't you like it?"

"I love it, but—"

"But what?" I said. "Come on." I grabbed his hand and pulled him.

"What are you doing?"

"Let's go and get another drink. Hey, Foster, Alice, we're going to get another drink. Okay?"

"Okay." Foster nodded. Alice smiled at me as she danced with my brother.

"Come on," I said to Oliver, looking back at him, a secret smile on my face.

"The bar is the other way," he said, frowning.

"Come on," I said. I pulled him to the corner of the room, where several couples were making out. I grinned up at him. "Hey, honey." I reached up and pulled him down for a kiss. I kissed him hard.

I could tell that he was surprised. But then he kissed me back. He pushed me up against the wall and growled against my lips. "You did not bring me to the corner of the club so we could make out."

"Yeah. Hello. I wanted you, and now I can have you."

"But Rosalie."

"What?"

"Your brother is in the same room."

"He can't see us. It's dark here."

"But still."

"Still what?"

"What if he sees your lipstick on my face or ..."

"Really, Oliver? Don't you want me?" I stared at him. I ran my hand down the front of his jeans and squeezed. He groaned as my fingers pressed against the hardness of his cock.

"Oh yeah. I want you," he said. He pressed his lips against my neck and sucked. I closed my eyes as I ran my hands down the nape of his neck and played with his hair. "Fuck," he said. I felt his hands sliding down my body and slipping under my dress. He moved his fingers toward my ass, and he squeezed. He paused slightly and stepped back. "Are you not wearing any panties?"

"Maybe not," I said, grinning at him.

"Fuck," he said, growling as he leaned forward and kissed me again, hard. I kissed him back and pressed my hands into his shoulders. I reached up and chewed on his earlobe and pulled on it.

"Fuck me," I said, whispering into his ear.

"What?" he said, kissing the side of my neck.

"It's dark. No one will know."

"Rosalie."

"Come on." I smiled at him. "How exciting and fun would this be?"

"I can't even put a condom on here."

"Well, you don't have to come inside me," I said, staring at him.

"Fuck, Rosalie."

I reached down and unzipped him. He groaned as I pulled his cock out of his pants. He grabbed me around the waist and lifted me up slightly. I wrapped my arms around his torso and my legs around his waist. He growled as he pushed me up hard against the wall. He reached down and positioned his cock between my legs. I leaned forward and kissed him. Lizzo started playing, and I grinned as I bounced from side to side in time to the music.

"Oh my gosh, Rosalie. What are you doing?" he groaned.

"What do you think I'm doing?" I said as I leaned down and pulled his head up to mine so that I could kiss him.

He kissed me back passionately. As my fingers played with his hair, I felt him thrusting inside me. I cried out, but thankfully, the music was so loud that nobody could hear. He plunged inside me. I could feel my body shaking with every movement of his.

"Oh fuck. Oh, Oliver," I said, "this feels absolutely ..." I bit down on his shoulder to stop myself from crying out as he pounded into me. I could feel myself coming against the wall on him. "Oh yes. Oh fuck me. Fuck me," I cried out, and then I bit down hard as I finally came, my body shuddering against the wall and his. He chuckled slightly and then groaned into my ear.

"Fuck. That's hot. I want to fuck you so badly. Rosalie, I want to fucking come in you, but I can't." Then he pulled out of me. He took a couple of deep breaths and let me down. "Fuck. I'm going to have blue balls," he said, shaking his head as he put himself back into his jeans.

"I'm sorry," I said, giving him a sweet, impish smile.

"Sure you are," he said, grabbing my hand. "But we should go back now. We must have been gone for at least fifteen or twenty minutes. Your brother's going to be wondering where we are."

"Uh-huh," I said.

We made our way back toward Foster and Alice when suddenly Oliver dropped my hand. "Hey, Foster," he said. "I didn't see you there."

"I was coming to figure out where you guys were." Foster looked at Oliver and then at me. "Did you guys get lost or something? Where are your drinks?"

"I drank it already," I said quickly. I could see that Oliver looked nervous. I felt bad.

"Okay. Well, let's go back and dance, and hope-fully, we can get going soon," Foster suggested.

"The night has just begun, Bro," I said, shaking my head. I ran over to Alice and grabbed her hands. "Let's dance," I sang at the top of my lungs. Alice grinned at me. We danced back and forth.

Foster looked at Oliver and shrugged. "I guess we'll be here for a long night."

"I guess so," Oliver said, nodding. I watched as he adjusted his pants, and I grinned to myself. I felt more alive than I had ever felt in my life.

Chapter 31

OLIVER

I watched as Rosalie and Alice danced their hearts out on the dance floor. Both of them were laughing and having an amazing time. I enjoyed watching them dance as it made me happy as well, though I couldn't ignore the feeling in my pants that felt like hard rock. My cock was ready to explode. I couldn't believe Rosalie had taken me into the corner and begged me to fuck her. It had been hot but so dangerous. If Foster had seen us, he would've killed me.

"You want to get another drink, man?" Foster asked as we just stood there looking at each other.

"Sure. Let me go and ask Alice and Rosalie if

they want anything," I said. I headed over to the two girls and tapped Rosalie on the shoulder.

"Hey," she shouted, giving me a wide grin.

"Hey," I said, stepping forward and talking in her ear. "You want anything to drink?"

"I'm good," she said, shaking her head. "Why? What are you getting?"

"I'm not sure yet, but hey, we got to be more careful, okay?"

She looked at me and frowned. "What? Say that again?"

I talked louder in her ear. "We got to be more careful. You can't be pulling me into corners and fucking me. That's dangerous territory. And I don't want to lose my balls tonight."

She stared at me for a few seconds and rolled her eyes. "Oh my gosh. Grow a pair, Oliver," she said, stepping away from me.

I looked over at Alice. "You want anything to drink?" I shouted.

"I'm good. Thanks."

She nodded at me, and I headed back to Foster. "They don't want anything else right now."

"Okay"—he shrugged—"cheaper for us." He laughed as we made our way toward the bar. "So this place is absolutely packed."

"I know. All these teens. They make me feel like an old man."

"Well, I don't think they're teens, dude." Foster shook his head. "You have to be twenty-one to get into this club."

"You know what I mean. College students. Unprofessionals."

Foster laughed. "Dude, you sound like our dads."

"I know. I'm an old man now, huh? Well, I'm an attorney, and you are a broker. I figure we're past our prime."

"Hey, speak for yourself," Foster said as he ordered two beers for us.

"So have you heard anything from Amelia?" I asked him curiously.

"No, but knowing her, I'm sure she'll show up soon."

"Tell me about it," I groaned.

"Oh, what's going on with you?"

"I got a couple of messages from Diana." I shook my head. "She can't seem to accept that it's over."

"I mean, is it really over?" Foster said, hitting me in the shoulder.

"What do you mean?"

"I mean, wasn't she like your friend with benefits? Why stop the benefits?"

"Because I don't want benefits with her anymore," I said quickly, hoping he didn't ask.

"Why not?"

I didn't want to lie to his face and say it was

because I was now fucking his sister. I knew that wouldn't go down well. "I mean, she was kind of hot. She was hot, but her personality wasn't all that."

"Yeah. Just like Amelia. What is it with these women?"

"I don't know. Maybe we have to find some women who don't have drama."

"Like who?" Foster said. "I wish they existed."

"Too true."

"I mean, look at Alice and Rosalie," Foster said, and I could hear my heart thudding. Oh fuck. He wasn't going to bring Rosalie up.

"What about them?" I said.

"I mean, Rosalie's my sister, and Alice is her best friend, and I love them both, but they are like drama queens of the world."

"They're not that bad," I said.

"Yeah, I know. They're good people." He handed me my beer, and we both chugged. "I guess we should get back onto the dance floor before they get themselves into trouble."

"Sounds good," I said. We walked back to the dance floor where we'd been before, but the girls were no longer there.

"Oh fuck. Where are they?" Foster said, looking around.

I looked around as well. And that was when I

saw them in cages high up in the air. "Oh shit. Foster, look."

I pointed up at the cage, and Foster followed my finger. Rosalie and Alice were dancing in the cage with two other girls, going absolutely crazy. I couldn't believe it. I was super turned on to see Rosalie's long legs and the way she was flipping her hair back and forth. But I could also see several other guys staring at them, which was not making me happy.

"What the fuck are they doing?" Foster said, heading over to the cages. "Hey, get down," he shouted up at them.

"I doubt they can hear you."

"Well, Rosalie will be in big fucking trouble if she doesn't get down soon."

"Dude, lighten up. She's twenty-two. She's having fun."

"Yeah. Well, I just..." He sighed. "Oh my God. I am like my dad. Aren't I?"

"You are. Yeah, you're her big brother and a great big brother, but she's not a kid anymore. She's gonna do what she wants, and she's going to make mistakes. And if she wants to dance in a cage, she can. You know who dances in cages?" Foster looked at me with a look, and I grinned. "Hey, I mean, as far as we know, she's not a stripper, right?"

"Very funny, Oliver." He shook his head. "Rosalie

and Alice, get down, please." The cage moved down, and Rosalie and Alice jumped out.

"Hey, there you are," Rosalie said, looking at me, licking her lips, and then turning to Alice. "That was so much fun. Wasn't it?"

"It was amazing," she said, grinning.

It looked like Foster was about to say something when a tall blond guy approached us and looked at Alice. "Hey, Zola?"

Alice blinked and looked up at him. "No, I think you have the wrong person."

"No, I'm pretty sure I recognize those sexy moves. You're Zola, right?"

"No, I'm Alice."

"Oh, well, nice to meet you, Alice." He held his hand out. "I'm Harry."

"Nice to meet you, Harry," she said.

"You want to dance?"

He grabbed her hand, and Alice looked like she was about to say no when Foster cleared his throat. "Hey guys, I think we should get going. I'm kind of hungry, and I figured we could get some food on the way back."

Rosalie looked at her brother's face and then looked at me and rolled her eyes. "Yeah, I'm sure that's why you want to leave now, Foster."

He looked over at Alice, who was smiling at Harry. "I guess my friends want to go."

"Pity," he said, giving her a seductive smile. "I wanted to get to know you better."

"Maybe next time," she said, with a flirty little laugh. "Bye."

She looked toward us, made a face, and grabbed Rosalie's hands. "Oh my gosh. That was so cool. That guy was so hot."

"Let's go, guys," Foster said in a monotone voice, and we all headed out of the club. "What the hell was that?" he said as we stopped, and then he looked back at me and sighed. "You know what? I don't care." He held his hands up in the air. "You can do whatever you want. But right now, I would really like to get some pizza. You in?"

"Sounds good to me," Alice said.

"Yeah, sure," Rosalie agreed.

I nodded. "I'm down." I watched as Alice and Foster started walking toward the pizza spot, and Rosalie stood next to me.

"So that was a lot of fun," she said. "Did you enjoy yourself?"

"I did, but you really have to be careful with..."

"Oh my God, Oliver, this is getting really annoying."

"What? I just don't want your brother catching us."

"You know what? If you're so worried about my brother finding out that you're going to be a stick in the mud and not want to do anything fun, then maybe we should call this whole thing off. Maybe we don't even need to do anything anymore."

I stared at her, feeling angry. I grabbed her hands and pulled her to me. "Stop right now," I said.

"What?" She was blinking, looking up at me.

"We're not stopping anything. I was just saying we need to be more careful."

"Or what?" she said, pushing away from me.

I grabbed her around the waist and pulled her to me. "Or I'll teach you a little lesson you'll never forget."

I slapped her ass lightly, and she gasped. "You're going to do that in the street with my brother just a couple of feet away."

"He's walking away from us," I said, giving her a small smile.

"Yeah, but what if he stopped? He'd really want to know why you were spanking his sister in the middle of the street."

"And then I'd tell him. You were being a bad woman."

I laughed as she rolled her eyes at me. "You are absolutely ridiculous. You know that, right, Oliver James?"

"And that's why you like fucking me so much." I pressed my lips quickly to hers and then pulled away.

"Now come on, let's go and get that pizza. I'm hungry."

"I'm hungry for more than pizza," she said, grabbing my hand and playing with one of my fingers. "I'm hungry for a lot more, if you know what I mean."

"Do not tempt me, Rosalie."

"Or what?" she said.

"Or I might just have to satisfy your appetite when we get back to the apartment."

"I bet you won't," she said. "I bet you're going to be a scared little boy."

"We'll see about that," I growled as we walked toward Foster and Alice. I knew it would be risky to fuck her with her brother in the next room, but I didn't care. I needed to teach her a lesson.

Chapter 32

ROSALIE

"Tonight was so much fun," Alice said as she lay on the air mattress in front of the couch.

"I know," I said, staring at her. "I'm so happy that you're here. This will be an amazing experience for both of us."

"I know." Alice bit down on her lower lip. "It's just so weird living in the same house as you, Oliver, and Foster."

I stared at her for a couple of seconds. "Um, I mean, we have stayed at each other's places all the time."

"Yeah. But not for significant amounts of time," she said. "And I've never lived with guys before."

"That's fine. It's not like we're living living with them," I said.

"I mean, you kind of are," Alice said. "So tell me all about what's going on with you and Oliver. It seemed like you had words earlier. I had to keep Foster distracted because I had a feeling you and Oliver were arguing about something."

"Oh my gosh. Oliver's so nervous about Foster finding out. We had a moment in the club, and he got upset because he thought it was too risky."

"What do you mean 'a moment'?" she said.

"Well, you know ..." I winked at her.

"Oh my gosh, you did not have sex with him in the club?" Alice's jaw dropped.

I giggled. "Shhh. Don't be loud, Alice. I don't want Foster to hear. Anyway, Oliver got really upset because he thought it was risky and la-de-da. And I basically told him that if this was too much for him and he didn't want to have fun, then maybe we shouldn't do it."

"Oh shit. And what did he say?"

"He said he still wanted to do it, but ... He's annoying me. I mean, I just want to have fun. I really like him, and I hate that I can't be spontaneous with him and touch him, kiss him, and do whatever I want to do."

"I know," Alice said. "That has to be really hard."

"I mean, part of it is fun and sexy, but the other part is really annoying." I sighed and heard my phone pinging. "Shit, who's texting me?" I grabbed it. "Oh my God. It's Oliver."

"What's he saying?" Alice said.

"Let me see." I opened it. "'Can you come to my room?' He wants me to come to his room."

"Are you going to go?"

I chewed on my lower lip. "I don't know." I texted back, 'What for?'

"Okay. So I just asked him what for. And depending on what he says, then I will decide."

"Girl. He probably wants to fuck you again," Alice said. "What do you mean, 'what for'?"

I started laughing. "Well, I wouldn't say no, but he has to work for it. You know?"

"I feel you, girl," she said.

My phone pinged again. "I have something for you," the text message read.

"He says he has something for me."

"Girl, you better go. And if it's a ring, I will absolutely scream."

"Alice, don't be stupid. He's not going to get me a ring." I started laughing. "You're so silly sometimes."

"Sorry. I just don't know what I was thinking."

"It's fine. Anyway, I'm going to go speak to him, if you don't mind."

"That's fine," she said, yawning. "I'm tired. I'll

probably be asleep by the time you get back. So don't rush back or anything."

"Alice," I said, laughing.

"What? I'm just saying take your time."

"Thanks, girl." I got up off the couch and twirled around. "How do I look?"

"As sexy as anyone could look in a T-shirt and shorts," she said.

"Thanks." I laughed and headed toward Oliver's bedroom. I tried to be careful as I walked past Foster's room because I didn't want him to get suspicious. I opened Oliver's door and walked inside. He was sitting on the bed, waiting for me.

"Hey," he said, looking up. He was only wearing a pair of black boxer shorts and no shirt.

I swallowed hard as I stared at his sexy body. "Hey ... What's going on?"

"I have something for you," he said, standing up.

"Oh my God. If you point at your crotch and say 'my big fat dick,' I'm going to walk out of here right now."

"No. Why would I say that?" he said, laughing. "Really, Rosalie?"

"What? I don't know. I feel like that's the sort of thing guys would say."

"Well, that's not what I'm going to say." He shook his head. I watched as he walked over to the side of the room and picked up a bag. He brought it back to me. "This is for you."

"What is it?" I stared at him in surprise.

"Open it and see."

I gingerly opened the bag and pulled out a large object wrapped in gold tissue paper. I unwrapped the tissue paper and looked at the item. It was a stuffed animal ... a dolphin, to be exact.

"There's something else in the bag," he said, smiling.

I looked in the bag again to see what I'd missed. I opened it. And it was a certificate from the World Wildlife Federation, saying, "Thank you for your generous sponsorship, saving the dolphins."

"What's this?" I said, looking up at him.

"I made a donation to the WWF in your name. I remember when we were kids, you said you always wanted to fight to help save the dolphins."

"Wow. You did that for me?" I said, surprised.

"Yeah. Do you like it?"

"I love it. It's so thoughtful."

"I wanted to get you something, and ... Well, I can't get you jewelry or anything crazy because your brother would want to know where it came from. But I thought a cute little stuffed bear and a donation in your name ..."

"Oh my gosh. Oliver, thank you." I stepped forward and gave him a hug and a big kiss.

"That was really nice. It's hard for me to be mad at you when you're nice."

"Hey, I don't want you to be mad at me."

"I know. And I'm sorry if you thought I was pissed off today or acting like an asshole. But what we did in the club was kind of risky, and ... well, could you imagine what would've happened if your brother caught us?"

I sighed. "No, I can't imagine what would've happened. But I wasn't thinking about him. I was thinking about us. I was thinking about how I wanted to be with you, touch and kiss you. And ... well, I want to do all those things right now as well."

He grabbed my hands and pulled me toward the bed. "I want to do those things, too. Do you really want us to stop whatever this is?"

"No," I said. "I was only saying that because I was angry and upset."

"Okay," he said, "because I don't want to stop whatever this is either. I know it's complicated. And obviously, it's not going to work like this forever. But for now, can we just try to make do?"

"Okay," I said. "We can."

We leaned back on his bed. I placed my hand on his chest and ran my fingers up and down his happy trail. "You feel so warm," I said.

"So do you." He ran his fingers down the side of my arm and pulled me toward him. He brought me over so that I was resting on his body. I placed my head on his shoulder so I could look at his face.

"I love the feel of you next to me," he said. He bent his nose to my hair and sniffed. "I love the smell of you. Does that sound creepy?"

"A little," I said, laughing, "but it's okay. I love the smell of you as well."

"So I was thinking that …"

"Yeah?" I said eagerly.

"We could just talk for a little bit."

"Oh? Talk … I thought you wanted to do something else." I slipped my hand into his boxers and felt around for his cock. He groaned as my fingers gripped him and moved up and down.

"Oh, Rosalie," he said, "that feels so good."

"I'm glad it does." I pressed my lips against his shoulder.

"It feels fucking amazing. But I don't want this to just be about sex or the physical."

I stared at him in surprise and laughed. "Really?"

"Really," he said. "Have you read any good books recently?" he asked me.

"I've actually been reading a lot of Agatha Christie," I said. "When I was young, I enjoyed watching the *Poirot* TV show, but I never read the books. And now I can't get enough of Miss Marple and Poirot. She was such a fantastic crime writer. I love them."

"Oh wow. You know, I don't think I've ever read Agatha Christie." He laughed. "But I did see that one movie. What was it called? *Murder on the Orient Express*."

"Oh, did you see the new one or the old one?" I asked him curiously.

"I'm not sure. It was quite good, though. The storyline was fun."

"Yeah. She really knows how to catch you."

"I love a good whodunit."

"Me too."

"I didn't know you were into mysteries," he said. "I thought you were just always about the romance."

"I'm an English literature major, Oliver. I'm not just all about romance. I mean, don't get me wrong. I love a good romance. I like romantic suspense or romantic comedy. I even got into mafia romance for a little bit."

"Mafia romance?" He laughed. "What's that?"

"It's these stories where the protagonist is attracted to, or maybe not even attracted in the beginning, but the hero of the story or anti-hero is a member of the mafia."

"Okay. And?"

"Well, of course they fall in love, but lots of crazy stuff happens in between."

"You are into mafia romance. That's crazy."

We laughed together. "I know. I never thought I would be into it, either. What are you into?"

"Honestly, I think the last book I read was *Huckleberry Finn*."

"Really? What made you read *Huckleberry Finn*?"

"I wanted to know why it got banned by schools."

"Oh, Oliver, you're funny." I pressed my hand against the side of his face. "This is nice. I really like just lying here and talking to you."

"I really like you lying here and talking to me too," he said, kissing my forehead. "And before you get all worried and nervous that I don't want to fuck your brains out, of course I do. But I want us to have moments that are about more than that. You know?"

"I know," I said, nodding, "and I like that. So okay. Tell me what your favorite piece of art is."

"Oh shit. You would ask me that."

"Why are you saying, 'oh shit'?" I giggled.

"Well, because I can only think of the *Mona Lisa* right now. I'm an attorney. I don't know art. What's your favorite piece?"

"I would say *Water Lilies* by Monet."

We just stared at each other for a few seconds, enjoying the moment of being together. And I realized that this was something special. This was something I craved.

Chapter 33

ROSALIE

"I'd like to get a caramel macchiato, please, and a blueberry muffin," Alice asked the barista at the cool little coffee shop we found a couple of blocks away from Foster and Oliver's apartment.

"What do you want, Rosalie?"

"Oh, I can get it, girl."

"No, it's on me."

"Are you sure? I know you don't have much money either."

"It's fine. We'll find jobs, and it will be cool."

"Okay. Well, could I get a vanilla latte please, and one of those cheese and spinach quiches?"

"Sure. Anything else?" The barista smiled politely at us. I wondered if she felt bad hearing that we didn't have much money. If she did, she didn't show it on her face.

"I'll actually get a cheese and ham quiche, as well," Alice added.

"The quiche Lorraine?" the barista questioned.

"Yeah. Thank you. Do you want anything sweet?"

"Girl, you can't spend all your money."

"It's fine."

"I mean, those chocolate croissants look good too."

"And she'll get a chocolate croissant. If you could heat it and the blueberry muffin?"

"We'll heat all the food. That's going to be thirty-three eighty-six, please." I watched as Alice handed her two twenty-dollar bills.

"You can keep the change for the tip."

"Thank you, ma'am, very generous of you," the barista smiled wildly. "You can have a seat. I'll bring the food and drinks to you."

"Thank you." We both smiled and headed toward a table near the wall with our laptops.

"This is really cool," Alice said. "I know I keep saying that, but it's just so different from Florida."

"I know. I feel like I'm in another world."

"We kind of are." She giggled. She opened her laptop.

"So how are we going to approach this?"

"I was thinking, you try one site, I try another site, and then we keep open the tabs for all the jobs that we think either one of us will be interested in. And then we submit our résumés."

"Sounds good," she said. "And what sort of jobs are we looking for?"

"I mean, I know Oliver and Foster said they want us to find ourselves and choose a career that we're really going to love and all that good stuff, but I think for now we're just looking for jobs, right?"

"Yeah." She nodded. "I think so. I mean, I don't really know what I want to do. I mean, I do know what I want to do, but I can't do it."

"Oh? What do you want to do?"

"I told you, I want to work for a TV show. I want to write TV scripts."

"That would be pretty amazing," I said, nodding, "and you're a brilliant writer."

"Aw, thanks, Rosalie."

"What? It's true."

"Do you know what you want to do?" she asked.

"Um, can I say be a housewife and sit and watch TV all day?" She started laughing.

"Oh my gosh. You did not just say that."

"I mean, I did, and it's only half true. Does that make it half less bad?"

"I guess so," she said, "but that's a long way off. You don't even have a boyfriend right now."

"I know," I said, smiling as I thought about Oliver.

"Unless Oliver is your man."

"No, no, no. It's nothing like that. Though, last night he was so sweet."

"Oh yeah, what happened when you snuck off to his room? Did you bow chicka bow wow?" She winked at me.

"No, actually. He gave me this cute little dolphin because..."

"Don't tell me he remembered how much you loved dolphins when we were kids."

"Yeah," I said. "Sweet, huh?"

"That is really sweet," she nodded. "And so you didn't give him thank you sex for that?"

"Girl, I wanted to give him 'hello, let's get it on' sex, but he wanted to talk, and it was really nice. We just talked about things we liked and were into and, you know, just sort of caught up after all these years."

"Oh, wow. It sounds like one of those first dates that you have at a coffee shop," she said, "where you get to know everything about the other person."

"Yeah. I guess it was like that, except we didn't

have to find out the basic things because we already knew them. We were just filling each other in on our likes and dislikes and, you know, just enjoying each other's company and laughing."

"Oh, that sounds amazing, Rosalie."

"It kind of was." I chewed down on my lower lip. "I think I'm really falling for him."

"Oh no," Alice said. "Is that a good thing or a bad thing?"

"I don't know. He's got much more depth than I remember as a teenager, but maybe that's because I have more depth now, as well. I mean, I appreciate that he's a fucking sexy guy. I like his personality, as well, like he's caring and he's funny and he's protective. Sometimes he's a little bit over the top and grumpy, but I like him in all his stages. Is that weird?"

"No, girl. I think you're falling in love with him." I looked at her and nodded slightly.

"I think you're right. I think I'm in love with Oliver James, and this time, it's not just puppy love." I sighed. "He was right."

"What do you mean?"

"He told me if we slept together, I would probably develop feelings for him. Bug, what am I going to do?"

"Well, do you want to tell him?"

"Are you joking, Alice? There is no way I can tell

him that I think I'm in love with him. He'll never sleep with me again. He'll probably move out of the apartment, and I'll be mortified. Do you hear me? I'll be absolutely mortified."

"Well, I don't want you to be mortified."

"I mean, I'm just going to have to figure something out."

"Like what?"

"Like just enjoying the hot sex we have, and maybe I'll see if I can go on some other dates to keep my mind off him."

"I thought you guys said you weren't going to date other people."

"No, we agreed not to hook up with other people. We can still go on dates so Foster and you don't get suspicious."

"Oh, yeah," she laughed. "I forgot that he doesn't know that I know."

"I know, and now I'm feeling guilty that I told you. I can't believe I couldn't keep my mouth shut."

"He has to know that you tell your best friend."

"Well, Foster's his best friend, and he's not telling Foster."

"True, but it's okay. I won't say anything."

"I know you won't, Alice"—I sighed—"but we should concentrate on looking for jobs because we need money, and I want to go shopping on Fifth

Avenue. I saw these new Louis Vuitton handbags, and I want one."

"Oh my gosh, girl, there's a Gucci purse that I saw." She shook her head. "I need fifteen hundred dollars ASAP." I started laughing.

"Then I guess we need to get to finding a job."

"I guess we do," she said with a small smile. I opened my laptop, and that's when my phone started beeping. I grabbed it and smiled when I saw that I had a text message from Oliver.

"Who's that?" she asked.

"Oh, it's Oliver."

"Oh, what does he want?"

"Oh, he wants to know if I want to go to lunch with him."

"Oh," she said, nodding. "Okay then, that's cool. You want to meet me later?"

"I'm not going, Alice. We just got here, and we just ordered food."

"But he wants to take you to lunch and..."

"Yeah, just because he said, 'Jump,' I'm not going to say, 'How high?' I mean, I'm glad he's texting me and wants to take me to lunch, but he should have asked me last night or this morning. He should have made plans in advance. I'm hanging out with you. This is our time."

"Are you sure?" she said. "I really don't mind."

"I know you don't mind, and that's why I love

you. You're the most selfless person I know, but we're having lunch together, and we're looking for jobs, and you just got to town. I'm not just going to ditch you."

"Oh, I love that you are that sort of girl," she said. "So many friends will dump you in a second for a guy."

"I would never do that to you, Alice."

"I know, and I would never do that to you either, Rosalie." I smiled.

"Okay, let me text him back." I typed in my phone quickly. 'Hey, thanks for the invite, but sorry, Alice and I are at a coffee shop. Enjoy lunch.'

He typed back, 'miss you.'

"Aw, that's sweet." I held up the phone and showed Alice. "He said he misses me."

"He's a really nice guy, Rosalie."

"Thanks," I said. "He really is. I don't think it's so bad if I distance myself a little bit, though. I don't want him to think I'm overeager, and I don't want to keep falling more and more in love with him, you know?"

"I get it," she said. "It's hard when you have strong feelings for someone and don't really know where the relationship stands."

"Yeah, it really is. Okay, let's look for these jobs."

Alice and I walked back to the apartment after our lunch, feeling pleased with ourselves. We'd sent our résumés to several jobs, and I was hopeful that at least one of them would call us.

"So what do you want to do?" she asked as we got to the apartment building.

"I don't know. Hang out, watch TV."

"Sounds good to me." We walked into the lobby, and that was when I saw Rich and his granddaughter, Maddie.

"Hi, Rich. Hi, Maddie."

"Hi, Rosalie," Maddie said, an excited look on her face. "How are you?"

"I'm good, thanks. I'm so surprised you remember my name."

"I remember it because it reminds me of a rose, and roses are my favorite flowers."

"Oh, I love roses too." I smiled. "This is my best friend, Alice. She's moved in, too."

"Hi, Alice. I'm Maddie, and this is my grandad."

"Hi. Nice to meet you, Maddie."

Rich stared at us and looked at his watch. "Can I ask you something, please, Rosalie?"

"Of course, anything. What is it? Is everything okay?"

"It is. I told my son that I'd look after Maddie this afternoon, but I forgot that I have a doctor's appointment. Well, I'm going to be having an MRI, and I don't really want to take Maddie with me."

"Oh, I can look after her if you want."

"Are you sure? I hate to impose and..."

"No, of course. It's fine. We'll just go to the apartment. We can play games."

"Can we play school, please?" Maddie said eagerly. "I love that game. I love school. I'm so good at my ABCs and 123s."

"Of course," I said. "Yeah, and we can make popcorn and have juice. I mean, if you're allowed."

"Yeah. Can I have some, Grandad?"

"Sure." He smiled at me benevolently. "Thank you so much, Rosalie. I should be back in a couple of hours."

"No worries. It's my pleasure. That's okay, right, Alice?"

"Of course. I love kids."

"You have a good doctor's appointment," I said. I reached down and grabbed Maddie's hand. "Come on, Maddie. You want to go play school and have some popcorn?"

"Yes, please, Rosalie." She grabbed Alice's hand, as well. "Alice, I like your hair. It's pretty."

"Thank you, Maddie. You have pretty hair, as well." We walked into the elevator and then made our way to the apartment. I opened the door to see if anyone was home.

"You want to sit on the couch, Maddie, and I'll make the popcorn and get you some juice?"

"Okay," she said.

"You sure this is okay?" I said to Alice. "I know you didn't sign up to be a babysitter."

"No, it's fine. She's really sweet, and we weren't doing anything anyway. We were just going to watch TV."

"Yeah, true," I said. "Thanks for being so understanding."

"There's nothing to be understanding about. I love kids." We spent the rest of the afternoon playing games with Maddie and eating popcorn, and then two hours later, her grandad arrived.

"Hi," he said. "Thank you so much for looking after her. I hope everything was okay."

"It was brilliant. I had an amazing time."

"I'm glad," he said, smiling. "Come on, Maddie. I've got to take you home in a little bit."

"Okay, Grandad." Maddie ran up to me and hugged me. "Thank you so much, Miss Rosalie. You are the best teacher ever."

"Thank you. I appreciate that," I beamed. "And you're the best student ever."

"I know. I get A's and gold stars all the time."

I laughed.

"You guys have a great evening."

"We will," Maddie said. Rich stood there for a couple of seconds.

"Hey, is everything okay?" I asked him, hoping he hadn't had a bad time at the doctor's.

"Yeah, everything's fine, but I was just thinking..."

"Oh?"

"Well, Maddie's school is looking for teachers and teacher's assistants, and I was wondering if you'd be interested."

"Oh, I would love to, but I don't have a teaching certification or anything. I just have my bachelor's in English literature."

"Then I think you'd probably be able to start as a teacher's assistant. And if you like that, you could get your certification." He nodded. "If you want, I can put a word in for you at the school."

"That would be so amazing. I am looking for a job right now."

"Okay, cool. Would you like that, Maddie? Would you like Rosalie to teach at your school?"

"Oh my gosh. That would make me the happiest girl in the world," she said. "Bye, Rosalie." She hugged me again and waved to Alice, who was sitting on the couch. "Bye, Alice."

"Bye, Maddie, so good seeing you. You too, Rich. Have a great evening."

"Bye."

Maddie gave me one last hug, and as she pulled back, I saw Oliver walking through the door.

"Hello," he said. "Rich, good to see you."

"Hey, Oliver."

"Hi, Oliver," Maddie said. "I was just giving a hug to Rosalie because she is amazing."

"Yes, she is," Oliver said, looking at Maddie and me. "To what do we owe the pleasure of your company?"

"Oh, I had a doctor's appointment, and I completely forgot, so Rosalie and Alice took care of Maddie for me this afternoon."

"Oh, awesome," Oliver said, smiling. "I hope it went well."

"It was amazing," Maddie said with a huge smile.

"Well, I'm glad. You guys have a great evening."

"You too, Oliver."

"Bye, Rosalie. Thank you once again," Rich said, sincerely, "and I'll put in a word for you?"

"Great. Thank you." I watched as they walked down the hallway, and Oliver closed the door behind him. He looked at me for a couple of seconds, a warm expression on his face.

"I didn't know you liked kids."

"I love kids."

"Awesome," he said, nodding. "I missed you today. I was hoping we would go to lunch. I had this steak restaurant I was going to take you to."

"Maybe next time," I said. "If you feel like asking."

"Oh, I definitely feel like asking," he said with a warm smile. "Hey, Alice.

"Hey, Oliver," she said.

"Well, I will go and change, and I'll come hang out in a little bit," he said. He whispered to me, "I wish I could kiss you right now. I want to feel the touch of your lips against mine so bad."

Chapter 34

O<small>LIVER</small>

"So I have a meeting at three thirty," I mumbled under my breath as I checked my calendar, "and then I have to meet with Kramer at four thirty. That should last about thirty minutes." I sigh.

That meant I wasn't getting home until around five thirty or six. I was missing Rosalie. I wanted to see her. She'd been so busy the past couple of days with Alice that we hadn't really been able to spend any quality time together. We hadn't made love in over a week, and, well, I didn't like that. I missed being able to hold her close. I missed being able to snuggle her. I missed listening to her laugh and how her eyes lit up in fire or mischief when she was teasing me or arguing with me.

"Fuck," I said as I sat back in my chair.

Realization suddenly hit me. I'm in love with her. I fucking love Rosalie Sloane. It hit me like a ton of bricks all at once, and I realized this wasn't something new or shocking. I'd been in love with her for a long time, but I'd let the feelings sit dormant in me. But now, now, there was no denying it. I loved her and wanted to be with her as more than a secret hookup. I didn't care if Foster got angry or upset or wanted to kill me. I wanted to date Rosalie. I wanted her to be my girlfriend and didn't want the secrecy. I wanted to be able to kiss her whenever I wanted. To hold her hand. To take her on dates. To sit and watch a movie with her. I wanted her to sleep in my bed so that the first thing I would see when we woke up in the morning would be her beautiful face.

I looked at my calendar again and debated canceling all my appointments so I could rush home and speak to Rosalie. But I knew that I couldn't. My job was important to me, and doing well was impor-tant to me, and the meetings I had were important. There was a knock on the door, and I sat up straight. I grabbed my pen off the table.

"Come in," I called out.

"Hi," Diana's sultry tone sounded in the room as

she walked into the office and closed the door behind her.

"Hi," I said, smiling congenially. "What's up?"

"I just came to see how you're doing, Oliver James," she said, biting down on her lower lip.

I watched as she started unbuttoning her blouse, and my eyes stared in shock. "What are you doing, Diana?" I said sharply as she slipped her heels off, unzipped her skirt, and let it drop to the floor. I saw that she was wearing a high black thong.

"What do you think I'm doing, Oliver?" she said as she finally unbuttoned her shirt and dropped it onto the floor. My jaw dropped in shock as she unbuttoned her bra and threw it at me. "I've come to offer you what you've been missing."

"Diana, please, no. This is not a good idea."

"Oh, but all the right decisions start out as not good ideas. You have to know that, Oliver."

And then I watched as she took off her thong and dropped it on my desk. She giggled slightly as she walked around the desk and stopped right before me. I stared at her naked body, at the look of seduction on her face, and realized I felt sorry for her. I realized that what I had with her meant absolutely nothing to me. All I could think about was Rosalie and the way she giggled, the way she pranced, and the way I just wanted to grab her and hold her and kiss her all over. As I stared at Diana's body, I felt like

I was staring at an image in a magazine or a biology textbook.

"Diana, no."

"But Oliver," she said, grabbing my hand and placing it close to her breast. I pulled it away quickly.

"Diana, put your clothes on and get out of here."

"You know you want me, Oliver. You can't resist. I know you can't. There's no need to make me pay for not wanting to be with you. But I've changed my mind. I've decided you're what I want after all."

"I don't want you, Diana. I told you that. We never had anything real. It was just sex."

"Exactly. And you used to love to fuck me. Remember what we did with those handcuffs and that whip that time?"

I sighed. "Diana, we had some fun, and we experimented, yes, but that was it. I have feelings for someone else now."

"Not that little idiot you brought to the award ceremony." She rolled her eyes. "The one who was flirting with Chad? She was practically all over him. Oliver, do you really want to—"

"Diana, I'm not going to tell you this again. Put on your clothes, and get out of my office."

"You know you don't mean that, Oliver. You know you've been missing this wet pussy," she said, and then I watched in horror as she squatted.

She turned around and pushed her ass up

toward me, and I looked away, feeling sorry for her. I didn't know why she was acting like such a desperado. I didn't understand why she was parading around like this.

"Diana, I don't want to have to report you to HR, but I will if you do not put your clothes on."

She stood up straight and looked at me, confusion in her eyes.

"You're really going to turn this shit away?" She stared at me in disgust. "You're a fool, Oliver James. You know that, right?"

I shrugged. "Maybe, but I don't want you."

I watched as she put her bra on and buttoned her shirt. She grabbed her skirt and put it on.

"You forgot your panties." I nodded toward the desk.

"You know you want them. You know you want to probably masturbate into them tonight."

I shuddered at the thought. I hadn't thought about Diana in months. And then another knock came on the door.

"Just a second," I called out, but it was too late.

The door opened, and there stood Rosalie. I stared at her, horror and fear in my expression. As she gazed at Diana and me, she looked confused and puzzled and then angry.

"What's going on," she asked, "exactly?"

"Nothing. Diana just came to—"

"We were just having a good time, young lady," she said. Diana pressed her lips against my cheek and giggled.

"Thank you for that, Oliver. I had fun, as always."

I turned to look at Rosalie. She looked close to tears.

"Rosalie, it's not what you think." I hurried toward her. "Please let me explain."

And then Diana came up behind me, her panties in her fingers held up in the air as if they were some sort of trophy. She laughed.

"Here you go, darling." She pushed them into my pants pocket. "I know you want my panties, like always."

"Diana!" I said, "Take your—"

"Don't be coy in front of your little friend, Oliver. She knows what we just did. I mean, why else would my panties be off and now in your pocket? Bye. Have a good afternoon."

And with that, she waltzed out of the room. I was seething in anger. I couldn't believe that she had just said that. That she tried to pretend that I'd hooked up with her when I wanted nothing to do with her.

"Rosalie," I said, grasping at her hands, but she pulled them away.

"Look, I'm sorry. I didn't even know you were

coming to the office today. You didn't tell me."

"I, I, I wanted to surprise you." A single tear rolled down her face.

"Surprise me with what? What's going on?"

She stared at me for a few seconds and shook her head.

"Nothing. Nothing's going on, Oliver. I don't want to do this with you anymore. I don't trust you, and I can't do this. I can't believe you slept with her. We promised. We promised we wouldn't do anything with anyone else."

"Rosalie, I didn't. I swear. I—"

"Yeah, right."

She ran out of the room crying, and I swore under my breath. My alarm started going off, and I realized that my meeting was about to start in a minute. I had two options. I could go to my meeting with a million-dollar client and keep my job, or I could skip it, run after Rosalie, and keep whatever we had going. I debated for half a second and then ran out of the office. Rosalie meant every-thing to me. I couldn't have her thinking for one second that I would ever cheat on her or do anything with another woman. Didn't she under-stand that she was who I lived for? That I loved her? That I wanted to be with her? I had to tell her, and I had to tell her now. There was no way I would let her leave this office building without hearing me out. I got to the elevator just as she reached it.

"Rosalie, please wait. I want to——" And then the doors closed.

I pressed the button, but the doors didn't open.

"Fuck it," I said.

I headed toward the stairs. I was on the twentieth floor, but I'd run down those stairs as if I were a sprinter at the Olympics. I needed to make sure I got to the bottom before the elevator. I needed to make sure I got to speak to Rosalie before she left. Because if she left, I had no idea what she would do. And I didn't want her to feel an ounce of pain for something that wasn't even real. I sprinted down the stairs. I felt out of breath, and my legs felt sore, but I kept going. I nearly tripped down one flight and steadied myself slightly, but I knew I couldn't stop. I had to keep going. I had to make sure I got there before Rosalie left. I got to the bottom of the stairwell, opened the emergency door, and ran into the lobby. I looked toward the elevator, but the doors were open. She'd already left. I looked toward the front of the building and watched as she walked out.

"Rosalie Sloane! Wait!" I shouted.

She stopped and turned back to look at me. I could see her face was red and puffy, and my heart broke.

"Wait!" I said as I ran toward the door.

She stood there for a couple of seconds and then started running.

"Fuck it," I groaned as I picked up my pace.

I was out of breath, but I wasn't going to let her get away.

"Rosalie!" I shouted as she was running down the street. I could see people staring at us, but I didn't care. Finally, I caught up with her and grabbed her by the shoulders.

"Please, Rosalie. Wait! Please let me explain! Please!"

"How could you, Oliver? How could you do this to me?"

"I didn't, Rosalie. I promise. Okay? She came in. She tried to seduce me, but I didn't want her. I was telling her no. I love you, Rosalie. I would never sleep with someone else. You're all I think about. Fuck, just an hour ago, I was thinking about how I wanted to get out of work because I wanted to see you because we hadn't had any quality time in ages."

"That's why I came to the office to see you too," she said. "I feel like we don't have any time with each other, and I wanted to come after my interview."

"Your interview?" I stared at her in surprise. "What interview? You didn't tell me you had an interview."

"I didn't want to say anything, but… wait, you love me?"

She stared at me with her jaw open, her eyes wide, and I nodded.

"I love you, Rosalie. I've loved you for a long time, and I'm such a dumbass that it's taken me this long to figure it out. But I don't want to do what we've been doing anymore. I want us to be official. I want us to make this real. I don't care what your brother has to say. You're important to me, and—"

Before I could finish speaking, she grabbed my head, pulled me toward her, and kissed me hard. I sighed in relief. She was forgiving me. I wrapped my arms around her and dragged her to me close as I kissed her back passionately. I couldn't believe that I'd almost lost her. I knew I never wanted to experience anything like that again. I knew we had to come clean about it all.

Chapter 35

Rosalie

I looked at Oliver with love in my eyes. I couldn't believe the various emotions that had passed through me in the past twenty minutes. When I'd walked in and seen Diana in his office, my heart had sunk. And when she'd pushed her panties into his pocket, I'd wanted to die. I had never felt more heartbroken in my life. I'd arrived at the office so excited to tell him my news, but then I thought he'd done the worst thing he could ever have done to me.

"So Rosalie," he said, cupping my face.

"Yes," I said, softly looking at him.

"I know that you've just graduated from college, and you're brand new to the city, and you might want to explore meeting other guys and going on dates and all that. And I understand that. I don't want to trap you. I don't want to make you commit to something you're not ready for. I will wait for you for however long it takes to find yourself and live your life and party and do all the things you..."

"Oliver, I don't want to meet other guys. I don't want to party if it's not with you. Don't you know I love you too? I've loved you since I was a teenager. I've loved you forever. Why did you think I stopped talking to you when I was seventeen? That kiss meant the world to me. I thought you were going to propose to me or something. And then I hear that you're calling me a fat pig or whatever." I started laughing hysterically. "I've always wanted to be with you, Oliver. It's always been you."

"You mean it?" he said with a warm, deep smile.

And I nodded. "Yeah, I do. It's you. You're the one for me."

"So does that mean you kind of love me too?"

"Yes, Oliver. I love you. I love you. I love you. I love you. I love you so much that I don't even know if there are words in the dictionary to express how deeply I feel."

His gray eyes shone at me. "Oh, Rosalie. You don't know how happy you've made me."

"Really? But what about Foster?"

"We'll tell him eventually," he said, laughing. "And when I say eventually, I mean soon. We just have to figure out how to tell him because I think it'll come as a bit of a shock, right? We argue all the time, and we're kind of like frenemies, and then we're going to tell him we're dating?"

"True," I said. "I guess he has no clue, and it will be a shock. Do we tell him that we've been messing around?"

"I don't know," he said. "Let me think on it." He pulled me into his arms and kissed me again. "I can't believe how fucking lucky I am that you came back into my life."

"I guess you should be thankful to my university."

"Why should I be thankful to your university?" He looked confused.

"Because if I didn't study English literature, I might have had a real job when I graduated. And if I had a job when I graduated, I probably wouldn't be living with you and Foster."

"Boy, two beers and three thumbs-up to your university and your stupid English literature degree."

I laugh. "Well, it's not that stupid because guess what?"

"What?" he said.

"I got the job."

"The job at the school?"

"Yeah. I'm going to be a kindergarten teacher's assistant. They loved me, and I loved them, and I saw Maddie and all these other kids, and it was amazing."

"Are you sure that's something you want to do?"

"For now? Yes. I'm probably gonna try to get my teaching certificate as well so I can be a teacher. It's weird, but I've always liked kids, and I don't know why I never thought about that as a career path."

"Well, whatever you want to do, I support you," he said. He wrapped his arms around me. "I can't believe it. We're the typical cliché."

"What's that?"

"An attorney and a teacher."

"Oh, is that a thing?"

"I don't know," he said, laughing. "I just know several attorneys whose wives are teachers."

"Ah, are you proposing to me, Oliver?" I started laughing as I watched the expression on his face change to one of slight shock. "I'm joking. Don't worry."

"I'm not worried," he said softly. He grabbed my hand. "You want to go back into the office? I just have a couple of calls to make, and then we can leave."

"Oh my God, I completely forgot you probably had work. I can just go home, and we can chat later."

"Nope. I'm not letting you out of my sight for the rest of the evening. I want to kiss you and touch you, and..." He sighed. "I guess that will be hard with Alice and Foster at home."

"I can call Alice."

"Oh? And say what?"

"I can tell her to tell Foster she's really interested in working at a brokerage and see if he wants to go for drinks to talk about it."

Oliver nodded. "That could be a really good idea."

"Yeah, and I'm sure she'd do it."

"But why would she do it? Wouldn't she be curious why you'd want her out of the apartment?"

I bit down on my lower lip. "Well, not really 'cause she kind of knows about us."

"What? Rosalie, how does she know?"

"I kind of told her when she got here. She's my best friend. We're girls, and we tell each other everything."

"Well, she can keep a secret because I had no idea she knew." Oliver laughed. "Okay, well, you want to call her and see if she can set that up? And then maybe we can have the evening together in the apartment."

"That would be really nice. I could make you dinner," I said.

"Ooh, what would you make me?"

"I don't know. I only know about six dishes, but all six are really good."

"Then yeah. Surprise me. Make me something yummy. And I'll figure out dessert."

"You mean you're not going to be dessert?"

"Oh, I'll definitely be one of the desserts," he said, winking as we returned to the building. I chewed on my lower lip as we walked in. "What is it?" he said.

"Nothing," I said quickly.

"Tell me, Rosalie. I can read you like a book."

"Well, Diana. Is she going to keep trying to seduce you? And..."

"I'm going to go to HR tomorrow morning. What she did was unacceptable. I felt embarrassed for her at first. But she crossed a line when she tried to pretend to you that something actually happened. I will make an official complaint, and if I have to, I will get a restraining order against her." He looked at me. "You are more important to me than anything else in this world, Rosalie. I will not let anyone come between us."

"Oh, my hero," I said, grinning at him.

"Well, you can keep calling me positive words like that any time of day."

"Oh yeah? I will then. And... Oliver?"

"Yes, Rosalie."

"Can I tell you something?"

"Um, you can tell me anything."

"So I was thinking..."

"Uh-huh. What were you thinking about?"

"I was thinking it might be really sexy if you say dirty words to me the next time we have sex."

He raised an eyebrow. "What? Where did this come from?"

"I don't know. But I was thinking about it the other night, and I was feeling really turned on, and I thought it might be cool if you whisper really dirty words to me when we have sex."

"Okay. Whatever you want. Anything else?"

"No, not that I know of," I said, leaning up and kissing him on the cheek. "I'm so happy I'm with someone I'm not afraid to express my desires to."

He looked down at me with joy in his eyes. "I'm glad you can express yourself to me as well. Anything you want to try, anything you want to do, you let me know. I'm here for it."

"Same," I said, "if there's anything you haven't done, though I guess you've done everything."

"Oh, there are a billion things I haven't done," he said. "I haven't joined the mile-high club. I haven't had sex in a foreign country. I haven't..."

"You don't have to list them all now, but I will definitely join the mile-high club with you. And I would love to travel with you. We can have sex every-where we go."

"That's what I'm talking about," he said. "I can

just picture it. France, England, Germany, Thailand, Australia, South Africa, Jamaica, Hawaii."

"Wow. We're going to be traveling a lot. I am not making that much money as a teacher's assistant, Oliver."

"Don't you worry about it, my dear. I will always have you covered." He pressed his lips against mine as we made our way into his office. "I love you, Rosalie. I've always loved you. And I will always spoil you and treat you and give you whatever you want. As long as I can afford to, I will do it."

"Why are you so freaking perfect?" I said.

"Um, do you really think I'm perfect?" he said, laughing as he sat down. "Because there are a billion different times you've told me otherwise."

"Well, maybe you're not perfect perfect, but you're perfect for me."

"You're perfect for me too, Rosalie," he said. "Now I better call Kramer because I blew off a very important meeting, and I need to reschedule some things. You okay for the next twenty or thirty minutes just looking at your phone or something?"

"I'm fine, honey. I'll call Alice and make sure she goes out tonight. Love you."

Chapter 36

ROSALIE

"This lasagna is absolutely delicious." Oliver licked his fork clean and took the last bite of cheesy bread. "You are an amazing cook."

"Well, you know," I said. "Are you finished?"

"I am."

Jumping up, I grabbed the plate from in front of him and carried it toward the kitchen sink. "What did you get for dessert?" I looked around eagerly.

"Your favorite," he said.

"My favorite?"

"Yeah, tres leches cake?"

"Oh my gosh, you really do remember everything. Where is it?"

"It's in the fridge."

"I didn't even see it." I hurried to the fridge and opened the door, and there on the second shelf sat a plastic container with tres leches. "Oh, my gosh. You are amazing."

"I got it from a Cuban restaurant in the village," he said.

"Oh, my gosh. Oliver." I closed the fridge door and walked over to him. He pulled his chair back, and I sat on his lap. I leaned forward and kissed him. I ran my fingers through his hair and stared at his hands and face. "You are just the sweetest."

"Well, hey, anything for you, Rosalie. And good work with getting Alice and Foster out of here."

"Yeah. Alice was happy to do it, but she's worried that Foster will take her seriously and want her to go back to school and do some accounting classes or something." I started laughing.

"Oh, no. Well, she can always tell him it was just a joke or something."

"Yeah. I guess. They'll figure it out. I don't want to talk about them right now." I reached for the top of his shirt and undid the button. "We have other things to do."

"We do, do we?" he said, looking at me smugly. "You want dessert one or dessert two first?"

"Dessert two, definitely," I said as I jumped off his lap and grabbed his hand. "Come on."

"Where are we going?" he said, looking at his bedroom door.

"Oh no. Today, we do it on the couch."

"The couch?" He raised his eyebrows.

"Yeah," I laughed.

"But..."

"But what?"

"Won't it be awkward?"

"No, because you'll be sitting, and I'll be on top."

"Oh," he said, his eyes lighting up. "So you want to be on top?"

"Oh yeah, baby," I said as I pushed him down on the couch. I then got on his lap and straddled him. I continued unbuttoning, then pulled the sleeves down and threw his shirt to the floor. I looked at his handsome olive chest and pressed my lips forward and kissed him. I felt his hands running through my hair, and I laughed slightly as he got his finger stuck. "I didn't brush it this morning," I said, laughing.

"Oh," he said, "It's a little knotty, eh?"

"Yeah." I gazed up into his eyes. "Why are you so amazing?" I asked him.

"I don't know if everyone thinks I'm amazing, but maybe I'm just amazing when I'm with you."

"Maybe," I said. I reached down and unbuckled his pants. "Stand up," I said, quickly getting off him.

"Wow, you're eager."

"Well, I haven't been with you in a while, and I'm really quite ready."

"Oh really?" he asked. "Just how ready?"

"You'll see soon." I winked at him, and he growled. He pulled his pants down and stepped out of them. I watched as he quickly got rid of his boxers as well. I stared at his cock, long and hard, and I grinned. I reached down and rubbed my fingers back and forth, and he groaned as I gave him a slight hand job.

"Fuck, that feels good."

"Oh yeah? How good?"

"You know how good," he said. He stepped forward and pulled my top off, and then I pulled my skirt down and my panties too. He whistled as he stared at my body. "You're fricking gorgeous."

Pushing him back down on the couch, I got into his lap and straddled him again. I could feel his hard cock between my pussy lips. And he groaned as he felt how wet I was there.

"Shit, you really are ready." He grabbed my ass and pulled me toward him. And I groaned as he rubbed me back and forth on his cock. His tip was rubbing my clit, and it felt amazing. My breasts bounced against his chest, and I leaned forward and kissed him. His fingers ran up and down my back, and his tongue slid into my mouth. And I knew I just wanted him then. I reached down and positioned him between my legs.

"Fuck me, please."

"Hold on," he said, reaching over and pulling out a condom from his pocket. I watched as he ripped it open and slipped it on. "Because I want to come this time," he said with a laugh. I just smiled and placed him back between my legs. I shifted slightly so that the tip of him was at my entrance. And then I lowered myself down little by little.

"Oh my gosh," I said, as he was finally completely inside me. He grunted in response, and I felt him moving my hips back and forth faster and faster as I bounced up and down on his lap. This felt different from the other times we had sex. And I couldn't believe just how amazing it felt. I grabbed his head and kissed him as I felt myself coming close to orgasm. He reached up and started playing with my nipples as he continued to move his hips, and I knew I was close to coming.

"Don't stop," he said as I bounced up and down faster and faster.

"I won't," I said. "I'm close." And then I started screaming as I felt everything inside me exploding in pure and utter bliss.

"Fuck yeah," he said. He gripped my hips and moved me up and down on his cock. And then I felt his body still and then shudder inside me. I collapsed forward and kissed him. He looked at me with happy, tired eyes. "That was fucking hot," he said.

"It was amazing." I slid off him and watched as he pulled his condom off and placed it on the floor.

"Fuck, that was hot." He grabbed my hand and pulled me back onto his lap, and I sat on it and looked up at him. He lazily played with my back. I could hear my phone beeping, but I ignored it. There was no one I cared to talk to at that moment.

"You're so beautiful, Rosalie," he said, staring at me with adoration and love in his eyes.

"You're so handsome. Oliver, I just can't believe it's real. I just can't believe we finally got together."

"Me either." He leaned forward and kissed me on the nose, and I grabbed his ear.

"You have the most beautiful ears," I said, studying them.

"I do?" He laughed. "That's a weird observation to make."

"I study each and every part of you," I said. My phone started ringing then, and I rolled my eyes. "Oh my gosh. I'm not getting it." I started laughing. "Whoever it is cannot take a hint. Just leave a message."

"I know, right? I hope it's not your ex Graham Cracker telling you he's back in the country and wants you back."

"Oh my gosh, it's not Graham," I said, poking

him. "Trust me, he's not coming back. And even if he did, I don't want him."

"Well, good, because you're mine, right?" he said suddenly. "You are my girlfriend now, right, Rosalie?"

"Of course. And you are my boyfriend, Oliver." I heard the door opening, and we both froze. Foster strode in with Alice behind him.

"What the fuck!" he exclaimed as he looked over to the living room. I stared at him in shock. Thankfully, Oliver acted quickly and grabbed one of the throw blankets from the couch and pulled it around me. And then he pulled one around himself. Foster strode over to us. "What the hell is going on here?" I bit down on my lower lip.

"I'm sorry," Alice said softly. "I tried calling and texting, but no one answered."

I stared at Oliver and sighed. "Well, at least we know it wasn't Graham."

He laughed lightly. "Foster, I'm sorry. Please don't be mad at Rosalie. It's my fault. I..."

Foster shook his head. "I just can't believe you guys would do this in the middle of the living room. All of us sit on that couch."

"Wait, what? That's why you're upset?" Oliver frowned.

Foster started laughing as he looked at us. "Do you think I'm stupid or something?"

"What are you talking about?" I stared at my brother.

"Dude, you guys aren't exactly CIA agents. It's been very obvious to me that you guys have been dating and hooking up and doing who knows what. Obviously, you weren't ready to tell me, so I pretended I didn't know. But obviously, you guys are getting serious." He paused as he looked at Oliver. "At least I hope this is more than just a sex thing. I didn't expect you guys to be having fun in a common room. I don't want to sit on that couch ever again."

"I'll get it cleaned," I said quickly.

"With whose money? I'm not paying to get it cleaned."

"I'll get it cleaned," Oliver said. "But, bro, you knew?"

"I knew," Foster said. "I'm not sure why you didn't tell me, though."

"Because I remember when we were younger, you told me not to even look at your sister and that no guy would ever be good enough and you'd kill any friend who dated her."

"Oh, that's when I was young," Foster said, "and Rosalie was young. I never meant you. Dude, you're like my brother. You're my best friend. I wouldn't have you in my life if I didn't think you were a good guy. I wouldn't be living with you. I never would've let you pick up Rosalie from the airport and stay with her while I was out of town."

"So you don't mind?" I said.

"I don't mind, Rosalie. I know you've been into Oliver forever. It's been so obvious. You always talked about him. And well, I figured if it was meant to be, it would be. And I guess it was meant to be."

"We're boyfriend and girlfriend," I said quickly. I looked over at Alice. Alice was smiling widely. "We're officially together now."

"Oh my gosh. That's amazing. Congratulations, Rosalie."

"Thank you. And well, do you guys mind kind of turning around while we get up so we can put on some clothes? I feel kind of awkward sitting in here with only a blanket covering me."

"Come on, Alice," Foster said. "Let's go to my room, and we can chat. You guys just knock on the door when we can come out, okay?"

"Will do," I said quickly. Oliver looked at me, and I looked at him, and we both burst out laughing.

"I cannot believe we went through all that," Oliver said, "and Foster already knew."

"I know! Can you believe it? We were sneaking around thinking we were being so covert and having these secret sex rendezvous. And it was all for nothing."

"Well, it wasn't all for nothing. It was kind of

fun," Oliver said as he gave me a kiss. "Now come on, let's go put some clothes on, and then maybe we can all order a pizza or something."

"Dude, we just ate."

"Yeah, but did Foster and Alice eat?"

"Oh, true. Maybe not. You mean to order a pizza for them?"

"Yeah, silly. I mean, I'm stuffed from all that lasagna and cheesy bread. Aren't you?"

"Well, yeah." I smiled at him. "I love you, Oliver."

"I know. And I love you too. And you know what is the first thing we're going to do next week?"

"No, what?"

"We're going to get you on the pill."

"Oh really? And why is that?"

"Because I want to be able to fuck you without a condom. If that's okay, of course."

"It's fine," I said, laughing as I reached up and touched his chest. "I mean, that's what people in relationships do, right?"

"Yeah," he said. "I'm so happy that you're going to be my girlfriend, and..." He bit down on his lower lip. "Well, nothing."

"What were you going to say? Tell me."

"I was just going to say that now that we're official and everyone knows, maybe you can sleep in my room?"

"I mean, do you think Foster will be cool with that?"

"We can ask him. It would get the air mattress out of the living room because then Alice could sleep on the couch."

"Sure," I said. "And hey, I know Foster's hooked up with plenty of women, so it would be a double standard if he said no to me."

"Exactly," Oliver said with a smile. "I would love to have you in my room. I've thought about waking up to you every morning for ages now."

"Me too," I said, loving that he'd also thought about it. "I'm so happy right now, Oliver."

"Me too, Rosalie. I love you."

Chapter 37

Rosalie

One Month Later.

"Look at this house, Oliver." I pointed at the screen. "This looks amazing."

"It really does," he said, staring at the first picture, but I could tell he was distracted.

"What is it?" I looked up from my position on his bed. He was standing by the window, looking out.

"I was just thinking that a year ago, I never would've imagined that I'd be this happy and living with you. It's just funny how life goes sometimes."

"I know," I said, beaming at him. Stretching my legs, I got off the bed and stood next to him. "I feel like the luckiest woman in the world if that means anything."

"It means everything," he said, turning to me, "though I guess we should go into the living room. I think Foster and Alice are waiting on us to play Monopoly."

"Oh my gosh." I laughed. "I forgot about that."

"And how is Alice liking her new job?" he asked.

"I don't think she's really liking it," I said. "I think she's going to quit, but that's okay. She can find something else she likes."

"I hope she finds something she loves as much as you love working with kids," he said, gazing at me with love in his eyes.

"Yeah, I'm really lucky. I'm so thankful to Maddie. I have to get her a present or something."

"Yeah, that would be nice. She'd really like that."

I squeezed his fingers. "And you told Foster, right?"

"Not yet," he said, "but I'm going to."

"You better tell him soon because I don't want him looking for a place thinking you're going in on it together when we're getting our own place."

"I know, but I just feel bad. I told him we'd invest in it together and—"

"Yeah, but we want to move in just the two of us."

"I know," he said, "and I'm glad you're finding

places you like. We can go to some open houses tomorrow if you want."

I shook my head slowly. "Depends on the time. I told Alice that I'd go with her to Greenwich Village. She wanted to check out this play in the park. I think it's Shakespeare in the Park or something?"

"Oh yeah, they have that every year. That would be fun."

"Maybe we can go on Sunday to the open houses then?"

"Yeah, that sounds good."

"You're so understanding."

"Well, she's your best friend, and I know you want to spend time with her. I'm grateful you're not one of those women who dumps their friends for their man."

"That's funny. Alice and I were talking about that very same thing a couple of months ago."

"When was this?" he said, frowning.

"It was after I started dating you. Don't worry."

"Okay, I was just checking," he said.

"It's so funny when you get jealous, Oliver."

"What? I'm not being jealous. I was trying to figure out if you were two-timing me when you first came to live with us."

"Um, we weren't official right away. So if I was seeing someone else, it wouldn't have been two-timing."

"Yeah, but you weren't, right?"

"No, I wasn't." I gazed at him, my heart constricting with love for him. There was just something about this man who made me feel complete. I had never felt such happiness before in my life. "Come on, let's go play Monopoly," I said, "before they call the police to see that we're okay."

He started laughing. "Ha ha. Very funny, Rosalie."

We made our way into the living room, and I could see Foster and Alice on the couch arguing about something.

"Everything okay?" I asked, frowning.

"Yeah," Alice said, overly chipper, but I could see Foster still had an unpleasant expression on his face.

"You okay, Bro?" I asked him.

"I'm fine," he said, shaking his head.

Alice looked at him and then at me and shook her head as if to say don't even bother. I wondered what was going on between them. Oliver had told me that he thought that Foster had real feelings for Alice, but I wasn't sure. I didn't want to tempt fate because the last thing I needed was for them to mess around and for Alice to get her heart broken. Alice wasn't like me. She was a sensitive soul, and I knew that a broken heart would completely break her.

"So I figured we could get Thai food tonight," Foster said, "right, Alice?"

"That's fine by me," she said with a shrug.

"Hey, there's something I wanted to say." Oliver cleared his throat.

I looked at him in confusion. "What is it, honey?"

"Well—"

"Oh my gosh, Oliver. Don't tell me you don't want Thai food," Foster said, rolling his eyes.

"No, that's not it. I just wanted to say that Rosalie and I are looking for a place."

"What do you mean you're looking for a place?" Foster looked confused.

"We're going to get our own little house together."

"Oh, okay." Foster looked at me and then at Oliver. "So I guess we're not investing in that brownstone anymore?"

"No, I'm sorry. I meant to tell you, but—"

"It's fine," Foster said. "When are you guys hoping to move out?"

"Well, we haven't even started looking yet. I just wanted to square everything away with you, and well, there was one other thing."

"What other thing?" I stared at him in surprise.

"Well…" He cleared his throat and looked toward Alice. Alice jumped up and ran over to the speakers.

"What is going on? I'm so confused."

Foster jumped up then as well and headed to his room. He came back with a bouquet.

"Wow. Those are beautiful," I said. "Who are they for?"

"They are for you." Foster gave them to Oliver, who handed them to me.

"I wanted him to hide them for me."

"Why are you hiding flowers?" I said, and then Air Supply started playing through the speakers, and my jaw dropped. "I love this song. I've always loved this song. In fact, when I was young…" I said, and then it hit me. "Oh my gosh, no. Wait, what?"

Alice stood next to Foster, and they both stared at me with huge grins. Oliver licked his lips nervously, and I watched as he stuffed his hand into his pocket and pulled out a little black jewelry box. He got onto his knee and looked up at me.

"Rosalie Sloane, I have known you what feels like all my life and to have known you is to have loved you. We first kissed when you were seventeen, and I've never forgotten how you made me laugh and lit up my life. And then we didn't speak for five years. I didn't try to get in contact with you because I wanted you to be able to experience the joys of college and of becoming an adult without me in it. I think I've always known that I've loved you, and a part of me has always known that you've loved me, too. And maybe that scared me, but I'm not scared anymore.

You are my girlfriend, the most wonderful, most important, most beautiful person in my life. I have loved you for what feels like a million years, and I will love you for a billion more. Rosalie Sloane, will you marry me? Will you make me the happiest man in the world?"

He pulled the ring out of the box and held it up, and I nodded. Tears were rolling out of my eyes. He stepped up as he pushed the ring onto my finger, and I grabbed him and pulled him to me.

"Oh my gosh, Oliver James. You are the most romantic, most sweet. Oh, I love you." I pressed my lips against his and held him close to me. He ran his hands down my back and held me close. I could hear sobs coming from the side, and I looked over and saw Alice crying with happiness. Foster was rubbing her back and giving her a hug.

"Oh my gosh, that was so sweet," she said. Oliver let go of me, and then Alice ran over and gave me a big hug. "Congratulations. I'm so happy for you."

"You knew, and you didn't tell me?"

"I can't keep a secret, you know that," she said with a giggle and then looked up at Foster.

"You knew, too?"

"I did," he said, grinning, "and I am super happy. My best friend is about to become my brother, and my sister is marrying the best guy I know. I'm over the moon."

"Thank you, Foster," I said. "I know we argue sometimes, and I get on your nerves sometimes, but you are the best big brother."

"I know," he said, grinning. He looked over at Alice. "And, hey, Alice, don't you worry. You can have Oliver's room when he moves out."

"Oh no," she said quickly. "You don't have to do that. I don't want to impose."

"No imposition. Any friend of my sister's is a friend of mine."

"Of course," she said quickly. "Of course." She looked at me, and I could tell from her expression that there was a sadness, but I wasn't sure what caused it. I'd have to find out from her later.

Oliver grabbed my hand and pulled me back to him. "So we're not actually playing Monopoly tonight."

"We're not? What? But—"

"I wanted to propose to you, and I wanted to celebrate the fact that we have officially lived in the same room together for a month, and we haven't killed each other."

"Yay," I said, laughing. "You're such a goof, Oliver."

"I know, but can I tell you something else?"

"Anything," I said.

"This past month has been the happiest of my life. Sometimes I wake up, and I just stare at you, and you make everything okay. If I'm having a bad day at work or if I'm stressed out about something else, all I have to do is think about you or call you or text you, and you make everything okay. You are the equilibrium in my life. You are the joy. You are the light. You are the peace, and I can't believe I got so lucky to find and be with someone like you. I can't believe I'm so lucky that someone like you would love me back."

"I feel the same way, Oliver. I can't believe I'm so lucky you would love me back. You are the most gorgeous, handsome, wonderful man I've ever met, and I've loved you since I was a girl, and I will love you until I'm an old lady."

"Promise?" he said.

"I promise."

The End

Thank you for reading The Edge of Falling. To read a bonus epilogue just for my newsletter readers, sign up here.

The next book in the series is Never Falling and features Foster and Alice. You can preorder the book here. Continue reading for a sneak peek.

. . .

Sneak Peek of Never Falling

Never Falling: A Best Friend's Brother Romance

Blurb

*D*id I perform a lap dance for my best friend's brother after a late night of partying?

Well, if sitting on his lap, singing out-of-tune pop songs, and then falling asleep on him counts, then yes.

*D*id I wake up in his bed with only his T-shirt on and spy on him getting dressed?

Who's asking?

．　．　．

*D*id I pretend to be interested in finance and becoming his new assistant just to make a move?

Of course not...I absolutely love all things about 3D's, I mean VD's...or is it CD's?

*F*oster Sloane is my best friend's brother. He's everything you want in a daydream fantasy. Golden brown eyes that seem to glow when they watch you. A teasing tantalizing smile that makes my heart beat faster than the timer on a stop-watch. And dark brown hair that just begs for my fingers to comb through it. If it wasn't obvious, I've had a crush on him since I was twelve. And now I'm twenty-two and I'm ready to make a move.

*O*nly Foster Sloane is not looking for love. He's the sort of man who puts his career above everything else. He wants to be a millionaire before he's thirty. He wants to learn to fly. And he only dates models and actresses. He's not interested in not so little me, with my size twelve jeans and larger-than-life personality. I've always known that he only sees me as his sister's best friend, hot mess Alice, but I'm starting to wonder if he's starting to see me as more.

You see there was this one text message, that lead to a phone call, which lead to me getting drunk and proceeding to give him the not-so-sexy lap dance. I'm not sure exactly where I'm headed, but as long as it brings me closer to him, I'm going for it.

Chapter 38

FROM: FOSTERSLOANE@KINGOFBANKING.COM
To: AlicePascal@firstuniversity.edu
Subject: Home Alone

*A*lice,

I just wanted to say sorry for leaving you alone in the apartment. I hope the creaks in the middle of the night aren't scaring you. Feel free to have friends over for dinner.

Foster

*F*rom: AlicePascal@firstuniversity.edu
To: FosterSloane@kingofbanking.com

Re: Home Alone

*H*ey Foster,
No worries. The apartment is amazing, and I'm still hanging out with Rosalie when she has time. My job search keeps me occupied. Where in Europe are you right now?

Alice

*F*rom: FosterSloane@kingofbanking.com
To: AlicePascal@firstuniversity.edu
Re: Home Alone

*A*lice,
Glad to hear the apartment is amazing. I am currently in Paris. At this exact moment, je mange le baguette et fromage. I hope I got that right. I'm trying to practice my French. I am in a cute apartment with a view of the Eiffel Tower. Such a beautiful city. Have you been exploring New York yet? When I get back, I will have to take you to my favorite pizza joint.

Foster

. . .

From: AlicePascal@firstuniversity.edu
To: FosterSloane@kingofbanking.com
Re: Home Alone

Hey Foster,
        Now I am officially jealous. Views of the Eiffel Tower. Wow or as the French would say Tres Bien...I think. I haven't taken any French since high school. All I remember is Je adore le chien, haha. Ooh, can't wait to go to the pizza joint.
        Alice

From: FosterSloane@kingofbanking.com
To: AlicePascal@firstuniversity.edu
Re: Home Alone

Alice,
        I hope that's not a hint that you're buying a dog. I really don't want dog poop in my bed when I get home. :P I'm flying to Rome tomorrow and will go on a tour of the Colosseum and pretend I'm a gladiator. How's the job search going? How are

my sister and best friend? Haven't heard from either of them in ages.

oster

From: AlicePascal@firstuniversity.edu
      To: FosterSloane@kingofbanking.com
Re: Home Alone

Hey Foster,
    I promise if I get a dog it will be a cute one, and I won't let it poop on your bed. Rome sounds amazing. Are you on vacation or working? HA HA. The job search is going meh...might have to sell my body for money, JK.
    Alice

From: FosterSloane@kingofbanking.com
      To: AlicePascal@firstuniversity.edu
Re: Home Alone

. . .

*A*lice,
Unfortunately, it is definitely for work. I have a two-hundred-page contract that I'm working on tonight with the company's CEO, so don't be that jealous. Please do not sell your body. I promise it's not worth the hassle. From someone who knows! Who am I kidding...I'd give it away for free.

Foster

*F*rom: AlicePascal@firstuniversity.edu
To: FosterSloane@kingofbanking.com
Re: Home Alone

*H*ey Foster,
Did you just call me? I was in bed sleeping and thinking of you standing on the street with a sign saying, "Have me for free," HA HA. I'm sure there would be plenty of takers.

Alice

*F*rom: FosterSloane@kingofbanking.com
To: AlicePascal@firstuniversity.edu
Re: Home Alone

. . .

*H*ey Alice,
     Glad I didn't wake you up. Was just calling to make sure everything was well. I forgot the time difference. Would you be one of the takers? HA HA. Or do you not like free items?
Foster

*F*rom: AlicePascal@firstuniversity.edu
     To: FosterSloane@kingofbanking.com
Re: Home Alone

*H*ey Foster,
     I plead the Fifth. There's no good way to answer that question as you're my best friend's brother! :)
Alice

Chapter 39

ALICE

My stomach was rumbling as I made my way to the coffee shop Alice had chosen for us to meet at. I looked at my watch to make sure I wasn't going to be late. I had about five more blocks to go, and I was wearing heels, so I couldn't exactly run. As I passed a boutique, I looked into the windows and saw some summer dresses that looked absolutely stunning. I stopped for a few seconds and stared at them, wishing I had the funds to treat myself to a dress. I let out a deep sigh and made my way back down the street.

I really needed to find a job. I really needed to make some money. I had been in New York City for three months now and was living with my best friend's brother, Foster. I bit down on my lower lip as I thought about Foster. He had been gone for the last month on a business trip, but I knew he was coming back this weekend. I wasn't quite sure how I felt about that. This would be the first time he and I were living alone without Rosalie and her fiancé, Oliver.

Rosalie was my best friend and had been since childhood. When she'd graduated from college, her parents had said she could either move back home or move to New York City to be with her brother. She elected for the latter, and she moved in with her brother and his best friend, Oliver.

Rosalie had a crush on Oliver since we were kids, and it turned out that Oliver also had feelings for her. It hadn't taken long for their chemistry to sizzle, and they'd gotten together. Now they were engaged and had just moved into their own brownstone in Chelsea.

I was slightly envious but super happy for my best friend, especially because she also figured out what she wanted to do with her life. She was working at a school as a teacher's assistant and was hoping to become a full-time teacher. She'd signed up to take classes to get her certification.

I followed Rosalie to New York City because I wanted to be with my best friend, and I'd always wanted to live in New York, but I hadn't been quite so lucky yet. I hadn't found a boyfriend, I hadn't even gone on any dates yet, and I still didn't know what I wanted to do for a living. I'd worked for a couple of weeks at a coffee shop but quit when the manager had cornered me in a back room and told me to get on my knees. I'd looked at him in confusion, and when I'd realized what he was saying, I'd shaken my head, alternated between laughing and crying, and left within a couple of minutes.

When I told Rosalie what had happened, she'd told me that I should find what I really wanted to do, and she'd lend me a couple of thousand dollars, which had been absolutely amazing of her, but I didn't want to take her kindness for granted. I knew I needed to find a job, and well, I also wanted to find a man. Well, that wasn't exactly true. I wanted Foster. I'd had my eyes on Foster since I could remember. Growing up with Alice and her brother, I had been around him for so many years. I'd seen his personality, and there was just something about him that made my heart race.

"There you are, Alice." Rosalie ran toward me from outside the coffee shop with a huge smile on her face.

"Hey. Sorry. Am I late?" I said, opening my arms and giving her a big hug. She looked absolutely radiant. She'd been really glowing since she and Oliver had officially started dating.

"Just a couple of minutes, but I know we're in New York, and I'm sure the subway had delays." She was so gracious.

"Thanks, girl. I actually got on an earlier subway. It's these heels." I looked down at my feet. "They hurt so bad but—"

"You want to look good because you're in New York."

"You got it," I said, laughing. "So how are things?" We linked arms and walked into the coffee shop.

"Amazing," she said, beaming. "Oliver said that I can have a destination wedding wherever I want. And," she said, grinning at me, "We're going to pay for all of my guests."

"Whoa, what?" My jaw dropped. "How?"

She shrugged. "I guess the brownstone didn't cost as much as Oliver had anticipated. And he knows that a lot of my friends are right out of college and can't really afford a destination wedding." She grinned at me. "And..."

"Yeah?"

"He said that..."

"What?" I said.

"We can do it within the next six months if I want."

"No way. What, Rosalie?" I gawked at my friend. "Are you sure you want to get married so quickly?" I paused. "Wait, are you pregnant?"

"No, silly." She giggled and hit me in the arm. "Though I'm sure Oliver would love to get me pregnant."

"Oh my gosh. Really, Rosalie?"

"What? I'm just kidding. You know I'm on the pill."

"I know. That's what I was thinking. So you're really going to do it in six months?"

"I don't know," she said, shrugging. "I need to decide where I want to do it. I was like, do I want to go to England or France or Hawaii? Or maybe even a safari in Uganda."

"Wow." I stared at her. "That's a lot of different options."

"Yeah. I was even thinking maybe the coral reefs."

"Which ones?" I said.

"Girl, there's only one to go to, the Great Barrier Reef in Australia."

"Girl," I said, mocking her, "do you know how much flights are to Australia?"

She started giggling then. "I know. I don't want to put Oliver in the broke house."

"He wouldn't mind," I said. "He loves you."

"I know, and I love him so much. So what about

you? How's it going on Tinder?"

I groaned. "Don't talk to me about Tinder. Why does every guy think you want to see his dick?"

"I don't know," she said, laughing, "but don't you kind of want to check out the goods before you get down and dirty?"

"I'd like a hello and a coffee first, please." I grinned at her.

She laughed. "That's true. So no potentials?"

"Well, there's this one guy, but..." I made a face.

"What?"

"He doesn't really ask me about myself."

"Oh, what does he talk about?"

"He will send me a message and... Hold on, let me bring it up." I pulled out my phone from my handbag and opened the app. I scrolled to my messages and looked for a message from Chris. "Okay. This is the last message Chris sent me."

"I'm listening. Is it X-rated?"

I rolled my eyes. "No, I don't even think he knows anything X-rated."

"Well, that's good, right?"

"Listen to the message, Rosalie."

"Okay. I'm listening," she said.

We both checked to make sure that we weren't about to be called next, but there were at least four people ahead of us in the line. "Okay. 'Hey, chica. How was your day? Mine was absolutely excruciating. I went to the gym and did cardio for about forty-five minutes, and then I was doing weights. Lifted two fifty. I'm hoping to get to three hundred, but I don't want to look like Arnold Schwarzenegger's son. Ha ha. Though I think I'm much harder than Arnold Schwarzenegger's son, don't you think? Check out my new pic, the third one, the one next to the Eiffel Tower. Do you think I look good? Do you think my jeans are too tight?'" I paused.

Rosalie was giggling. "Oh my gosh. Um, I don't know what to say to that."

"Girl, he goes on for another paragraph talking about himself."

"Well, he is trying to engage you, right?"

"How is he trying to engage me?"

"He's asking you questions."

"He's asking me questions like, are his jeans too tight? Girl, he..." I shook my head. "You're not even going to believe this."

"Oh my gosh. What?"

"Listen to this bit." I skimmed through the message to find the sentence I was looking for. "Okay, listen to this. 'So I have a question for you. I was thinking about French kissing. I know, random. But do women like it when men get a little bit of saliva in their mouths? Does it make them feel sexy, or is it yucky? Just want to know so the next time I go on a date, and I end up French kissing. Ha ha. Hope it's you. Then I will know what to do.'"

Rosalie's eyes were wide, and she was laughing hard now. "Oh my gosh, Alice. I'm so sorry."

I could stop myself from laughing as well. "Girl, this is what I have to deal with. Like maybe Florida was better. I don't remember all these losers in Florida."

"Girl, you weren't swiping when we were in Florida."

"I know, but still."

"So what did you say to him?"

"What do you mean what did I say to him?"

"What was your response? Do girls like a little bit of saliva in their mouth when French kissing?"

"Ew. Rosalie."

"What?" She laughed. "I'm going to tell you one thing, though, that I thought I would never say."

"What's that?"

She lowered her voice and looked around. "Okay. You have to promise not to be grossed out, right?"

"I guess. What is it?"

"So when Oliver comes—"

"Yeah?"

"I like to swallow."

I made a face. "Wait. What are you talking about?"

"When I'm giving him a blow job, I like to swallow. Is that weird?"

"Um, yes. That's gross." I made a face.

"Maybe it's because I love him, but it just really tastes like..." She bit down on her lower lip. "Okay. I'm not going to say that it tastes like champagne or anything. It does have this kind of salty taste, but it just makes me feel really connected and closer to him."

"Um, okay. TMI, Rosalie."

"I'm just saying, when you love someone, you just want every part of them."

"I guess so." I sighed. "I mean, it's not even like I have that worry or concern right now. No one is even in the running."

"Well, once we get our coffees, and they're on me, by the way." Rosalie gave me a look. "And then we can swipe, and I'll check out your profile to see if everything looks good."

"Sure," I said. "That'll be fun.

"And how's the job stuff going?" she asked.

"It's not really." I sighed. "I just have no clue what I want to do."

"Have you thought about going to some auditions?"

I shake my head. "No, because that's not going to pay the bills. I'll be lucky if I—"

"Rosalie?"

"What, girl?"

Rosalie was giving me a weird look. "Alice, you have to go for your dreams. Because if you don't, you'll never know if you can achieve them. Reach for the stars. Maybe you'll make it to the clouds."

"Since when are you such a philosopher?" I asked.

"Since I became a teacher, or rather teacher's assistant. Did I tell you that my certification classes start next week?"

"Oh, awesome."

"I'm so happy."

"I know. Me too."

"Oliver and I were talking, and he was like, 'Maybe you could homeschool the kids.' And I was like, 'No, the kids are going to a regular school.'"

I laughed. "So when are you guys planning on having kids?"

"I think we'll wait a couple of years. You know I want to have a large family, and it turns out Oliver does too."

"Aw," I sighed.

"Hey, girl. I'm sorry. I've been going on about Oliver way too much. I didn't mean to be inconsiderate or insensitive to your feelings."

"Oh my gosh, Rosalie, stop. You're totally fine. I love hearing about you and Oliver. And I just hope that I can meet someone so that when you're ready to have kids, I can have kids as well around the same time. And they can be best friends, and well, you know that would be the dream."

"Yeah it would," she said.

I didn't tell her what I was thinking inside, that I hoped her brother would be the man to make all those dreams come true.

Chapter 40

"Good morning, sir. Where are you traveling to today?" The lady behind the counter gave me a winning smile, and I smiled back.

"Hi. Good morning, Matilda. I'm actually flying to JFK in New York."

"Oh, long way. You're American?"

"Yeah."

"Very nice. I've always wanted to go to New York," she said in what I assumed was a Northern British accent. "So can I see your ID please, sir? Your passport?"

"Sure." I handed her my passport. She opened it. "Foster Sloan. What a nice name."

"Thank you." I nodded.

"So Mr. Sloan, I see, oh, you're traveling in business class today, sir."

"Yes, I am." Her eyes widened, and she preened.

"Well, very nice. I currently have you in seat 2B. Is that the seat you would prefer?"

"Yeah, that works, unless there's a better seat I don't know about."

"Well, I try not to tell too many people this, but 3A is actually the best seat on the plane."

"Oh, is it available?"

"Let me check, sir." She punched some buttons into the keyboard. "Well, it's currently occupied, but I could change seats for you."

"Are you sure? I wouldn't want you to get into trouble."

"Oh no, it's fine, sir," she said. "So Mr. Sloan, what have you here in sunny, old London?"

I laughed at her comment, as it had been raining for the entire week I'd been there. "Actually, I've been all over Europe. I'm in banking and, well"—I shrugged—"just meeting with directors from different companies my brokerage is thinking about investing in."

"Oh, wow. That went completely over my head, but very nice. Okay, sir. I've got you in 3A." She handed me back my passport. "I'll print out the tickets for you. Are you checking any bags today?"

"I will be checking one suitcase, please."

"No problem. And, of course, that's free, seeing as you are one of our preferred customers."

"Hey. Well, I'm glad to hear that I'm preferred." I gave her a warm smile.

She giggled slightly. "Sir, I don't normally do this, and I could get in trouble, but my break is coming up in thirty minutes."

"Oh, okay."

"And you don't have to go through for a good hour, so..." She paused. "So that would give us thirty minutes."

"Ah, really?" I said, knowing exactly what she was intimating.

"Yes. I mean, I don't know if you are married." She looked at my left hand.

I wiggled my fingers and shook my head. "No, I'm not married."

"You're not engaged or have a girlfriend?"

"Nope. Nothing." I thought about Amelia and shuddered.

"Oh no. You are engaged then?"

"No, I was seeing someone casually, and she might've been crazy."

"Oh. Well, I mean, this wouldn't be anything really, except for thirty minutes of fun." She winked at me. "I mean, there's the mile-high club, and then there's the airport club."

"Yes, there is," I said, grinning at her. "And you're suggesting we join which one?"

"Well, I can't get on your flight today, so the mile-high club's out, but I can take you to a private area reserved only for employees. And well, you look like you could really make a girl come in thirty minutes."

I stared at her, surprised at her words, shocked even at how forward she was being. I wasn't sure what to say. Matilda was an attractive middle-aged lady, maybe even slightly younger than middle-aged, and I appreciated that she was shooting her a shot, but I was actually excited to go home and just relax. I didn't want to ruin my months-long abstinence for a quickie in an airport with an unknown lady.

"I think I'm going to have to pass only because I have some work to do, but it was very nice meeting you today, Matilda."

Her face crumpled, and she looked disappointed, but then it changed quickly. She stiffened her shoulders and nodded. "Well, you're very welcome, sir. Have a nice flight."

"My bag?" I said quickly.

"Oh, yes. Put it on the scale, please." Her tone changed, and I felt a little sad that she was taking my rejection so personally, but I had decided to forego casual sex for the time being. Having gone out with someone who was slightly crazy made you do something like that. It made you rethink your life choices.

Alice's head suddenly popped into my thoughts and I shook my head quickly. It had nothing to do with Alice. I knew that. Yeah, she was beautiful, and yeah, we had history, but she was my sister's best friend, and I knew my sister would kill me if I did absolutely anything with her. I also knew that I wasn't like Oliver. I wasn't looking to settle down. I wasn't looking to get married. I wasn't looking to start a family. Not now and I wasn't sure if I ever wanted to. I knew that anything short of a full commitment would not be right for Alice, and it certainly would not be approved by my sister. I was going to have to talk to Rosalie soon because Oliver had just texted me about the possibility of a wedding being in South Africa on a safari. I rolled my eyes as I thought about my crazy sister and her antics. Only she would plan to have a wedding on a safari.

"Is there anything else, sir?" Matilda's voice interrupted me from my reverie.

"No. Sorry, I was just—"

"Well, you have a good day. Other customers are waiting."

She cut me off and I nodded. "You, too, Matilda."

"Next, please," she said, looking away from me, and I moved off to the side.

"Well, that was interesting," I said to myself as I made my way to passport control.

I loved Heathrow Airport. There was always something to do. There are so many stores to look in, restaurants to try, gifts to buy. As I waited in line, I realized that I hadn't got anything for Alice or Rosalie and decided to stop and get a present for them both. I hadn't seen them in over a month now, and well, I was missing them.

I'd been really glad that I'd been assigned this project in Europe, right when Rosalie had moved out because I wasn't sure what was going to happen with Alice and I living together in my apartment. Granted, she had taken over Oliver's old bedroom, but still it was something new for us. We'd been quite close when we were younger, closer than even Rosalie knew. When she'd gone to college, we'd had an unspoken agreement that we wouldn't keep in touch as often as we had. And while that had hurt me, I'd known it was for the best. I knew she had to grow as a person. I knew that she needed to live her life and enjoy it. I'd seen her casually here and there, and we'd said hello and goodbye and given each other hugs, but we've never had the depth of friendship or relationship that we'd had when we were younger. Now she was back in my life on a permanent, or at least semi-permanent basis, and I didn't know how that would go.

As I walked to find something to eat, I realized that I was nervous. I was nervous about living with Alice, and I was proud to be able to tell her that I'd only concentrated on work. Now I wasn't sure how that would come up in conversation. It's not like you just went home and knocked on someone's door like, "Hey, guess what? I haven't had sex in ages. Not even when a lady asked me for casual sex in the airport. Did you know airport sex was a thing?" Like Alice would look at me as if I were crazy.

I let out a deep sigh. I wasn't sure if letting Alice live with me had been the right decision for either one of us. I wasn't sure if it would bring up painful memories for her. I wasn't sure what we were letting ourselves in for. I wondered if she'd still want to sneak into my bedroom and spend the night. I wonder if she still had nightmares.

ou can preorder the book here.

Acknowledgments

Thank you to Amanda, Penny, Andrea, Susan, Donna, and Lisa for all their feedback with this book. I hope you loved reading The Edge of Falling as much as I loved writing it.

Printed in Great Britain
by Amazon

85909006R00251